Chasing the Case

The First Isabel Long Mystery

Joan Livingston

D1359625

CROOKED
CAT

Discover us online:
www.crookedcatbooks.com

Join us on facebook:
www.facebook.com/crookedcat

Tweet a photo of yourself holding
this book to **@crookedcatbooks**
and something nice will happen.

For my family

About the Author

Joan Livingston is the author of novels for adult and young readers. *Chasing the Case*, published by Crooked Cat Books, is her first mystery and the first in a series featuring Isabel Long, a longtime journalist who becomes an amateur P.I.

An award-winning journalist, she started as a reporter covering the hilltowns of Western Massachusetts. She was an editor, columnist, and most recently the managing editor of *The Taos News*, which won numerous state and national awards during her tenure.

After eleven years in Northern New Mexico, she returned to rural Western Massachusetts, which is the setting of much of her adult fiction, including *Chasing the Case* and its sequels.

For more, visit her website: www.joanlivingston.net. Follow her on Twitter **@joanlivingston**.

Acknowledgements

I extend my appreciation to anyone who encouraged me to write. You know who you are.

Also, I offer special thanks to Laurence and Steph Patterson, of Crooked Cat Books, for taking a chance on me, and Miriam Drori, my editor who helped make my novel better.

Praise for Chasing the Case

"Written with meticulous attention to the details mystery readers relish and a welcome playfulness, this novel zips along like a well-tuned snowmobile."

Anne Hillerman
Author of the *New York Times* bestselling
Chee-Leaphorn-Manuelito mysteries.

"A smart, fast-paced mystery, with a savvy and appealing protagonist who knows her way around the backwoods of the New England hilltowns."

Frederick Reiken
Author of *Day for Night,*
The Lost Legends of New Jersey,
*a*nd *The Odd Sea*

"An intriguing, clever plot, witty dialogues, a quaint setting, and believable characters, this novel is a page-turner to the very end."

Teresa Dovalpage
Author of *Death Comes in through the Kitchen,*
A Girl Like Che Guevara,
and *The Astral Plane*

"*Chasing the Case* is a fascinating look at a small-town mystery with rich memorable characters weaved masterfully into a yarn that could only be told by someone who lived that life once upon a time. Fortunately, the story stays with you long after you finish the last page. An enjoyable and satisfying read."

Joseph Lewis
Author of *Caught in a Web* and the *Lives Trilogy*

"Take a trip to the land of pot roast and murder. I did, and I liked what I read."

Craig Dirgo
Author of *The Einstein Papers,*
The Tesla Documents,
and *The Eli Cutter* series

Chasing the Case

The First Isabel Long Mystery

Dead Cat

My name is Isabel Long. You may know of me, at least if you live in these parts. I was the managing editor of the local paper, the Daily Star, for almost fifteen years until the bastard who owned it sold out to a big chain. I shouldn't really call him a bastard. He's a decent enough guy. But he walked away from the newspaper that had been in his family for three generations with a couple of million bucks in his bank account, lucky him, and abandoned us to a corporation.

I remember the morning he called everyone into the pressroom to give the news. He claimed nothing would change. We had nothing to worry about. I turned to my assistant editor and muttered, "Open wide. You won't feel a thing."

I was right. He was wrong.

A month in, we were told by the publisher, who still had his job then, we all had to reapply for ours. He pulled us into his office one by one. Of course, these things are always done on a Friday. They don't like ugly scenes in the middle of the workweek.

I sat across from George at his desk. I looked him in the eye. He had a hard time doing the same.

"Isabel, I hate to do this to you," he said.

"Then don't."

"I know it's been a bad year for you."

"Tell me about it."

"Please, Isabel, you're not making this easy."

"Why should I? I worked my tail off for this paper for thirty-one years, as a reporter then an editor. I ran the newsroom for the last fifteen. Now I'm getting the heave-ho."

"No, you're not. You just have to reapply."

"So, what are the odds they'll hire me back at what I get paid now?"

"Do you want me to be honest or lie?"

"What do you think?"

His head moved in a slow sideways roll.

"God's honest truth, I haven't a clue."

"Be straight with me, George. What'll happen if I don't reapply?"

"You can kiss this job good-bye."

That's what I liked about George. Being an old Yankee, he never tried to make bad news sound good. I'm the same way although I grew up in the eastern part of the state, and unlike George, I may be a New Englander, but I'm not a Yankee. My grandparents came over on the boat from the Azores and Madeira islands. My last name before I got married was Ferreira. George's folks were on the Mayflower or some other Yankee vessel. My folks fished and worked in sweatshops. His bled blue when they got a paper cut.

"What does that mean?" I said.

"You can collect unemployment for a while."

"Any severance pay?"

He cleared his throat.

"I believe there'd be a, uh, modest payment considering your length of service here."

"Enough to buy new shoes?"

"Depends on where you buy them."

"I am guessing more like Payless than Versace."

George's head was rolling still. He knew my humor by now.

"No, not Versace but a lot better than Payless."

I thought it over. If Sam, my husband, were still alive, we would've talked it over that night. But he's part of my bad year, the start of it really. He died in his favorite chair while watching a basketball game on TV. That was November 8, twelve days from today. No one suspected the skinny guy would go from a heart attack. I couldn't do anything to get him back when I found him. Too bad. He's one of the good ones. I miss him like hell.

I was too ticked off to accept the deal.

"Tell them I said no."

"You sure?"

"Have you ever known me not to be sure?"

He smiled one of those smiles that leak sadness from inside.

"Okay, go see the ladies in the office. Consider this your last day."

"So soon, eh? I get it. They don't want me poisoning the pool. Let me get my stuff, and I'll be out of your hair."

"Uh."

"What is it now?"

"I have to go with you to your office when you do it."

"They're afraid I'll take some pencils and a pica pole? Jesus, I'm glad I'm not gonna work here anymore."

George frowned. "I know."

Later, George tried not to make me look too criminal when he accompanied me to my office. He sat in my chair while I went through the drawers and shelves. I already had a box I snagged from the pressroom when the HR director thought I went to the women's room. As I took what belonged to me, I kept getting interrupted by my staff, who said nice things and even hugged me, all for the first time. I liked things to be at a professional distance. No drinks after work with the underlings or anything like that. But I was touched they wanted to say good-bye. I was a decent boss. I treated my staff fairly, and they knew I had their back. I was the mother wolf of the newsroom. No one touched my pups.

I wasn't about to ask any of them if they would be reapplying for their jobs. I bet the ones with young families and college debt would, but I didn't want to know. And I didn't want them to think I'm the only one with convictions.

I made cleaning out my desk seem as boring as possible. I wanted George to lose interest in what I was doing. I already stashed the photos of Sam, our daughter and two sons, and our granddaughter who was born in May, the only happy thing that happened so far this year. I had some desk art, silly stuff like

5

pinecones, shells, and a jar of sea glass. I'm nuts about stuff like that. There wasn't much in the drawers I wanted to take home: my lunch bag, thermos, and purse. I'm not a hoarder. I opened each drawer, gave their contents a quick assessment, and then let them slide shut. I didn't even take a pencil or pad although I should've out of spite.

George woke up a little when I removed a couple of manila folders from the bottom drawer.

"What's that?"

"Clippings. I'm gonna have to get a new job sometime."

He nodded. I was pleased he believed me. He wouldn't want what was in those folders to leave the newsroom. They were for cold cases like the one that happened twenty-eight years ago in Conwell, the hilltown in Western Massachusetts where I live. A woman, Adela Collins, disappeared, and the cops were too incompetent to figure out what happened to her. I shoved the folders in the box.

That happened four months ago. I can't even read the Star and what the new owners have done with it. At least, I don't think about the paper all the time or get pissed off about it, just some of the time, like right now while I bury this cat.

The cat's called Marigold. My husband named her because she's an orange tabby. I prefer black cats because they're mysterious and talk a lot. But one of the kids, Matt, brought her home when he found her on the side of the road, and of course, he left her behind when he moved out. Marigold was definitely Sam's cat. I fed her before I left early in the morning for the newsroom. I cleaned her litter box and let her in and out whenever she wanted. But that cat would see Sam, and she'd jump in his lap like she was in love. She decided to hang around for a while after he died. She didn't give me the same love, but enough love, so honestly I didn't feel slighted.

This morning, I found Marigold beneath a bush where she went to die after I let her outside. There were no marks on her. I don't think it was from a broken heart, just old age.

I dig the shovel's point into the earth. I chose a spot in the backyard away from my vegetable garden. Damn, it's cold for late October. The ground isn't frozen yet, thank goodness, or

I'd have a problem today. I'm in a sweatshirt and wearing gloves. I swear I see snowflakes when I glance up from my digging.

I hear a tap at the kitchen window. My mother's face is in the glass. Ma came to live with me this summer. Her name is Maria Ferreira. She didn't want to be on her own, and I'm her kid with the most room, lots of room, actually. She's been a widow a few years. Having your ninety-two-year-old mother move in could be a pain, but not my ninety-two-year-old mother. She hasn't lost her edge. She stays up past midnight, later than me, watching TV and doing puzzles. I got her interested in some of the stuff in our dinky town, plus there are the kids and granddaughter.

Ma still drives. She's got a heavy foot like she's behind the wheel of the getaway car in a bank robbery.

The other day I told her, "Ma, you're moving a little bit fast."

She joked, "No, it's the car."

I laughed.

I let her drive me around, so she doesn't forget. That will change this winter. My commute to the newsroom was at times an adventure, snow, and the worst, ice. Sometimes I had to find a place to sleep in the city. The road crews do their best, but the weather can be unpredictable and fast.

Ma checks my progress. I asked her not to come outside because it's so cold. I give her a wave and keep digging.

I bend to chuck rocks from the hole. I'm about two feet down and aiming for four. I don't want anything getting to Marigold like coyotes or coy dogs, whatever in the hell they are. At least, she's on the small side, so I aim for depth and not width.

It's moments like these when my body is doing something that I start thinking. Like I said, I stopped reading the paper because it's turned into a bona-fide rag. George lost his job after all even though he dutifully reapplied. Some of the others, too, are gone after the new owners shrunk the staff. They don't cover the little towns like this one anymore. Conwell is a one-stoplight, one-church, one-school, one-store, and one-bar kind of town with about a thousand people. But even so, a lot goes on that's newsworthy. I should know. My first job was covering it.

I didn't grow up in Conwell, but I've always taken an interest in what goes on here, but not in that obnoxious way most newcomers adopt. They want to shut the gate after they've moved here. But back to the topic, the one bar and one store don't advertise. So, why bother writing about the town unless something really big happens, which is hardly?

I met George for coffee one day. His job only lasted a couple of months before they brought in someone from the corporation, a relative of the CEO. George is trying to find something else. He has a daughter in college. I told him to use me as a reference. He said he would do the same.

"By the way, Isabel, what was really in those folders you took?" he asked when we were about to leave the coffee shop.

"Like I told you, clippings."

"Yeah, sure." He chuckled. "You're up to something, aren't you?"

"Maybe."

"I just knew it."

My unemployment checks will run out soon. I have to find something else, too. I probably should've started earlier, but things got complicated with my mother moving here. Besides, I always work close to deadline, an occupational hazard to being a journalist, I believe. Ma chips in, and Sam did have life insurance, so I have money in the bank. The house is paid off anyway. I could likely do some freelance, but now that I'm out of the news biz, I don't want anything to do with it. I could even file early for Social Security in a few years, but I'd like to hold off if I can. Uh-huh, I don't look my age, do I? Neither does my mother. She looks maybe seventy-two. That makes me hopeful I inherited her genes.

Damn, it's cold. I'm repeating myself. The snow falls steadier. I have a sizable pile of dirt. I dip the shovel into the hole and eyeball the depth. I figure I have at least a foot to go. I've reached a rocky patch, but if I need to, I'll get the crowbar from the shed. That's the way Sam would do it, so I follow his advice. The crowbar is hanging where he left it.

Sam was a master woodworker although he was too humble to say that about himself. Anyone who hired him to build a staircase or do finish work in their house always got more than their money's worth. He did the same when he built this house.

His workshop was in the basement. I could hear him banging around down there, building something beautiful. I haven't had the heart to do anything with his tools. Sometimes I take my coffee down there, especially the first months after he was gone, just like I used to when he was alive. I'd bring him a cup. He'd light up a cigarette, the only place in the house he smoked, and tell me what he was doing.

Yes, I miss him like hell.

We met in Boston, got married pretty fast, and started having kids. We moved to Conwell with the first, Matthew, because we wanted to raise him in the country, and then had two more close together. After taking a break to be with the kids when they were little, I started writing for the Daily Star as a correspondent, covering my town and the ones around it. I got paid, first by the inch, and then by the story. I used to be a reporter in Boston, not the Globe or Herald but something a lot smaller and now nonexistent – a victim of the big crash in 2008 and the rise of online news. At the Star, I went from correspondent to staff reporter to editor, and as I joke, clawed my way to the top, where I liked it until the paper got sold.

Sam and I made a good life here for our kids and us. He was a trustworthy guy, a little deaf from the power equipment and used to keeping things inside. But he was kind, hardworking, and a great dancer.

Yup, it still hurts.

The crowbar does help. I'm making progress. It's a good thing because the snow hasn't let up. The flakes still melt when they hit the grass, but that won't last if the snow keeps going. I didn't know it was supposed to snow, but then I stopped watching the weather report. When I was commuting into the newsroom, forty minutes in the morning, when there's no traffic, and fifty in the afternoon, when there is, that is, when the roads are clear, I was a fanatic about the weather. I left at 6:10 a.m. because I knew the highway crew had made the first sweep of the hill in front of our house at 6 a.m. for the early morning commuters. The next town over did the same because of the steep hills there. I traveled through four towns. I knew every bump and grind on that route.

If this snow amounts to anything, it could be a pain for the nighttime commuters, especially if the temperature drops and ices the roads. The first winter storm is always the worst. Everyone forgets how to drive in the stuff. The last storm is the second worst. The snow is wetter because it's likely spring and the road crews are sick of plowing. But they're hardworking guys, mostly rednecks. I see them at the one bar in Conwell. It's called the Rooster Bar and Grille. I always say hello.

Sam and I went dancing at the Rooster most Friday nights. Our song was "Brown-Eyed Girl" because I am one. No one can sing it like Van Morrison, but we didn't care. Sam would swing me back and forth. I gave him the lead. Oh, Sam.

I chop at the hole. Ma is on the deck. She has a coat draped over her shoulders.

"You have a call," she tells me.

"Thanks. Just take a message, Ma. I want to get this done."

She goes back inside.

So, what have I been doing for the past four months besides feeling pissed and a little sorry for myself? I helped Ma with her house and the stuff she's accumulated for seventy years. She doesn't want to sell the house, so she's renting it to a granddaughter, my brother's kid, who is married. It took weeks to clean or give away a lot of it. What she couldn't part with is stored in her house's attic or cellar. Course, we took some with us, so she'd feel at home. I gave her the downstairs bedroom, which is next to a bathroom. It's been good to have Ma here. Not many people would say that about their ninety-two-year-old mother, but I can.

Seeing how things can add up, I cleaned out my house, save for Sam's tools in the basement. I started reading books again. Then there are my kids, Matt, Alex, and Ruth, who live close enough, so I can see them whenever I want, and that granddaughter, Sophie, Ruth's girl. It feels good to hold someone that small in my arms again.

I've been back to the Rooster a few times, but not on a Friday night. I have a beer or two, talk with people about what's happening in town and around here, and about sports, everybody's favorite topic at the Rooster, especially Boston sports. Woe to the Yankees fan who admits it, or as I like to say, the only thing worse than the Yankees is a Yankees fan.

But with two weeks to go on unemployment, I've got to think about a job. Since I can't leave my mother alone too much, the pickings are slim if I want to work close to home.

I drop the shovel. The hole is deep enough. I use the edges of the towel the cat is lying on to lift and lay her gently inside. I fold its edges over her before I shovel the dirt, first a sprinkle then larger scoops, until her body is covered with a nice mound. I top the grave with the stones I picked from the hole. I'll find more later.

I stay there for a moment and thank the cat for being the loving animal she was, especially for Sam. If I could have figured it out, I would have buried her at the town cemetery with him. It would only have been fitting.

The snow is sticking. I grab the tools to put in the shed. My job is done.

Kale Soup

The kitchen smells like kale soup. Ma's been busy. Long before kale became the foodie thing to eat, we Portagees ate the green. No kale salads for us. No kale smoothies. We cook the kale to death in soup with white beans, potatoes, chorizo pork sausage, and cubed beef. That's the way my mother makes Caldo Verde, and we eat it three days in a row. The soup only gets better, well, as long as it's refrigerated. Being one of those natural food nuts who prefers not to eat red meat, I skip the chunks of beef when I make the soup, and if I have to use sausage, then it's turkey or chicken instead of pork, which horrifies my meat-loving mother. I figure if it makes my ninety-two-year-old mother happy, I can eat a soup with pork sausage and beef cooked in it.

"Smells great, Ma," I tell her as I slip off my boots at the door.

Behind me the snow is coming down hard for October. I have yet to see the strobe of a highway department truck moving down the hill in front of our house. But I will if the temps drop.

I check the phone message. My assistant editor called. I suppose he got shit-canned, too, and wants a reference. Maybe he needs advice. I'll call him later.

Ma is watching an old movie. I had a dish installed on the roof, so she could have all the shows she got on cable back home. I also turn the heat on instead of just running the woodstove. I want her to feel at home. I still get the paper delivered, so she can do the crossword puzzle and Sudoku, which I can never figure out. She plays solitaire, too, but on a tablet. They help keep her mind sharp.

"Do you always get snow this early?" she asks without taking her eyes off the TV's screen. "It's not even Halloween."

"Sometimes one sneaks in," I tell her. "It'll probably all melt tomorrow. The kids will be able to go trick or treating and have their party at Town Hall like they always do. Actually, one year we had a snowstorm on Halloween. It was a mess."

"Really?"

"Uh-huh. Hey, I'm gonna wash up before dinner. I'll make a fire later."

There are two bedrooms upstairs. Sam and I had the one on the right. I use the one on the left for an office and a guest room, for whenever we have overnight visitors. I have a crib in here for Sophie when I watch her, which is twice a week when her mom needs to go to the office. The rest of the time Ruth works at home.

I wash first. My face in the mirror is still red from the cold. I don't know if I would call myself beautiful. Interesting-looking is more honest, with smooth skin I'm proud of, damn high cheekbones, and brown eyes on the big size. I used to have dark brown hair, but now it's mostly silver after I decided to stop dyeing it. I'm taller than my mother by several inches and thin for someone who worked at a desk job so long. I also don't look like Ma. I definitely take after my father's family, especially when I see old photos of his sisters.

I check my email and Facebook. There's nothing to respond to, but I hit "like" on a couple of friends' posts. I mean what can I say about a person who writes nonstop about her dogs, all eight of them? I see one friend was foolish enough to pick a fight over national politics. I have a couple of friend requests. Uh, later. I tap the manila folders beside my laptop. These are the ones I stole from the newsroom on my last day there. They do contain clippings, from when I was the hilltown reporter, notes and police records.

I flip open the top folder. The headline on the first story says: "Conwell woman missing." It has a photo of Adela Collins, not a very good one, but it's what her family gave the cops. Here is my lead:

"Police are investigating the disappearance of Adela Snow Collins, 38, a Conwell native, who was reported missing Tuesday, Sept. 15 by her family when she failed to show up for work at the town's only store."

It was my first front-page story. My coverage won me an award in the ongoing series category, a second, but, hey, still an award. It happened twenty-eight years ago, when I was still kind of green. I was surprised the then-editor let me handle it on my own, but by then I already had proved to them the locals would likely talk with me more than some city reporter.

The police never found Adela Collins or why she disappeared. Their mistake, I believed from the start, was to treat her as a missing person and not consider that something criminal could've happened to her. Women don't just disappear in a town of a thousand people. Neither do men. It still bothers me. That's why I copped the folder. I found it the other day in the box I brought home from the newsroom and left in a closet. Like I said, I was busy moving my mother. I was happy to make the discovery.

I'm going to sit down and read everything. Maybe there's something I missed. Certainly, the cops did.

Everyone in Conwell knew Adela Collins. Her parents owned the Conwell General Store forever, well, until ten years after her disappearance, when their son took it over. Adela ran the cash register five days a week. What did she look like? She was one of those soft-bodied women. Middle height. Longish, brownish hair. I can't recall if her eyes were green or blue but definitely not brown.

We weren't friends, but we always found something to talk about when I went to the cash register, or I saw her at a town event. She was nice to my kids, which counts a lot. I knew, but didn't include in the story, Adela had a teenage marriage, and then a second marriage to a mean drunk that produced one child, a boy, before they got divorced. Dale was ten when Adela went missing. I see him now and then. He lives in his mother's house, which used to be her grandmother's, within walking distance of the store. That's why it was odd she didn't make it to work that day. All she had to do was go a few hundred yards or so. And when her father went to see her, thinking she was too sick to answer the phone, he found her car was missing, too.

The dog was inside the house. Her pocketbook, with her wallet, was on the kitchen counter.

The family took it hard. Adela was gone and nothing more. Things just fell apart for the Snows.

Sam and I weren't friends with the Snows, but in a town this small you know everyone, even the part-timers, who live most of the time in New York or Connecticut, and the nut cakes, who hide out on the way-back roads. We know what they look like and drive. We give a wave or a friendly toot of the horn.

Yup, we hilltowners are nosy, and I am probably nosier than most. I inherited that from my mother, who'd drive to a fire scene in our hometown if it was close or look up someone's address in the town's directory when the paper reported they were caught doing something they shouldn't have. I liked to tell my reporters I inherited the curiosity gene, how I turned being nosy into a profession, that and always being last minute, that working close to deadline I mentioned before.

I hear my mother calling. She's at the bottom of the stairs. She likes to eat early. I don't mind.

I shut the folder and give it a pat.

"Coming, Ma," I tell her.

The soup's great, naturally. I tear off chunks of the bread I bought at the bakery in the city. It's not Portagee bread, but it's close enough. I dunk the chunks in the broth. Ma does the same.

"Are you going to get another cat right away?" she asks.

I forget Sam's cat kind of became Ma's cat. Marigold took to her lap right away. I wasn't offended. The cat and I had an understanding. I was her loving servant. Just like the meat in the soup, it's not too much to get another cat if it makes my mother happy.

"Sure. I'll check the board at the store," I say. "If there's nothing, we can go to the shelter in the city soon to pick one out. A kitten would be nice. It could grow up with Sophie."

Ma smiles. She likes that idea. We eat and don't talk for a while. I'm thinking about Adela Collins and the folder upstairs. I'm not finished eating, but I set down my spoon.

"I want to ask you something," I say. "You know a little bit about the town already. A woman who lived here all her life disappeared twenty-eight years ago in September. She used to work at the store when her parents owned it. One day she just didn't show up. Two months later, a couple of local guys hunting deer found her car on an old logging road in the woods on the next town over, Wilmot. But she wasn't in it. The doors weren't locked. It was the first day of shotgun season."

My mother's head tips to one side. Besides being a nice kind of nosy, she's read tons of detective novels and watches the same kinds of movies.

"Tell me more about her. What's her name?"

"Adela Collins. She lived with her son, Dale, not far from the store. He's still in town. She was the store's cashier. People liked her. I never heard anyone say anything bad about her even before she disappeared. She was divorced twice, but both were a long time ago. I sometimes saw her at the Rooster. That's the bar in town."

"What about the son?"

"Dale was only ten when it happened. He doesn't seem the child killer type to me. He went to live with his grandparents, but then he inherited his mother's house. He's kind of a sad sack."

"What do you mean?"

"I don't know if I've ever seen him smile. He doesn't stick with one job too long."

"What about the cops?"

"They treated it like a missing person's case. At least the seven years are long past, so the family could officially declare her dead and take care of the paperwork."

"When was the last time anyone saw her?"

"Her son was sleeping over at his grandparents' house that

16

night, so it would've been after she left the store and walked home. It was a Monday evening. People said they saw the lights on at her house. They were still lit when her father came to check on her the next morning. Get this. Her dog was inside. Her purse was on the counter. Nothing was taken."

My mother sits back in her chair.

"Why are you so interested?"

"You know why. Patsy."

She presses her lips as she nods.

"I suspected that much. It's hard to forget something like that."

"Uh-huh. But I also was a reporter when Adela disappeared. It was really hard on the people who loved her. Besides, how could a woman in a town this tiny disappear into thin air? Now that I have some time, I'd like to find out." I catch my breath. "So, what's your opinion?"

She pauses.

"Well, there are a few possibilities. I'd probably rule out her going for a walk in the woods and getting lost." She continues when I nod. "She could've taken off somewhere and gotten a new identity. But if she did, why would she leave a son that young behind? I think it's easier to do that in the movies and books anyways. It doesn't make sense, but it's still a possibility if she had one of those midlife things."

"A midlife crisis?" I say.

"I read about it in a magazine." She smiles. "Or she could've killed herself somewhere people couldn't find her after she dumped the car in the woods. Or someone could've killed her. It could've been an accident or on purpose. Maybe it was a stranger. Maybe it was somebody she knew. Maybe they still live here, or they could've moved away."

I smile when I hear my mother use the word "dumped." Like I said, she reads a lot of mysteries.

"That's a lot of coulds and maybes."

"What are you going to do?"

"I have a folder upstairs with every piece of paper I could get my hands on at the newsroom about this case. I'll talk with the people who were close to her."

"That was almost thirty years ago."

"Uh-huh, twenty-eight. But people have good memories here cause not much goes on, and this was really huge for this town."

"Be careful, Isabel."

"Don't worry, Ma." I dip my spoon into the bowl. Through the living room windows, I see the strobe of yellow lights as a highway truck makes its first pass down our hill. "This is really good soup by the way."

Lloyd

I call Lloyd, who was my assistant editor at the Daily Star. The number he gave my mother is his cell. He answers right away. Of course, I'm still in his contacts.

"You working tonight?" I ask him.

"Yeah, we're a morning paper now you might have noticed," he says.

"How's that working out?"

"We had to make some, uh, adjustments. I'm the regional editor now. The new managing editor said he didn't need an assistant. It's okay."

I liked working with Lloyd. He wanted to learn, so he didn't mind doing grunt work. He's married with two young kids. From what I hear, he's one of the few survivors during the change in regime.

"What can I do for you, Lloyd?"

There's a bit of silence from the other end of the line, except for newsroom static.

"We're missing some folders in the morgue. They contain info about some of the cold cases in our area. We were wondering if you might know what happened to them."

"Cold cases?"

"Yeah, like that woman who went missing in your town."

Now I have an ethical dilemma. Do I lie or admit I took them? I know for certain, because it used to bug me, the files are a mess in the newsroom's morgue, which admittedly is an odd name for a library. I had a hard time finding hard copies of clippings and photos, old black-and-whites when they were still processed by chemicals in the darkroom. It all depended on who was the newsroom librarian then, a position I doubt still exists. Also, reporters would take stuff to their desks and not bring them back. I used to get after them about that.

What the hell, I've made my decision. I'll dodge it.

"Gee, I wish I could help you," I tell Lloyd. "You really can't depend on that filing system. Your best bets are the hardbound copies in the morgue or the microfiche at the library. I've used both."

"Yeah, it'd just be easier with the folders since that was before we had our website," Lloyd says. "My understanding is they had copies of documents. And I can't Google anything."

"Need them for something special?"

"We have a new eager beaver cops reporter who's thinking of doing a series on cold cases. That woman from your town is one of them."

"When's that coming out?"

"Don't know. Maybe in the new year. He's also covering the courts and social services beats. We have to make do with a lot less now."

"I hear you, Lloyd. Well, good luck to you."

Dinner at the Rooster

Friday night I take Ma to the Rooster. I don't know if she's ever been inside a bar, never mind eaten in one. My parents never drank because their fathers did. But I tell Ma at this time of night, which is 5 p.m., of course, the Rooster is more like a restaurant than a bar, so she agrees.

"Now you'll really get to know the town," I tell her.

"That's what I'm afraid of," she says.

The place is a quarter full when we get there, mostly guys off from work and not willing to go home yet, or they're here for the night, and people like us who came to eat. I find us a table in the row alongside the windows.

The Rooster is more like a shack in the woods, but it's *our* shack in the woods. Rustic pine boards line the walls and photos of sports teams – Boston sports teams, naturally – are hung everywhere. There are a few wide-screen TVs placed strategically high. Jack Smith, the owner, with his sister, Eleanor, has already gotten some of the guys to move tables outside to make room for the dance floor and the band that'll play later tonight. Right now, people are feeding money into the jukebox.

Jack, who's in his sixties, has owned the bar longer than I've lived here. Before that, he was a truck driver. He's considered one of the good guys in Conwell. His sister started cooking when Jack decided to expand food offerings at the Rooster beyond jars of pickled eggs and bags of chips.

Eleanor didn't get enough oxygen when she was born, so her brain doesn't function normally. She grunts "Hi" when she greets people, but that's about it although once we did have a short conversation about raising goats. She's got a nice moon-shaped face and a silly giggle, if she ever laughs, which is rare.

She doesn't mind working long hours cooking for her brother. Frankly, I don't know what else she could do for a job. Before she started at the Rooster, she helped her mother and father on their farm when they were still alive. They raised livestock, like pigs, goats, sheep, and cattle. They supplied eggs at the general store. Until the father got too old, he and Eleanor sold firewood. I hear she's good with a chain saw. The hard way the Smiths ran their farm makes me think there's nothing glamorous about working the land.

Jack and Eleanor live next door to each other only minutes from the Rooster. It's actually the same house where they grew up. The house has been in the family always, and way back when, it was divided into two apartments.

Eleanor doesn't drive, so on the nights the Rooster serves food, which is Thursday through Sunday, Jack asks someone trustworthy to mind the bar while he runs her home. Other times, one of the drinkers will volunteer because they know it guarantees a beer on the house when Jack returns.

As we wait for Jack to take our order, drinkers stop by the table to say hello and ask how I'm doing. I used to see them all much later on Friday nights. Sam and I aren't rednecks, but I used to joke we were made honorary ones. He worked alongside so many of them. I wrote stories about them and the things they love to do like truck pulls, raising hogs, and hunting.

"This is my mother, Maria Ferreira," I tell them. "She lives with me now."

Ma says hello to each one. I don't expect her to remember any of them although I do give her a reference point for each, like this is Frankie, he works on the highway crew, or this is Will and Lisa, their daughter is best friends with Ruth. You met Charlie when he delivered our firewood. "Remember how I asked him if he was bringing me the self-stacking wood this year?" I say although she doesn't get the joke.

She sips a diet soda while she checks out the menu. I have a beer, something on tap that's fancier than Bud. For years, I didn't drink alcohol in front of her and Dad. Then one Thanksgiving at their house, Sam and I brought a bottle of wine, and that kind of broke the ice.

I tell her, "I wouldn't order the fish and chips. It's not like fish and chips back home."

Ma nods. She knows what I mean. We always go to a place there that gets its fish right off the boat.

She still does the Catholic thing of no meat on Friday, so I tell her to try the linguine with shrimp. That's what I'm ordering. Ah, yes, the Catholic thing. Ma was raised a Protestant because of her father, a really long story, but she converted when she married my Dad. I dropped being a Catholic a long time ago, but now I drive her to Sunday Mass at a church in the city on Sundays. I even join her. I go through the motions, saying the responses, but I skip communion because it's been decades since I went to confession, and heaven knows, I've done my share of sinning since. I try to hit the folk Masses. They move faster. Going to Mass is like having meat in kale soup and installing the TV dish. If it makes Ma happy, it's not asking too much of me.

Jack takes our order. He's a big bear of a guy, rather good looking, with dark hair still even though he's gotta be in his mid-sixties or older, and it's not dyed. He'd have too much pride for that. He's got a square jaw and brown eyes that are on the large size. I don't think he's ever been married. A steady gal? I don't think so, but then again I've been out of the loop.

He's in a rush, but I introduce him to my mother. He warns us our order may take a while.

"Eleanor's cranking out the food as fast as she can," he says. "We're a little backed up. Busy night."

"Busy is good," I say.

He grins.

"You got that right, ma'am."

The place is filling fast. I check out who's here with whom. Over the years, I've seen a few romances begin at the Rooster although they don't typically last very long. It's the place where separations are formally acknowledged when one half of a couple shows up consistently alone or with a new person. It can get awkward at times.

People may give up their partners, but they stay true blue

to the Rooster. There isn't another place in town to drink, except at home.

Dale Collins, Adela's son, sits at the far end of the bar. He's in his late thirties, the age his mother was when she disappeared. He keeps his hair to his shoulders in a bona-fide mullet. There's some gray to it, and he has that haggard look of a smoker and a drinker. He wears the standard country boy issue, a flannel shirt, jeans, and a John Deere cap on the back of his head. He drinks by himself.

I bend forward because I don't want to yell and you kind of need to in a bar this noisy. It was almost impossible carrying on a conversation with Sam at the Rooster. I may as well have announced whatever I was going to say to the whole bar, so he could hear.

"Ma, turn around slowly like you're gonna look at the jukebox," I tell her. "Check out the man sitting at the end of the bar near the ladies room. That's the missing woman's son."

My mother nods then turns. She does a fine job of not making it obvious. She's back facing me.

"What's he do?" she says.

"Not much, I think. Handyman stuff."

Jack's back with our order.

"We've got a band tonight," he tells me.

"We'll probably be gone by then," I say.

"Tomorrow's our Halloween party."

I smile. Sam and I went to a couple of those. We even dressed up. One year, Sam went as Hank Williams and I was Patsy Cline. Not many people bothered with costumes that year, so we felt foolish at first, but we got over it fast. You don't put on airs at the Rooster.

"Oh, yeah, 'fraid I won't be coming," I say. "Maybe next year."

Jack and my mother make small talk. That's when I notice Dale Collins isn't alone. A guy has taken the stool beside him. He's maybe in his sixties or seventies. It's hard to tell, but he has some serious country miles on him. He and Dale are talking. I don't recognize him.

"Who's that with Dale at the bar?"

Jack glances over his shoulder. He doesn't care about being subtle. It's his bar.

"That's his father, Bobby. He was living in Vegas. Just moved back to town, I hear. I don't think he's stayin' with Dale though. I'm kinda surprised to see them together."

"He's really aged."

"I suppose. Dirty living will do that to ya," Jack says. "He split a long time ago, a couple of years after Adela went missing."

I smile. I feel I might be pushing the line if I ask more questions.

"Thanks for the grub. It looks real good."

He grins.

"I'll tell the cook."

We dig in. I don't believe Jack's sister, Eleanor, makes the sauce from scratch or adds much to what's in the jar or can, so I douse it with the bottle of hot sauce on the table to give it some flavor. It's not Boston North End Italian, but it's not too bad. My attention keeps drifting toward Dale and his father. They're talking still. They order another round, Bud for Dale and something dark in a glass for Bobby. People seem to be avoiding the man. I don't see any slaps on the back or welcome homes from anybody.

I still haven't gotten a chance to read everything that's in the folder I copped from the newsroom. I took care of Sophie the day after the snowstorm. Then Ma and I went into the city to do grocery shopping yesterday. She got her hair cut at the place I go and complained about how much it cost even though it was my treat. We also stopped by the animal shelter. We got a kitten, all black, my request, although Ma picked her out. She named her Roxanne, which I like. I'll let her be Ma's cat.

My mother leans forward.

"You keep staring at that guy," she says.

"Am I being that obvious?"

"To me, you are."

I lean forward, too.

"Check this out. Dale has been joined by his long-lost

father, Bobby."

Ma turns as Bobby Collins gets to his feet. His voice is loud, but he's too far away for me to understand what he's saying. Dale yells back. Bobby jabs a finger at his son. One of the guys in the crowd goes over. He blocks my view, but minutes later, when he finally moves, Bobby's gone and Dale picks at the label on his beer. Bobby's smart. Like I said, there aren't many places to drink, so it's best to be on good terms with Jack, who won't tolerate fights in his bar.

"What's that all about?" Ma asks.

"Don't know."

After my second beer, I go to the bar to ask for our check. Ma's doing okay, but I warn her it's going to get real loud soon. Musicians are carrying instruments and speakers through the back door. I recognize the band. It's called the Cowlicks, which always brings up a lot of dirty remarks from the guy drinkers, but I guess all the good names have been taken. The Cowlicks are kind of the house band since it plays at the Rooster once a month, at least it did when Sam and I danced here, mostly covers of good old boy standards. Loud covers.

Behind the bar, Jack looks swamped, but he's smiling. When I tip forward, I see Eleanor hustling in the tiny kitchen. She wears a matronly apron and covers her hair with a hairnet. I'd say hello, but I don't want to startle her.

"Can I get you another beer?" Jack asks me.

"No, I'm driving. I'd like to pay up."

He goes for the stack of tickets.

"Sure enough."

That's when I notice the small hand-written sign next to the bottom row of liquor bottles that says, "Help wanted."

"Is that sign for real?" I ask.

Jack's head is down as he figures the tax on our bill and writes the total.

"Help wanted? Yeah, I need an extra hand behind the bar. Know anybody?"

"I might be interested."

I say the words even before I think them through. I wait for Jack's answer. He eyes me.

"Huh? You used to run a newspaper."

"Not anymore, and frankly, I'm done with the news biz. Besides, I can't have a job in the city and leave my mother alone too much. She's ninety-two."

He gives Ma a steady look.

"Really? Wow," he says. "You ever tend bar?"

"Yeah, once. But, Jack, how hard could it be? This isn't exactly your martini and frozen pina colada crowd. I'm guessing most of your customers drink beer out of a bottle. Mostly Bud or Bud Light, maybe Michelob, if the guy thinks he's a stud. I know how to use the tap, so a guy doesn't just get foam in his beer, but it still has a good head. Pouring a shot or booze on the rocks is a no-brainer. I make a good gin and tonic, or vodka and tonic, no sweat. I can mix a margarita. Anything else, I can find in the mix book."

He chuckles.

"I guess that answers my question," he says. "You'd be great with the customers. And I know you wouldn't take shit from anyone." He pauses. "I can only pay a buck above minimum wage, but the tips are good, especially on a night like this."

"Okay. What are the hours?"

"I need help on the weekends, as you can see, and sometimes one or two other nights, so I can have some time off, or around the holidays when we're super busy. You really sure you wanna do this?"

I smile. "Let me think about it and get back to you tomorrow. That all right?"

"Uh-huh. Works for me. Nobody else has expressed interest. Well, one guy did, but he'd drink me broke."

"I bet."

The parking lot is a lot fuller than when we arrived. The customers try to squeeze their vehicles close together, since the town won't let them park on the road. It can make for a tight fit, especially in the winter when they arrive on snowmobiles. I swear all the dents in my Subaru are from drunks opening the doors of their pickups and cars at the Rooster.

"That wasn't too bad, was it, Ma? I mean the food's not like you make, but it's okay."

She holds her purse in her lap.

"It was nice to go out for a change."

I back the car carefully to avoid hitting any fool rushing to get inside. The snow melted the other day, but I can feel there's no turning back to any real warm weather until spring, and even that might take a while. What's that old joke? There are two seasons in Conwell: winter and the Fourth of July. The first time I heard it, from a local, of course, I laughed. Now I say it to visitors and newcomers to make them laugh.

The ride home is short, just three miles or so downhill, but I crank up the heat for my mother.

"I see they're looking for a bartender at the Rooster," I tell her. "I'm thinking about it."

"Work in a bar? You're really interested in that?"

"Unemployment runs out real soon. It's close to home, and it would only be part-time, two, maybe three nights a week. Would you be okay being home at night if I did that?"

She nods.

"I was alone before I moved in with you. Besides, it's close to home and only a few nights a week."

I smile when she says home. I'm glad she feels that way.

"Besides, I have an ulterior motive," I say.

"What's that?"

"A bar is a perfect place to get information, you know, about Adela Collins. People tend to talk a lot when they drink a little. You saw what was happening tonight between Dale and his father."

"Like I said before, Isabel, be careful. I didn't like that man's look. That Bobby fellow."

I agree with my mother as I turn into our driveway.

"Here we are," I tell her. "Home sweet home."

Box of Papers

I fetch a couple of logs from the cellar to feed the woodstove. I poke the coals with a shovel to get them lively and open the damper. It makes my mother a little nervous I keep a fire going when we're not home, but I tell her we did it all the time, especially when we didn't run the furnace. I give her the okay to turn up the heat when I'm not home, which isn't too often these days.

But Ma likes the fire. I moved a comfy chair with a footrest near enough, so she can feel the heat coming off the stove. She finds the new kitten, Roxanne, and pulls her onto her lap. The TV is on already with one of her shows.

I bring the folder, a large notepad, and a pen from my office upstairs to the kitchen table. I open a beer.

Here's the first story I wrote.

Police are investigating the disappearance of Adela Snow Collins, 38, a Conwell native, who was reported missing Tuesday, Sept. 15 by her family when she failed to show up for work at the town's only store.

State police, who were called to assist the Conwell Police Department, issued a statement they are treating her disappearance as a missing persons case and at this time, do not suspect any criminal activity.

Her father, Andrew Snow, said in an interview he became concerned when Collins wasn't on time because she was always prompt even during bad weather. "She only lives three hundred yards from the store," he said.

Snow said he walked to his daughter's house on Booker Road when she didn't answer the telephone despite his calling several times. He said he thought maybe she was ill

although she seemed fine the day before.

But Snow said he couldn't find his daughter or her car in the garage. Her purse was on the kitchen table and her dog was inside the house.

"That's when I called the police," Snow said. "This isn't like my daughter at all. The last time I saw her, I was locking up the store. She always tells us where she's going especially if she's leaving town, and she didn't say anything. We're all so worried for her. Please, if anyone knows anything, call the state police."

Customers at the Conwell General Store also expressed concern for Collins, who has worked in the family's business since she was a teenager. She grew up in Conwell and attended local schools. She has one son, Dale, 10, who was staying overnight at his grandparents' house, according to police.

"You couldn't ask for a sweeter person," said Thomas Macintyre, who works on the town's highway crew. "We've known each other since we were kids. I hope she's okay."

Franny Goodwin, who was Collins' first-grade teacher, says she can't recall anything like the woman's disappearance happening in the small town.

"We only have a thousand people living here," she said. "How can a woman just up and disappear? You tell me."

State Police say anyone who may have information about Collins should call the barracks in Vincent.

That story appeared on the bottom of the front page. Like everybody else, I heard Adela was missing the afternoon before and called the editor to give him a heads-up. I remember him asking, "Missing? She's only been gone a few hours."

"It's not like she took off shopping or went out for breakfast and didn't tell anybody," I told him. "You don't know the woman like we all do. She'd never not show up for work or take off like that."

"Don't you have to wait twenty-four hours?" he asked.

"Only on TV," I told him. "The woman comes from a prominent family in Conwell. They own the only store. People are really worried."

"Okay, get me something for tomorrow."

Those days I used a company-issued laptop, which sounds fancier than it was. The screen showed seven lines, and all I could do with it was write and send a story over the telephone line when I plugged it into the socket. It was a couple of years before I got an actual computer. I bought it myself. It had DOS, and that was it. I only knew two people then who had email, imagine that.

The editor didn't change a word.

I kept with the story through the week, but the trail was dry from the beginning. A few of the locals said they saw her walking home after the store closed. One guy said he stopped to offer her a ride home as a joke, but she laughed him off. She wore a blue print dress and a black cardigan sweater. She had sensible shoes. None of them were found in her house when her family looked. But her suitcases and clothing were still there, as was her purse on the kitchen counter.

That week, people here and in the neighboring towns drove everywhere looking for Adela's car or any sign of her. By the time the cops gave in to pressure and called the local search-and-rescue team, it was too late to use the dogs outside her house because the scene had been contaminated. The team leader, a guy named Red, told me if the cops had called right away, the dogs could have told them exactly where she had gone when she left her house. If everybody hadn't walked and parked all over the damn place, the team could have seen if there had been more than one set of tires in the driveway or on the roadside. It didn't help that it rained one of the days.

"But they never do," Red told me. "We could've helped find that gal."

Irma Snow, Adela's mother, sat by the phone, waiting in case she called. All would be forgiven, I suppose, please come home. After all, Adela did run off on her eighteenth birthday to elope with her boyfriend, John Albright. Both families talked them out of it when they got back and had the marriage annulled.

I even heard a couple of people speculate Adela might have gotten kidnapped, which I felt was rather far-fetched. It's not like the Snows had big bucks. But I suppose if somebody had called with a ransom request, her parents would've been ready.

Adela's son, Dale, who folks said was really broken up, didn't want to leave the house, but ended up living with his grandparents. He was too young to be on his own. The story was that he blamed himself for not being home that night. He last saw his mother at the store. Word was she kissed him and told him to call her in the morning before he left for school. He did as he was told, but she never answered.

I wrote a profile of Adela, which we ran with photos her parents entrusted with me. Her mother was too upset, but Andrew, a true New England stoic, talked about her being in 4-H, how she was so good with the customers. The Sunday before Christmas she arranged for one of the regulars, usually Jack Smith from the Rooster, to play Santa. She handed out candy then and at other holidays like Easter and Halloween.

I kept after the state cops for updates until they got so irritated I was told by the sergeant at the Vincent barracks, "If there's something new, miss, we know how to reach you."

Even my editor got tired of the story until two months later, when during shotgun season, deer hunters found Adela's car on that old logging road deep in Wilmot. Andrew Snow insisted the cops call in the search dogs again, but the scent was long gone. The dogs didn't find anything decomposing in the woods, which brought hope to some.

But the discovery of Adela's car in such a remote spot was a really bad sign. The state cops had nothing new to say, except they would have the car towed to test for prints. Later, they reported they found prints from Adela and her son, plus some that were not identifiable. Eventually, they released the car to Andrew, who had it towed to a junkyard and crushed. He couldn't bear to look at it.

I hated going inside the store those days. It was so damn quiet like it was a funeral home, and it kind of was because her family was taking it so hard. My kids were young then, and I cringed when they ran happily through the aisles. No one talked about Adela in front of her parents, who got their daughter-in-law, Jamie's wife then, to work part-time at the register. Irma Snow handled it the rest of the time, but I could tell she didn't have it in her. It was about the time she started looking unwell, and months later, we heard about the cancer. She lasted two years, her death accelerated likely by the disappearance of their daughter.

One day, weeks after the car was found, almost Christmas, Andrew Snow took me aside in the store.

"Have you heard anything?" he asked

"I'm so sorry," I said. "I wish I did."

I flip through the papers. I did an update months later, which really only said the police and everyone else in town didn't know what happened to Adela Collins. I wrote one on the year anniversary, and seven years later, when she was officially declared dead. I assigned a reporter to write the story of the memorial service. I was an editor then.

I read the police reports and clippings from other papers. The Boston paper summed up the story in three graphs. The reporter called Conwell a quaint hamlet, whatever that is.

Ma switches channels on the TV in the living room. I forgot for a moment she's there. I check the clock on the stove. It's only eleven. The night is still young for my mother.

I sit back and recall what it was like in Conwell then. Wherever I went, people wanted to talk about Adela's disappearance, whether it was at a board of selectmen's meeting or a kids' soccer game. They mentioned her ex-husband, Bobby, the drunk, as a possibility. Maybe he and Adela had an argument. The state cops did interview him, but he was excused because he supposedly had an alibi.

Or maybe someone broke into her house like those punk kids who hit homes during the day when people were away working in the city.

One woman, who was a supposed friend, said Adela was depressed. If so, she hid it well.

I didn't print any of the speculations.

Naturally, people were pissed the cops weren't doing more.

They put up signs all over the hilltowns and in the closest cities. The Snow family pledged a reward. Of course, the kooks called. One woman who claimed to be a psychic said Adela's body was buried somewhere on Mount Greylock, the highest mountain in the Berkshires. Another, a man this time, claimed she drove to New Mexico and jumped off a bridge there.

Then people started getting really pissed it was taking so long to find out anything about Adela.

"Shit," I say, slapping the table.

"You okay in there?" my mother calls.

"Yeah, yeah, Ma, I just remembered something."

"Is it something good?"

"Oh, yeah," I say, and then I rush upstairs to my office.

I push open the folding doors to my closet, where I have stacks of boxes instead of clothes. I eye the writing on the outside of each one and smile. The box I want is on the bottom. It contains the notebooks from my early reporting days, when I was a correspondent and worked from home. I was told I should throw them out after I'm done with a story, so no one can legally request them in case there was a libel suit, but that's never been a problem with me. I didn't cover many stories that involved lawyers.

Besides, my handwriting is so hard to read. I mean, I'm scribbling as fast as someone speaks, often without looking at my notebook, so the shelf life for readability is pretty limited. I used to have perfect cursive, thanks to the public school teachers who taught me the Palmer Method, but as I often told my staff, journalism ruined my handwriting.

The box is filled with notebooks, including two legal pads. I had a system. If I was doing a person-to-person interview, I used a reporter's notebook. If I did a phone interview, I wrote on a legal pad. I also jotted down my observations. They were only leads and not print-worthy, totally off the record. I grab the legal pads and shove the rest of the notebooks back in the box. Someday I may have a bonfire in the backyard but not yet.

I take a chair in the living room, where the light is better for reading.

"What do you have there?" Ma asks when I am back downstairs.

Ma watches the news. The kitten is already a fixture on her lap.

"Old notes. I hope I can find some clues in here."

"Good luck with that."

At least, I can read what I wrote. In the days, weeks, and months after Adela went missing, I kept these notes, dated even, and I congratulate myself for doing that much. I flip to the last page on the second notebook. It's only filled halfway. My last notation is dated seven years after Adela disappeared. Her father and brothers held a memorial service now that she could be declared officially dead. Everything was done to try and find her, or so the cops said. At least the service brought some degree of closure.

The memorial was held at the Conwell Congregational Church, where the pastor, who was new in town, tried hard to make it pleasant for the family. Irma, her mother, was long dead. Adela's father, Andrew, had aged. His hair was white, and he didn't smile as much as he did before all of this started. Dale, who had just turned 17, stood beside his grandfather with his head down. Adela's brother, his wife, and ex-wife, plus their kids were there. So was half the town.

Afterward, a reception was held across the street at Town Hall. I came as a resident of Conwell and not as a member of the press. I couldn't bring myself to cover the event. I must have written these notes when I got home because they're rather extensive. I have a list of who attended. Bobby Collins is at the bottom. I heard he flew in from Vegas for the service, which gives him points in my book.

I shake my head. I need to start at the beginning, but I'm too tired. I tell Ma I'm going to bed.

"Don't stay up too late," I joke.

"Don't worry. I will," she says.

Who Says What

I'm up early drinking coffee, my first today. The kitten's fed. Ma's still asleep. I have two legal pads in front of me on the kitchen table.

I've already gone through half of the first pad. Most of the conversations I recorded first are of disbelief that something like this could happen to Adela and in our town, as if being such a rural place should make it immune to big city crime. I note old-timers claim no one has ever been murdered in Conwell although there have been bad accidents when someone got killed, including a few drunks, and someone said a guy died from a gunshot during hunting season that may or may not have been intentional, but nothing was ever proven. There have been a number of suicides in the usual manner, a gun to the head, pills, or a running car in a closed garage. Here's a tip about obits. If it says, "died suddenly," and there isn't a request to send donations to a heart fund or any other place like that in the obit, you know the recently deceased offed himself.

People do leave town in a hurry, but it was expected of them. They likely owed money, got into some trouble, or ran off with somebody else's wife or husband.

I don't mark up the pages. I am in a reading mode. I want to take it all in first, the mood and suspicions townspeople had. I am amused by my own interest. Morbid might be a good word. Obsessed would be another.

As was my habit then, there's only writing on the front page and thankfully in pen. Here's a sample.

MARY ALLEN [NEIGHBOR]: I heard Adela's car leave her driveway when I was going to bed. What time? It

couldn't have been too late. Maybe ten or earlier. Our houses are really close together, so the headlights on Adela's car flashed across my windows. The car was moving too fast for me to catch even a bad look. Besides the leaves were still on the trees, so it blocked my view of the road. But I saw enough. I thought it was odd at the time. Adela never drove that fast. I figured I would ask her in the morning what happened. Maybe someone was real sick, like her parents or the boy, and she was going to the hospital. No, I didn't see another car or pickup. I did tell the cops about it by the way.

VIRGINIA WOODSON: I was leaving the store when I saw Adela and her ex, you know Bobby Collins, arguing outside the store. It was a week before she was gone. It sounded like they were fighting about money because she said, 'you never gave me anything for Dale, so don't come around thinking you're gonna get anything from me cause you're broke.' He grabbed her wrist, but she yanked it away and went back inside. Her head was down when she passed me. I could tell she was embarrassed. Bobby Collins sure looked pissed before he drove off in that beat-up pickup he had. He's a drunk you know.

MY ENTRY WITH A STAR: Cops say Bobby had an alibi that night. He was with Marsha Dunlop.

I know the woman. My mother would call her a Floozy. I would say she was a good-time gal although if you saw her now, fat with raggedy, gray hair and missing teeth, you wouldn't think so.

On the third sheet, I drew a map of the village where the store and Adela's house was located. Nothing has changed since. The lots are too small there to build any new homes. I even worked by scale on the road and neighboring houses.

I drew a similar map after they found her car. I went to the spot, hiking in, because the car I had then was too low to the ground to risk it bottoming out. Plus, as I remember, I doubted there would be a wide enough spot to turn around, even a three-point turn, and I sure as hell didn't want to back my car two miles, which was the distance to the road.

I knew exactly where to go thanks to a couple of the volunteer firefighters who joined the cops that day. As a reporter, I found out fast the cops are a tightlipped bunch, but the firefighters tend to be a friendly group that loves to chat. I got more from them. I couldn't use any of it on the record, but it helped me head in the right direction.

It had snowed a few days before I hiked that logging road, so I saw the footprints of other people who also made this trek. Mostly, they were made from work boots. Maybe they were from hunters, and I was glad I wore an orange vest and cap I found in the house. Even so, I was taking a chance being out in the woods since it was still shotgun season. Or maybe they were just people being nosy like me.

Of course, the car was long gone, towed to the state police barracks in Vincent to check for fingerprints and whatever they could find. The boot prints took me right to the spot. I walked a bit around the area. I was told by my chatty firefighter friends the road led to one of the branches of the Brookfield River. The Brookfield is one of those rocky New England rivers. If it hadn't been for shotgun season, I wonder how long it would've taken for someone to find Adela's car.

I see my notation: Did the cops walk to the river?

I didn't that day. I hadn't told anyone what I was doing, not even Sam. I probably would've been all right, but I had an uneasy feeling. I mean a missing woman's car ended up here.

The next weekend, on a Sunday, when hunting is not allowed, I talked Sam into going with me. We walked to the river's edge a couple of miles more, passing one of the snowmobile trails that run through woods, useless without a lot more snow on the ground.

Sam kept waiting for me to give up.

"There's nothing here, Isabel," he said.

But Sam was a good sport as I searched among the rocks for any signs and took photos of the scene. I didn't turn the photos in to the Star because I was on my own time. The paper did run a few I shot like the one of the crowd gathered on the side of the road, hoping for news.

Another photo showed Andrew Snow walking with the local chief. He had been called about the car. Andrew's head was down. I hated to take the shot, and I got some grief for it from the locals, but I was hoping it would stir someone's guilty conscience. Andrew told me later he was okay about it. I still have all the photos I took. I found them in an envelope at the bottom of the box after I carried it downstairs to the kitchen table this morning.

I surprise myself that I held onto all of this stuff. I go through phases where I toss stuff out, purges really, especially old notebooks since I can barely read what I wrote anyway. I can remember leaving a notebook at home and calling Sam from the newsroom, so he could read a section out loud, and he'd tell me, "Sorry, Isabel, I can't make heads or tails of any of this." Frankly, I had a hard time, too, if I waited too long to read my notes. I've already taken a peek at the reporter notebooks. That's true about them. But I was more careful about writing on the legal pads, thank God.

On one page of the pad, I created a family tree of Adela's kin. At the bottom I wrote: First husband, John Albright, moved to Florida, so he's out of the picture.

Another page has a list of everyone who claimed they saw her the day before she was reported missing. Most said it was just another ordinary day in Conwell. Adela was as friendly as usual. Nothing seemed amiss. I actually shopped at the store earlier that day. Adela asked about the kids. She liked the story I wrote about one of the old-timers who still logged with horses. He gave the photographer and me a ride through the woods.

But then I find this notation I marked with stars. It's on a page with the title: SUSPICIONS. It only had two listed.

LEE KELLEHER: I stopped at a bar in the city. I was meeting up with some people because it was a co-worker's birthday. Adela was sitting in a booth. She had a half-finished cocktail in front of her. I was as surprised to see Adela, as she was to see me. She looked like she was waiting for someone. It was a Tuesday, which seemed an

unusual day to be out drinking rather far from home. I kidded her about meeting a man. Adela told me she went shopping and decided to relax a bit. I didn't believe her. It was maybe a month before she disappeared.

ANONYMOUS PHONE CALL: A man tells me to check the building permits and board of health records for the cellar holes and septic systems issued that year. They'd be good places to stash a body. His voice was low and gruff, so I couldn't recognize him. From the background noise, he was calling from a payphone.

The payphones at the store and near Town Hall are long gone now that cell phones mostly work up here. But no one had them when Adela went missing.

Ma's bedroom door opens. She's already dressed as she makes her way to the bathroom. I have the coffee machine she brought from her house ready for her. I can't stand the stuff it makes, but she does. My coffee is too strong for her. Hers is too weak for me.

"Still reading that stuff?" she asks me when she's done and in the kitchen.

"I've only begun," I tell her.

Saturday Morning

I'm mostly home all week, but out of habit, I keep to the Saturday routines I had when I worked. I call it the Conwell Triangle: the dump, the library, and the general store. The first stop, naturally, is taking the trash and recyclables to the transfer station, which is open two days a week only. The town dump was done and covered by dirt per order of the state before Sam and I moved here.

I see Jack Smith, the owner of the Rooster, two pickup trucks back. I've given the job enough thought and figure what the heck, I'll try it out. I can always quit. What's the saying about a restaurant? As soon as you hire someone, they're walking out the door. It's probably double for a bar. Maybe they're sprinting. But I would make sure I left on good terms with Jack if that happens. I like drinking at the Rooster.

I park my car out of the way after I toss our trash bags into the compactor.

"Be right back, Ma," I tell her. "I see Jack, you know, the owner of the Rooster. I'm gonna tell him I want the job."

"I figured as much," she says.

Jack lowers the window when I walk toward his pickup. He's got a full load in its bed.

"Hey, Jack, is that job still available?" I ask.

"Yup, haven't hired anyone since last call," he jokes.

"Well, I'm interested if you'll hire me."

"Sure, I'll hire you." He nods. "How about coming in Thursday around four, so I can break you in before Friday?"

"Works for me."

"All right, see ya then." He tips his head forward. It's his turn to dump. "Gotta go."

I'm heading to my car when I see Andrew Snow alone in

his station wagon at the end of the line. I can't imagine one old man living alone creates much trash. He probably has a small bag in the trunk unless he's picked up drinking. He stares straight ahead, waiting to move his wagon another vehicle length. His face is serious. Maybe he looks at everyone he meets and wonders if they might be hiding something.

I know what I have to do. Before I go snooping around, I've got to tell Andrew I want to solve his daughter's mystery. I owe him and his family the heads up. Besides, I will need their consent and cooperation. Maybe they'll have useful information.

Andrew's okay would go far in town. Anyway, it's the decent thing to do. If I were a reporter doing a story, I wouldn't bother, but this is different.

I tap on my mother's window.

"One more," I tell her.

"You're getting as bad as your father," she says.

I know what she means. Dad was Mr. Sociable. We'd all be in the car waiting for him to finish his errand, which took a lot longer than necessary because he'd stop to talk with one person then another. There were no quick stops with Dad.

"I promise I'll make this fast," I say.

"I've heard that before," Ma says.

Andrew's car moves forward one space. He rolls down his window when he sees my approach.

"Hello, Isabel, how are you? I heard you aren't with the paper anymore."

"Yes, the Star's got new owners. Lots of changes. It's been four months."

"I also heard you have your mother living with you."

"That's true, too."

I smile. The general store, especially its backroom, is gossip central. Early in the morning, before it opens, a bunch of old guys sit on benches, drinking coffee and chewing the fat. Once, when they teased me about working for the Daily Fart, I got them laughing their heads off when I said, "Well, then you Old Farts should all get subscriptions."

And although the Old Farts don't know it, that's the name I

call them. I even capitalize it.

The backroom hasn't changed since Jamie Snow took over the store although now Andrew drops in for a visit, or so I heard from Sam, who used to dash in there for a cup to go. I'm sure the folks deliberated over bad coffee about the end of my career at the paper. My mother? She got maybe a sentence or two.

"How does your mother like it here in Conwell?" Andrew asks.

"So far, so good."

I pause, working up to what I want to say. When I was a reporter and had to talk with someone who wouldn't be an easy interview, I called it a deep-breath phone call. I'd take a deep breath and punch the numbers before I changed my mind. Right now, I'm just going to get to the point fast.

"Andrew, I was wondering if I could meet with you."

"Meet? What for?"

"I've been thinking of investigating what happened to Adela. I know a lot of time has passed, but I've never forgotten her. I just want… "

He looks straight ahead, and then at me. Everything on his face slopes downward.

"Twenty-eight years ago."

"I'm sorry."

"She's dead. It's official. We knew long before the seven years were up. I felt it. Irma felt it, too. I believe it shortened her life quite a bit. The family hasn't been the same since."

His voice fades on the last words.

"I'd like to do this with your blessing. Just so you know, I'm on my own. I'm not a reporter anymore or a private eye. But I always felt the cops could've done a much better job."

He mulls it over. He has two spaces open in front of his car, and a driver in back beeps the horn of his pickup for Andrew to move up. I walk alongside as his car rolls forward.

"How about tomorrow, say one at my house?" he says finally.

"We should be back from St. Anne's by then. I take my mother to Sunday Mass there. Would you mind if I brought her along?"

"Not at all." He cranes his head. "Is that her over there?"

"Yes, it is. I'll see you then. Thank you."

"You're welcome," he whispers.

I apologize to my mother when I get into the driver's seat.

"What was that all about?" she asks.

"He's Adela's father, Andrew. He's my first interview tomorrow. You can come, too." I turn the key. "Mostly, I wanted his approval. No one else is gonna talk with me unless they're sure it's okay with the family, especially him."

"Good thinking," my mother says. "Where next?"

"How about the library? It's time I got you registered there. You can get a stack of those steamy romance novels you like."

My mother laughs.

Go for a Ride

Ma starts one of her new books as soon as she gets settled back home. I go over my notes. I see a notation about the weather that September: sunny and unseasonably warm. We hadn't had a killing frost yet.

But other than that, I'm not getting anywhere fast, as my mother would say. The rest is more of the same. Why Adela? How could something like this happen in Conwell? Of course, quite a few had Bobby Collins high on their suspect list, alibi or not with the Floozy. I definitely feel I should put the woman on my list.

That's when I get a good idea.

"Hey, Ma, how would you like to go for a ride?"

"What for? We just came home," she says. "I'm getting into this book."

"I want to show you Adela's house and the road where they found her car. That way you have it in your head where they're located. You might see something I don't."

Her eyes are off the book. I sense she is interested.

"Oh, why not?" she says.

We start at the Conwell General Store, the town's official business hub, unless you count the Rooster. Sometimes people will try opening a gift shop or restaurant, that's happened twice since I lived here, but they don't last. Conwell doesn't get that many tourists. Those who've lived here all their lives go out for bar food, burgers and such, like they serve at the Rooster. Unless it's a super important occasion, they don't want to drive too far to eat and drink. The newcomers will make a night of it in the city, however.

The general store is strictly a place of convenience, for

stuff like milk, deli meat, and booze, although some of the old-timers who hardly leave town depend on it for more than that. The rest we buy at the grocery store in the city, a forty-five minute trip one way in good weather, or an hour if you shop at Whole Foods. The store does have a post office and a gas pump, again for the convenience because you pay a lot more than you would at a gas station in the city. The Rooster had pumps long ago, but Jack Smith gave them up about the time he started serving food. The state shut down that part of his business because the underground tanks were too old. Jack didn't want to spend the bucks to replace them, so he had them removed. Plus, he said it was a pain going out to pump gas when he had a bar full of drinkers.

Of course, I wrote about it at the time. The headline for that story was: "No gas at the Rooster Bar and Grille." The Old Farts in the store's backroom loved it. Jack Smith gave me a pleasing grin the next time Sam and I drank there.

I park the car behind a pickup but keep the motor running.

"Okay, Ma, you've been to the store, but this is where Adela opened the doors at 8 a.m. sharp. Her father got here an hour earlier, and the Old Farts use the back door to fix themselves coffee and get a donut."

My mother nods.

"Old Farts. Only men, right?"

"Yeah, but back when Adela was here, it was a different group of men. The Old Farts change over the years depending on who's retired and who's kicked. I'm awfully fond of the latest group." I put the car in drive. "Now I'll show you where Adela lived."

I take a left onto Booker Road and count three houses out loud before I stop on the shoulder across the street. I point.

"That's the house. The white one with the porch," I say.

"Looks kind of shabby," Ma says.

"It wasn't like that when it belonged to Adela. She kept it painted nice. There were flowers in the front. See the garage? That's where she parked her car."

The garage door is open and hanging rather crookedly. I can't remember when I last saw it closed all the way. The bay is filled with junk, lots of metal and old furniture, so Dale parks his pickup in the dirt driveway. His mutt, tied near the side door, barks at my car.

"That's not very far at all. Did she have a dog?"

"Yeah, Andrew found it in the kitchen."

"So, it's likely Adela or somebody made sure it wasn't left outside," Ma says. "Either they liked the dog or they didn't want it to bark and follow them."

"Good points. They found her purse, too. The wallet inside had money, her credit cards, and license."

"Hmm, that's odd. So robbery wasn't the motive." Ma turns around in her seat. "The houses are close together here. Nobody saw anything?"

"It's supposed to have happened after dark. One woman told me she heard Adela's car leave maybe between nine and ten. She lived in that green house to the left. She died years ago. Her daughter has the house now."

"The neighbor heard only one car?"

"That's what she said. She saw the car's headlights. Maybe there was another vehicle. It could've been parked on the road and left another time. See? This is why I wanted you along."

Ma makes a satisfied smile.

I pull into Dale's driveway and wait for a pickup truck to pass before I back into the road.

"Did the daughter live there at the time?"

I shake my head.

"She moved in after she inherited the place. It's a much nicer house than the one she and her husband had."

I head north. We pass the Rooster, maybe a mile away. The parking lot is empty. Some guy in a pickup toots his horn as we drive by. He works with Charlie, the guy who delivers our firewood, a Rooster regular. I toot back. It's common courtesy here.

"See that house on the left?" I say a couple of miles later. "Jack and his sister, Eleanor, live there."

"That's an awfully big place."

"Well, they divided it in two a long time ago. Eleanor's part is on the south side. See where the glassed-in porch is?"

"They're both single?"

"If either of them were ever married, it was long before we got here. I doubt Eleanor had a husband. She's kinda simple. Jack? I don't know. I tell you what. I'll let you know after I've worked at the Rooster a while."

Ma nods. She's into this field trip.

I keep going. Here the land is mostly wooded with an occasional house tucked inside the trees. We pass two mobile homes. The town outlawed them a long time ago. If anybody had a mobile home before the law changed, it was grandfathered, so it could stay. I believe these two, which belong to members of the same family, have outlasted anyone's expectations for longevity.

We reach the sign that says "Entering Wilmot." This town is dinkier than Conwell. It doesn't even have a store or gas pumps although there is a town hall and church.

Some guy in a pickup is on my ass, but I have my eye on the odometer. The spot I want is 1.7 miles from the town line. The truck zooms past with a lot of noise, probably to make the point I'm driving too slowly. No one is on the road when I reach our destination, and I steer left into an opening in the woods. I stay in the entrance of what was likely a logging road or maybe it was a town way at one time and no one built on it. It's on state forestland now.

"This it?" Ma asks.

"Yes, the car was left about two miles in. We're not going to walk it, but I wanted to show you the entrance."

"Why leave a car here?"

"Good question."

"But somebody found it a couple of months later?"

"Yeah, hunters. The road goes all the way to a good-sized river. The woods are pretty thick here."

"Hmm, it would seem someone was hoping the car wouldn't be found right away."

"But if it was somebody local, they knew hunters would go this way eventually."

"What if it was Adela?"

"The car went as far as it could go before it bottomed out.

If she did kill herself, she would've waited in her car until there was enough light, or maybe she had a flashlight, and then walked far into the woods. I mean really far so no one could find her. She could've even crossed the river at a low spot. It's been years since I went back there, so I've forgotten what it's like."

"Did she own a gun?"

"Good question. I'll have to ask her father."

Ma studies the road.

"You said there's a river. What else?"

"There's a snowmobile trail that cuts across it. I think it's about a half-mile beyond where the car was left."

"Snowmobile trail?"

I forget the town where my mother lived, and where I grew up, has never had enough snow for snowmobiles to run, but it's a popular and fun mode of transportation here in the winter.

"Yeah, the rednecks love driving on the snow. They built this huge trail system in the woods. Sam and I used to go snowshoeing on them. It was something else being in the middle of nothing, hidden away like outlaws. I can see why the guys like it. Well, women, too."

"You and Sam felt like outlaws?"

I laugh.

"Not really. We'd park at the Rooster, strap on our snowshoes, and head out on a trail. There're a bunch of trails that meet up in the parking lot."

"This one, too?"

"Oh, yeah, I hear it goes all the way to the Vermont border. Seen enough?"

"Uh-huh."

Andrew Snow

Andrew Snow's home is a sweet old colonial in Conwell's central village that's been in his family for generations. It's within walking distance of the Conwell Congregational Church, Town Hall, and elementary school. The village has two nice lines of antique homes, but it's not the oldest part of town. At one point, the town was first settled on what is still a dirt road, but for unknown reasons, it got moved to where it is now. I am guessing there was some sort of feud, which is a way of life here.

I can think of a few active feuds, all over some slight that may seem miniscule to others, but something big enough, so there's no going back to being friends and family. In one, a woman was involved. In another, someone got slighted in a last minute change to a will. Then there are those feuds between the natives and newcomers who can't keep their opinions and city manners to themselves. They don't want to hear chainsaws buzzing at 7 a.m. or smell pig shit in their backyard.

But I digress.

I knock on the side door. Ma stands beside me. No one ever uses the front. That door is strictly for show and hanging Christmas wreaths, one of the first lessons I learned here. A scruffy little mutt barks behind the door. Then I hear Andrew say, "Coming."

He clutches the dog, some shaggy thing, when he opens the door.

"Don't mind Jasper," he apologizes. "He'll settle down. He's just excited to have company."

"I can see that," I say.

When I was a reporter, I always asked ahead of time if the

50

person had a dog I should know about. I kept an arsenal of dog bones in my bag just in case. Only once did I think I was going to get bitten, but the guy called off his mutt in time. Andrew's dog is just another little dog that thinks it's a big dog. I've met several men just like him.

"Hello, Mrs. Ferreira," Andrew says. "Nice to finally meet you."

We follow Andrew into the kitchen. Photo albums and a scrapbook are on the table.

"Would you like some coffee?" he asks. "I've got some made. It's better than the store's."

I manage not to say something quick and stupid like "thank God."

"Yes, I would. Thank you. Ma?"

"Milk and sugar, please."

"I think I have that fake sweetener if you prefer," Andrew tells her, but Ma waves him off.

"Just milk for me," I tell him. "Can I help?"

"No, no, I'm fine. Just sit there."

We slip off our jackets as the man pours our coffee into cups. He places a spoon in each. He goes for the carton of milk in the fridge then sits across from us. He takes a sip of his coffee, which he drinks black.

Andrew slides the photo album across the table. It's one of those old leather-bound albums. Somebody glued a card to the front with the words "Our Adela" written in cursive. I bet Irma put the album together.

He opens to the first page and likely the first photo taken of Adela.

"She was a beautiful baby," he says with a fondness in his voice.

"She sure was," Ma says.

Andrew turns the pages, giving us the rundown: when Adela began walking; her first day at school; Halloween parties and Christmas mornings. As a reporter, I learned old Yankees weren't so quiet after all. They do take a while to warm up though. I liken them to a lawnmower that's been sitting a while. You need a few cranks to get the mower started, but once you do, it purrs and does its job.

I let Andrew ramble. Together we watch Adela grow up, become a young woman, and then almost middle-aged at family barbecues and holiday parties. The album's final photo was at the store. She's talking with Andrew. It's a candid shot.

"This is the last one I know of. One of the newcomers took it and gave it to us after Adela left us. He was just going around town with his camera."

I lean to take a closer look. A man is in the background, watching the conversation between Adela and her father.

"Hey, that's Jack Smith from the Rooster," I say.

Andrew bends closer.

"Yup, Jack," Andrew says. "The newcomer tried to take pictures in the store's backroom, but the guys back there wouldn't let him."

We both laugh. Ma doesn't, but then she hasn't had the Old Fart experience yet.

"That doesn't surprise me," I say. "The guy must have been really new in town to think he could get away with anything like that."

Andrew studies the last photo for a moment.

"So, what can I do for you?" he asks.

"Like I said yesterday, I am interested in solving Adela's disappearance," I say, choosing the words I practiced with Ma on the ride here. "I know she's been declared officially… "

"Dead," he says.

"Yes, dead. As you recall, I covered the story when it broke. I stayed with it until there was no more news. But I still think about what could have happened to your daughter. I know I'm not the only one. And if someone is responsible, we should know that, too. I have some free time to put into it."

Andrew clears his throat.

"It's a tragedy to believe someone is dead when you don't know for sure. We had to do that to settle things legally, especially since the house was in her name. Then we could give it to Dale."

"I remember."

"Did you hear we hired a detective?"

I glance at Ma.

"No, I didn't."

"We wanted to see if Adela had turned up somewhere else. Irma was still with us then." He pauses. "That detective couldn't find anything anywhere."

"I find it hard to believe she'd go somewhere else and hide out," I say. "It doesn't make sense. She had a son. She was close to her family."

"I agree. No money was ever taken out of her bank account before she disappeared and after. Could she have set aside money somewhere else? That's highly unlikely. But you never know." His head turns side to side. "As painful as it sounds, I would've preferred Adela was fed up enough to take off."

"Was she upset about anything?"

He takes a sip of coffee.

"Adela wasn't too happy we had a buyer for the store. You look surprised. We kept it a secret, which is nearly impossible in this town. It was a couple from Connecticut. They were going to pay top dollar. But after the bad publicity about Adela, they got cold feet. The deal fell through."

"That's too bad," my mother says.

Andrew nods.

"I think Adela was worried about getting another job. She didn't want to commute to the city. She never finished high school after she ran off with John Albright. She stayed back once in grade school, so she was a junior when she turned eighteen. She felt bad about not having that diploma. She mentioned taking the GED. It would've been tough for her to get anything decent without it. Irma and I told her we'd help her out if she wanted to start a business."

As I listen to Andrew, I note there's no emotion in this part of our conversation.

"Anyway, Jamie now has the store. He bought it from me. Of course, I gave him a good deal. It helps with Social Security. You sure don't make a lot of money running a general store."

"I can see how Adela would be upset about your selling the store but not enough for her to hurt herself," I say.

His head shakes a bit.

"When it comes down to it, I guess we only have a couple of options. It hasn't been easy coming to that conclusion. Do I believe my daughter is dead? In my heart, I do. Did she do it herself or was it somebody else? That I haven't figured out."

I read Ma's mind about my next question.

"Did your daughter own a gun?"

"No, I don't think so."

I glance at Ma. She stays quiet, her plan all along. But that answer eliminates one possibility. I seriously doubt someone would hike into the woods and down pills.

"Andrew, before we go any further, I have to know if you mind me doing this, asking questions, and snooping around."

"What if I say I would mind?"

The reporter in me wants to say, "Hell, I'd do it anyway."

But I can't.

Anyway, I believe Andrew is just testing me.

"Then I'd drop it."

He blinks.

"You know, it really bothered me the way the police treated this case. Even the staties came off as a bunch of dumb hicks. I remember telling one of them, 'how would you feel if this were your daughter?' He told me he was sorry. It was all he could do." He rubs his clean-shaven chin. "My answer is that you have my blessing. I will bring it up in the store's backroom, so that will get things rolling pretty fast."

"What about the rest of the family?"

"I already mentioned the possibility to Jamie. At first, he was against it, but he's okay with it now. I think he's afraid what you could find out about his sister."

"What about Dale?"

"I can talk with him."

"Thanks. I still have all of my notes, and there are papers I took with me when I left my job at the paper. I'm going to make a list of people to interview."

"You going to see Bobby Collins?"

I blow air.

"Not sure about that one. It might be tough."

"He was living here when it happened. He and Adela weren't on the best of terms. He'd be at the top of my list of suspects. I told the police that."

"My notes say he had an alibi," I tell him.

"That woman? He could've paid her off. It wouldn't have taken much."

I nod. He's talking about the Floozy.

"Andrew, could you tell my mother and me about that morning you went to Adela's house?"

He clears his throat as he sets down his mug.

"Adela always walked through the side door at 7:45. I could set my watch by her arrival." He pauses. "I waited five minutes, ten minutes, then I called her house phone. We didn't have cell phones back then. There was no answer. The machine didn't even pick up."

He shakes his head.

"I was a little bit annoyed since we had to open the store. I kept calling. I called Irma at home. Now I was getting a little worried. Irma was, too. She said she'd go to the store first thing. I remember her saying, 'This isn't like Adela. Maybe she's real sick. Why don't you check on her?' I don't know why I didn't tell her to stop at the house, but now I'm glad I didn't." He stops for a second. "So, I walked over. The first thing I noticed the garage door was open and her car wasn't there. I couldn't remember if she took it to Ed's garage to be fixed. Course, she could've stayed overnight somewhere else, you know, with somebody. Or maybe she went somewhere and was late getting back. Maybe she got a flat tire or her car broke down. All these thoughts went through my brain."

He takes a sip of his coffee.

"I was surprised to see her dog, Lucy, was inside. She wanted to go outside really bad so I figured Adela hadn't been here for a while. I called out loud, but Adela didn't answer. I went upstairs to her room. The bed was made. I went from room to room. Nothing. That's when I saw broken dishes on the kitchen floor. It was like someone took their dinner and smashed it on the floor." He sighs. "Then I found her purse on the kitchen counter. I looked inside. Nothing seemed missing.

The wallet had about sixty dollars." He whispers, "That was a bad sign."

I glance at my mother.

"What did you do next?"

"I called the store to see if somehow she might be there, but Irma said no. I asked if Adela said she had plans today and we just forgot. Irma said no. As I added things up, I started to feel a real panic coming on. Something wasn't right. I started calling people she knew like her brother. I called Ed's garage. He said Adela's car wasn't in the shop. Irma kept calling the house from the store. I just didn't know what to do." His head shakes side to side. "I had to get back to the store. Irma couldn't handle it all by herself. I called our daughter-in-law for help. Next was Chief Ben. He stopped on his way to work. But there wasn't anything he could do. He told me to notify the state police if she wasn't back by noon."

My mother's face is pinched. My heart feels the same way. Twenty-eight years later, Andrew hasn't gotten over those moments.

But all I could muster was, "Oh, Andrew."

"I ended up going back to the store. Irma was beside herself. I stayed behind the deli counter. I kept hoping and praying she would walk through the front door. I asked anyone and everyone if they'd seen her. Nobody. I even called Bobby Collins. That shows how desperate I was. He didn't have a clue." His voice caught. "The state police came. I could tell they weren't taking this seriously. I remembered when you called me. I was grateful you did. Thank you." His head keeps shaking no. "Irma and I dreaded Dale coming back on the bus. How do you tell a ten-year-old boy his mother is missing?" He sighed. "You just can't. It was one of the hardest things I've ever done. The little fellow cried and cried. I cried with him."

No one speaks for a minute. We just absorb his words.

"The days after weren't any better," he whispers. "And then those hunters found her car."

"Why do you think it was left on that logging road?" I ask.

"I walked that road after they found her car and looked around. I've been back many times. I couldn't find a thing."

"The police released her car to you. Was there anything inside that was unusual?"

Andrew hums.

"This may sound odd, but before I had it crushed, I put everything I found in a box. I still have it somewhere in the attic. When I find it, I'll call you. I have your number. Maybe you'll see something the rest of us missed."

"Please do," I say. "One more question for today, and then we'll go. Was Adela seeing anybody?"

"A man? Adela kept quiet about those things. She didn't enjoy all the gossip after she made mistakes with the two she married. When you work in the store, you hear so much of that. You try not to eavesdrop, but you can't help it. People really should be more careful what they say in a public place." His head swings back and forth. "I know Adela did go out with men. Sometimes she'd mention she was seeing somebody, but she always added it wasn't serious. Anyway, when your daughter gets to a certain age, you're on a need-to-know basis."

"Thank you for meeting with us, Andrew," I say. "Let me know when you find that box."

"I will." He presses his lips together. "Who are you going to talk with next?"

"I believe I'll try the old chief next. He's been retired a long time, but maybe he remembers something."

"I hope you get him on a good day. It's been hard on Sadie and the family."

"I heard about the Alzheimer's. But it might be easier for him to remember something that happened long ago than today."

"You're probably right about that." Andrew pauses. "You were a good reporter. I appreciated how you handled this story about my daughter. We all did. I'm also sorry about Sam. He was a great guy."

"That he was," I answer. "It'll be a year November 8."

Andrew clicks his tongue.

"Imagine that."

Old Farts

On Tuesday, I meet Ruth at the general store, where she is dropping off Sophie for the day. Normally, she brings the baby to my house, but she's going in the opposite direction, and this will save her time. I already have a car seat, a monstrous thing, permanently fixed to the back seat of my Subaru. Besides, I have other business to attend to here.

Sophie's wide-eyed and smiling when we make the transfer.

"I might be a little late," Ruth says.

I eye the bag she tosses onto the back seat.

"That's okay. It looks like you packed enough to hold her a while."

Ruth is off after a quick kiss. I'm still holding the baby. It's only seven, so the store isn't open although pickups and big-ass cars for the Old Farts already in the store's backroom are parked along the side of the road. I glance around.

"Oh, what the heck," I tell Sophie, keeping in mind Ruth doesn't want me to swear in front of the baby. She'd be pissed, ha.

I shut the car's back door with a swing of my hips and walk with Sophie toward the store. We don't lock our cars either, except when we go to the city. You've got to trust your neighbors. Besides, most of them have mutts, the best alarm system in the country. We haven't had a dog in years. After the last one died, I told Sam, no more. Dogs become too much a part of the family, and when they go, it's like losing family. I did ask Ma if she wanted a dog. So far, she says no, but it might be nice if I'm working nights and she's alone. It might make her feel safer. I'll have to bring it up again.

I hear the Old Farts yakking it up when I step inside the

side door and walk along the shelves holding canned goods, jars, and boxes. They go silent when they see me. I know every one of them, retirees with nothing better to do than get up early and drink coffee while they chew the fat in the store's backroom. There are six main Old Farts: the Fattest Old Fart, the Skinniest Old Fart, the Serious Old Fart, the Old Fart with Glasses, the Bald Old Fart, and the Silent Old Fart. Of course, they don't know that's what I call them.

There are others who drop in, the Visiting Old Farts, but these six are the Old Fart regulars. Then there are the blue-collar workers on their way to a job site. This is only a pit stop for them. Actually, two carpenters pass me on their way out. Sam's worked with both of them. They say their hellos and ask after me.

The Old Farts are likely the biggest gossipers in town, worse than any group of women, I wager. Sam told me they bring up a topic, say a touchy decision the board of selectmen made or a recent divorce in town, and weigh the details they know or suspect. They thrive on being the first to break the news. It's almost embarrassing how excited they get, Sam said. As a former reporter I can relate to the thrill of breaking news, but I had to attribute every fact. I used the word "alleged," which is unlikely in the Old Farts' vocabulary.

There are no females back here, except Sophie and me. They show up later in the morning, the women who drive school bus, or who are married to one of the Old Farts and have come to pick something up at the store.

"Isabel, what are you doing back here?" the Fattest Old Fart asks.

"I felt like bothering somebody today," I answer. "I don't get to do enough of that anymore."

The Old Farts laugh.

"No, really, why are you here?" the Bald Old Fart on the opposite bench says.

I sit on a bench beside the Fattest Old Fart. I unzip Sophie's snowsuit, so she doesn't get overheated.

"I wanted to see what I've been missing all these years," I say. "Go ahead. Don't let me stop you. This is my granddaughter by the way, Ruth's little girl. Her name's Sophie. Try not to swear in front of her. Ruth doesn't want her picking up any bad habits."

"Cute baby," the Serious Old Fart says.

I look around as if it's my first time here.

"Gee, this is awfully cozy back here. I'm an early riser, too. Might be a nice way to start the day, getting all the town news."

They glance at each other. I'm having fun pulling their legs. Actually, I'm supposed to meet Andrew Snow. He called last night to say he found the box containing the contents of Adela's car.

A few have guessed I'm teasing them. They snicker.

"So, what were you talking about when I came in?" I offer.

"About getting a vasectomy," the Skinniest Old Fart says just to see my reaction, I'm certain.

"I wouldn't think any of you would have to worry about that," I fire back.

More laughter.

"Nah, we're talking politics," the Fattest Old Fart says. "But while you're here, I've got a question for you. How's your detective work going?"

I glance around to see if Jamie Snow is within earshot. He's on my list of people to interview. I'll work up to it because he's a little on the sensitive side. But he is Adela's brother, and from what I recall, they were pretty close. I'm going to slowly reel in my answer. I don't want to offend Jamie, and I'm certain whatever I say inside here will get back to him anyways and who in the hell knows who else.

"You're talking about Adela, of course. I've just started. I'm going through my notes I kept back then, plus some records I have, and I've already talked with Andrew. I have a lot more to go. If any of you know anything that might be useful, give me a holler. My number is in the book. I would keep it confidential."

The Old Farts nod although I doubt if I'll get a call from any of them But then again, maybe it was one of the Old Farts who wasn't so old then who called me twenty-eight years ago to suggest looking at the permits for buildings and septic systems.

Last night, I printed a road map of Conwell off the Web and marked all the addresses where a new structure or addition went in, the same with the septic systems. I have it hanging on the wall in my office upstairs. I've also taped a map of Wilmot, photos I have of Adela and crime scenes like her house, the store, and where her car was found in the woods, just like I've seen in the cop shows and movies. I figure I can stare at the wall to see if it inspires a hunch. Her killer, if it comes to that, doesn't have to live in our town. But I've decided to exhaust my local options first before I go totally nuts on that idea.

"Heard you've got a job at the Rooster," the Fattest Old Fart asks as if he's the group's spokesman.

I get it. They want me to know they're keeping tabs on me like they do the rest of the town.

"You heard right," I quip. "I start Thursday. I think it'll work out fine, especially since my mother lives with me now. Do any of you have questions about my mother? I can set you straight about her if you do."

The Old Farts chuckle on cue.

"Go ahead," the Skinniest Old Fart says.

"My mother's name is Maria Ferreira. She's widowed and ninety-two. She worked for years in a school cafeteria. She likes to read and used to do a lot of art projects. Now she lives with me because she'd rather not live alone and the feeling is mutual. Besides, I have the space. Anything else you fellows want to know about my mother?"

"She's ninety-two? Really? She doesn't look it," the Bald Old Fart says.

Beside him, the Silent Old Fart nods. Maybe he talks when I'm not around, but I've never heard him utter a word.

"Uh-huh, people say that all the time."

Jamie Snow walks from the store into the backroom and stops when he sees me. He's the spitting image of his dad when Sam and I moved here. From what I can see, the men in the Snow family are short and thin-boned. Their hair goes white early. They have faces as craggy as New England rock. Adela clearly took after her mother's side of the family.

"Isabel, would you like some coffee?" Jamie asks.

"I'm fine, Jamie. I'm supposed to meet your father this morning. I was a little early. I figured it was warmer for the baby to wait inside here than my car."

Everybody's face swings my way. Now they know for sure I was taking them for a little ride.

Jamie nods.

"Well, here he is. Hey, Dad."

Andrew walks empty-handed into the backroom.

"Son. There you are, Isabel," he greets me. "These gentlemen weren't bothering you, were they?"

"I think it was the other way around, eh, fellows?"

There's a round of low laughs.

Then the Fattest Old Fart says, "By the way, the Daily Fart really stinks to high heaven now that you left it."

I zip Sophie's suit and get to my feet.

"That's sweet of you to say. See you guys."

I leave with Andrew, which I'm sure gets everybody's tongue wagging. Local news trumps national news any day.

"Were you waiting long?" he asks when we're outside.

"Just long enough to make those guys nervous I'm going to make a habit of it."

He chuckles.

I follow him to his car, which he parked behind mine. He lifts a cardboard box from the back seat.

"There's more in here than I remembered, but frankly, I don't know how useful any of it will be. Some of it's just trash, but I kept it anyway."

I nod. "We'll see about that."

Andrew stows the box in the back of the Subaru while I'm fixing Sophie into her seat.

"She's a real cutie," he says when he's done.

"Yes, she is. Thanks for the box. I'll return it to you when I'm done."

Andrew touches my arm and looks directly in my eyes.

"I know you're doing this out of the goodness of your

heart. I appreciate it. But I really hope you can see this through to the end. I want to know what happened to my daughter." He pulls a white handkerchief from his jacket pocket to wipe tears from his face. He mumbles, "Sorry."

"Don't be sorry." I pause. "When I was a girl, it happened to someone I knew. My cousin, Patsy, was a couple of years older than me. Someone took her when she was riding her bike." I shiver as I recall the feelings I had then. I glance at Sophie to calm me. "It's not the same, I know. But she, too, was suddenly gone. I believe you can understand how her parents felt, how I did. She and I were close. It hurt so much."

Andrew sniffs.

"Oh, Isabel, that's such a sad story." He takes a deep breath. "And they never found her?"

I feel the tears coming on, too.

"At first only her bike, but they found her remains when a wooded area was cleared for a subdivision years later," I tell him. "But they never caught whoever did that to her. They say most of the time it's somebody the victim knew. I hate to think that about my cousin. But I'm guessing it's true about Adela, too. I can't believe a stranger did this. Do you?"

We don't speak for a while. Sophie, good baby that she is, babbles in her car seat.

Andrew clears his throat.

"Isabel, I want to make you a business proposal. I'd like to hire you."

"Hire me?"

"I'll gladly pay you a thousand for the time you spend on my daughter's case. I could give you half now. I know it's not a lot…"

I feel myself smile again. I know I need to let him do this, and I welcome the gesture.

"Well, that would make me a full-fledged detective," I say. "If you don't mind, I prefer that we keep this arrangement between us. I don't want people getting the wrong idea."

"Certainly." He's smiling, too. "How about I write you a check now?"

"No, no, let me solve the case first."

The Box

I wait until Sophie takes a nap before I check the box's contents. Just to be on the safe side, I grab a pair of latex gloves although I suppose other people, including Andrew and the cops, oh maybe, touched this stuff when they went through the car. Still, I've watched enough crime shows to know this is proper procedure. I even have a pair for my mother, if she is so inclined to join me. I cover the kitchen table with a plastic sheet. Yeah, my kitchen isn't exactly the FBI's forensics department, but what the hell.

Andrew says he saved everything that was in the car, except the spare tire. The cops didn't take a thing, or so they said. Here's what I found: a black baseball cap; receipts; an ice scraper; the car's owner manual; a Rand McNally map book of the United States; newspapers; food wrappers; junk mail; one pearl earring; pantyhose with a large run; a pair of women's black dress shoes; leather gloves; coins; a dollar bill; a jack; and a tire iron.

I arrange them on the table.

Ma says behind me, "What's all of that?"

"It's the contents of Adela Collins' car."

"What's that man's cap doing there?"

I lift the black baseball cap. It's in a style that isn't adjustable, so it must be old. When I unfold the cap, I know it's large enough to even fit my gigantic head without my trying it on.

"It can't belong to her son, Dale. He was only ten when she disappeared. I don't think he's got a particularly large head either. He takes after the Snows with their little pinheads. And I've never seen Adela wear something like this. She was too ladylike for that."

64

"What about her ex-husband?"

"Nah. You saw him. He's got a regular-sized head."

"Well, that's something," Ma says.

"I agree. I'm going to go through the papers and write down info for each one, like the date and where it came from."

"Good idea."

I organize the receipts in chronological order. It appears the last time Adela cleaned out her car was a few months before she disappeared. July 9 is the date of the first receipt for gas from Cumby's, that's Cumberland Farms to you who don't live in New England. Actually most of the receipts are for gas stations, restaurants, or a store in the city. I write the info on a new yellow pad.

But then I find a receipt for a motel. It's called the Shady Grove, although its nickname was the Shady Grope, because it was rare anyone stayed there overnight. Just a few hours would be enough, maybe less under certain circumstances. The motel was located off the interstate until it got torn down twenty years ago, and a national chain built a four-story hotel in its place. Even if it were still there, it happened so long ago no one would remember what happened August 20, the date on the receipt. That's clearly a dead end. Still, what was Adela doing there?

The receipt says cash, so I don't know if Adela or somebody else paid for it. It was a Monday night. I have a calendar I printed off the web, which makes it easier to keep track.

I leave the newspapers for last. Of course, it's the Daily Star. They're folded neatly as if someone was going to stick them in a newspaper tube along the side of the road. I flip through the pages. I think maybe one or two people on staff then still work for the paper. The papers are from July, August, and the first weeks of September. My weekly column, Around the Hilltowns, is on the front of the B section. I hated the name, how mundane, but the managing editor then wasn't a person with a lot of imagination. At least, he didn't tell me what to write.

"Here, Ma, I used to write these when I was a reporter," I

tell her. "You might recognize some of the people I wrote about."

My mother starts laughing at the first one about two cousins who were the truck pull kings of the hilltowns.

"I bet these two go to the Rooster," she says.

"You win that bet."

It's fun to read these columns again. I recall how much fun I had writing them. In one column, I wrote about a woman who grew enough pumpkins, so the kids at the elementary school could carve jack-o'-lanterns when Halloween came around. Then there's one about people pilfering rock from stonewalls along the roads. I was starting then to get a feel for what community news was about and enjoying being the so-called hilltown expert for the Star.

I use my phone to snap photos of my columns, for the hell of it, and the front page of each edition. I shoot the receipt from the Shady Grope before I stick it in the plastic bag with the others. I take photos of everything, even the useless panty hose, before I return them to the box. I place the earring in a small bag and the money in another. I study the baseball cap, inside and out. If there were any hairs stuck to it, they're long gone. The wool on the brim is worn on the right side of the visor, likely from its owner's fingers. I go through the road map and owner's manual, but nothing is written inside.

Ma lingers.

I decide to change the subject a bit.

"You don't mind my taking money from Andrew Snow?"

"I think it's a good thing. It means he trusts you'll get him the answers he wants."

I lift the man's cap and search inside again. All I see are sweat stains. I sniff, but any smells are long gone.

"Well, as my partner, I'll be giving you a cut."

My mother laughs. "We'll be partners in crime, but on the good side."

"By the way, I told Andrew Snow about Patsy."

Ma sighs. We haven't spoken about Patsy at length in a long time. Make that a long, long time. "I can still hear my brother crying for her. It was awful."

"Yeah, I was only a kid, but I still remember what it was like. Maybe that's why I'm so interested in Adela." I pause. "What do you think happened to Patsy?"

"Something really bad. And whoever did it, got away with it," she says. "I'm glad you're doing this."

I replace the baseball cap.

"Hey, Ma, I was wondering if you'd like to have a dog. It could keep you company while I'm working."

She hums.

"I haven't had a dog in years. Let me think about it," she says.

I go upstairs to check on Sophie, who is still zonked out. I dial Andrew's number in my bedroom. He picks up right away.

"Well, I found a couple of interesting things in there," I tell him. "There's the hat, of course. No offense, but it looks larger than anyone in your family would wear. And I can't imagine Adela having one."

"I don't know who it could belong to."

"There weren't any loose hairs inside. Either the person was completely bald, but if that's true, he had a huge head. More likely, any hair fell out a long time ago."

Andrew hums as he thinks it over.

"You said you found something else."

"A receipt to a motel. The Shady Grove. It says cash."

"I see."

There's silence on the other end of the line. I feel awkward telling Andrew his daughter probably shacked up with some guy in a motel where you pay by the hour. Yeah, she was in her late thirties, but still.

"When do you want me to return this stuff?"

"There's no rush."

Thursday at the Rooster

I get to the Rooster at 4 p.m. sharp Thursday and park my car next to Jack's pickup. He's divvying up cash at the register when I step inside.

"Howdy, Isabel," he says as he shuts the register's drawer. "You can stow your stuff in the kitchen."

Eleanor is in the kitchen, cutting up onions for burgers. It's strictly burgers and fries on Thursdays and Sundays. The full menu is served Fridays and Saturdays. She wipes the tears from her eyes. I could ask her how she's doing, but I can already see. The fumes from the onions burn like hell.

"Hi, Eleanor, those are some strong onions," I tell her.

She nods and keeps wiping her eyes with the side of her hand. It probably doesn't help she's got onion juice on its skin.

"Yup," she gasps.

"Jack says to put my stuff back here. Oh, never mind, I see where."

I stuff my scarf and gloves in the sleeves of my coat, and then hang it and my purse on a hook between Eleanor and Jack's things. Jack is switching on the neon signs that advertise beer in the windows. He returns and reaches beneath the bar for a white apron.

"You'll want one of these," he says, giving it a toss. "That way the customers will know you're workin' and not drinkin' with 'em."

I smile. I like the way Jack puts it.

"Yeah, we wouldn't want to confuse them."

He tips his head.

"Come on over to the other side," he says.

I slip behind the bar with him. I take a look at what I would see from this vantage point, probably a lot of mischief after people start getting loose from their drink. Just like Andrew Snow said about eavesdropping in the store, I bet it happens here, too. I tended bar once at one of the failed restaurants when we were building our house. I learned about a bartender's ears then. You hear things, but whatever they are should stay at the bar.

"Okay, first thing I gotta show you are the lists," he says.

"The lists."

Two sheets of paper are taped behind the bar and beneath its overhang. Jack points.

"This one is for the people on probation. They did something to tick me off, so they get kicked out for six months. You can see I've written the date they can come back. But you only get two shots at being back in my good graces. Here, I have this list for people who just can't abide by the rules. They can never come in the joint even if their mother died and they're holding the wake here." He chuckles at the joke. "If they show up, and I'm here, I'll ask 'em to leave. If I'm not, and you're on alone, get one of the guys to back you up."

I study the lists as Jack talks. I recognize all the names. Most are men. One of them got caught selling dope in the parking lot. He's out permanently. So's the guy who came to the Rooster so drunk, he wiped out a couple of cars in the parking lot.

There are a few women, including one I witnessed going bonkers one night. She just kept getting drunk too fast and was awfully friendly with men in their pickups outside. She's on her second probation and due back next month.

"Sure enough," I say.

For the next forty minutes or so, Jack shows me where everything is, what costs what, and how to give Eleanor the food orders.

"Ya gotta give my sister some room," he tells me out of Eleanor's earshot. "She doesn't like anyone looking over her shoulder. She likes her space. It might spook her if you suddenly talk."

Jack has me practice using the tap, which only takes me a

69

couple of tries before I get it right. He says he'll change the keg since it's so heavy, and if he isn't around, the customers will have to drink from a bottle.

"It's a good idea to make a sweep of the tables to collect the empties. I'll probably handle that in the beginning. Or we can take turns. It can be tricky when a band's playing. You don't want to get knocked down, so you gotta have eyes in the back of your head." He kicks at a couple of cartons on the floor next to the beer cooler. "The empties go in here, and when it fills up, I'll show you where to bring it out back."

I understand about clearing the empties. Sam and I were in here one night when one of the guys on the out-forever list picked a fight and, yes, the weapon of choice was a broken beer bottle. I think the fight was over a bad car the victim sold to the beater. They were even cousins.

"Anything else?"

"Yeah, no tabs unless I say so." He grins. "Just be friendly to the customers. You'll do fine."

"Thanks for the vote of confidence."

Our first drinkers are a couple of regulars, stopping by after work before they head home for supper. Jack made a run to the store before it closed, so I'm going solo. Plumbers, they worked on a few jobs with Sam. I remember they came to Sam's funeral. So did a third of the town, which made me sad about losing him and happy they all cared, too.

"What are you doin' here?" one of the guys asks me, as they take the stools.

"Working," I say with a big smile. "What can I get you two guys?"

"A couple of Buds," one says.

"Really, you're gonna be tending bar?" the other says.

"Mostly on the weekends. Jack needs a little help. I could use a little money."

"Yeah, I heard about that."

The other one reaches into his back pocket for his wallet.

"I'll get this one," he tells the other. "Heard somethin' else. You really gonna find out what happened to Adela?"

"I'm gonna try. It's been a long time since it happened. But

70

I do have Andrew's blessing."

"So he told us. We were in the backroom."

The other guy shakes his head.

"Damn shame."

That's the way it goes all night, which is not as busy as a Friday or Saturday, but enough that there's a steady stream. It's the right night to break me in. The drinkers all ask what I'm doing. They tell me a story about Sam or if I wrote about one of their pals or family, or even them, they bring that up. Two people mention my mother. Of course, many know what I'm doing about Adela.

Sometimes Jack joins the drinkers at their table, and later after the kitchen closes, he drives Eleanor home. She shuffles behind the bar and says "yup" when I tell her I'll see her tomorrow.

The place clears out by ten. I clean up behind the bar, wiping down the counters and hauling a carton of empties out back. Jack brings full ones to load the coolers, so they'll be ready for a big Friday night. A band called the Lone Sums is playing. I'm not kidding. Yeah, all the best names have definitely been taken.

"Wanna cold one?" Jack asks. "You get one on the house."

I fold my apron and tuck it on a shelf beneath the countertop. His hand is on a tap. He remembers which kind of beer I like.

"Thanks."

I take a stool. Jack sits beside me.

"Did I hear right you're lookin' into Adela's case?" he asks.

"Yes, I am," I say into the glass before I take my first drink. "Andrew Snow says it's okay."

"I heard that, too," he says.

"Kinda hard to keep a secret in this town," I say.

"What do you think you'll find out?"

"I haven't a clue. You knew Adela well. Didn't you grow up here in town?"

"Yeah, we went to school all the way through. She was a year or two younger, but we hung around the same crowd until

71

she took off with John Albright. I never understood what she saw in him."

"I probably won't be able to solve this mystery. I mean it's been so long and people have died or moved away. But I want to try. If you can think of something, let me know."

We shoot the shit for a while, and after I finish my beer, I head home after Jack reminds me tomorrow will be a busy night. For the first time ever, I unlock the door when somebody is inside. I thought my mother would feel safer. She's watching TV with the kitten in her lap.

"Your clothes smell like hamburger grease," she tells me.

I sniff a sleeve.

"Yeah, I hang my coat in the kitchen."

"So, did anyone spill the beans tonight?"

I laugh.

"I believe it's a bit early. But it seems like the whole town knows what I'm doing. Andrew did a good job spreading the word. What are you watching?"

"An old movie with Gregory Peck. Wanna watch?"

"Oh, it's 'Roman Holiday' with Audrey Hepburn. I like this movie."

The Floozy

It's Friday night and I'm behind the bar, fetching Buds for two guys who want a fun night out. They order four because two women wait for them at a table. I flip the caps, toss them in the can at my feet, and slide the cold bottles across the countertop toward them. One of them has the dollar bills curled in his hand.

"Keep the change," he says.

"Thanks. Enjoy yourself.

They leave me an extra buck, which appears to be the standard tip for a round. I know Sam always did. I stuff the buck in the tip jar with the rest of the bills.

The Rooster is full. My station is behind the bar. Jack is on the floor, taking dinner orders and carrying the food out as fast as Eleanor can dish it out. She and I only spoke a few words. She grunts when I ask how she's doing. She grunts, too, after I ask about her dogs. I get the feeling she's not happy I'm working here, but that doesn't seem to be the case with Jack, who keeps up a friendly banter whenever he passes. Jack grins and winks. He's what I'd call a big tease.

I pop caps off beer bottles. The King of Beers reigns supreme at the Rooster. I've only had two requests for beer on tap by newcomers, of course, and I was pleased I got them done correctly.

I call home once to see how Ma is doing. She tells me she and the cat are fine. She's watching an old movie. I say I'll be home around eleven. I would tell her not to wait up, but that's not necessary.

The music started a half-hour ago and the Lone Sums are stinking up the place. I didn't think you could blow a song like "Sweet Home Alabama," but these guys are doing just that. Just wait until they try "Free Bird." Somebody always requests that one, usually one of the young drunks, who'll shout it from across the room just for the hell of it.

"These guys play here before?" I ask Jack when he brings a tray of empties behind the bar.

"Nah. I doubt if I'll bring 'em back," he says as he drops the bottles into the carton at our feet.

"They're pretty bad. But I guess if you drink enough you can dance to almost anything."

"You and Sam were quite the Rooster dancers."

"Yeah, we had a lot of fun here. Did you get all the empties or should I make a sweep?"

"We're okay. Keep pourin' beer and smilin'. The customers like it."

I do just that for a woman who stands in front of me. She went to school with my kids and asks about them. She wants a Bud Light. A woman waits behind her. I haven't seen the Floozy this close in years, but now that I work at the Rooster, I suppose I will. Her name is Marsha, if you recall. I remember when she used to be okay-looking with a decent figure she stuffed into tight jeans, with a bit of a muffin top above them, but she still turned heads among the guys looking for an easy lay. Now Marsha has racked up some serious country mileage. When she opens her mouth, I see gaps where she's lost teeth. Her dry, gray hair is pulled back in a ratty ponytail.

"Hey, Marsha, what can I get you?"

"Bud," she tells me.

I grab a bottle and flip the cap in one swipe. She fishes for bills inside her jeans' front pocket. I swipe the bar with a rag while I wait. She gives me the exact amount.

"Heard you're snoopin' around about Adela." She snorts. "She's no angel, you know."

"That so?" I weigh what next to say. "You knew her well?"

She takes a slug from the bottle.

"Well enough. Whatcha doin' that for?"

"No one knows what happened to her. I want to do this. The family said it's okay."

"You talk to Bobby?"

"Not yet, but I hope to," I say with semi-conviction. "I

understand he said he was with you all night."

"What's it to you?"

"Maybe you and me could have a talk some time."

Her face twists as she gives me an extra-hard stare.

"What for?"

"You lived in town then. Maybe you remember something you didn't tell anybody. It might help. Well, think about it."

"Bobby's not gonna like this at all."

"You still see him?"

"Yeah, I seen him."

"Enjoy your beer."

She scowls as she backs into the crowd. I don't have much time to think about our conversation. I'm too busy pouring beer and shots, plus the rare glass of house wine, which comes in a gallon jug, so it can't be too good. I help Jack clear tables.

Around 9:30, Eleanor comes from the kitchen, dressed in her coat and hat. She stands there waiting, I suppose, for Jack to notice she's ready to leave. She watches the crowd. I let her know Jack's unclogging the toilet in the men's room, but I can't tell from her face if she's really listening.

"You ready to go, Sis?" Jack asks when he's back. "Isabel, I'm gonna run Eleanor home. Think you can handle this crowd?"

"No sweat," I tell him.

Remembering Sam

Sunday the kids and I meet at Sam's grave. Ruth and her husband, Gregg, bring the baby. Matt and Alex come alone. They have girlfriends, but none so serious they would bring them to their father's gravesite, never mind dinner at my house. I told Ma she didn't have to come. It's colder than a witch's you-know-what and snowing lightly, just flurries really. Plus the ground is rather uneven.

She was okay with it.

Sam's ashes are buried in the highest section of the cemetery far away from the tall, tipping graves of the town's earliest families, those that date back a couple of centuries. His granite headstone says: "Samuel Long, husband, father, and a damn good carpenter." The owner at the memorial store in the city tried to talk me out of using the words "a damn good carpenter," well specifically, "damn."

"Mrs. Long, it is highly unusual to use that word," he told me. "What would people think?"

"That he was a damn good carpenter, which he was," I answered. "I already checked with the town's cemetery commissioner, and he said it was fine."

Actually, the commissioner laughed when I told him. He agreed Sam would like it, and it might start a colorful trend in Conwell. Besides, damn wasn't such a bad word considering what people say these days, and darn just isn't good enough.

"If that's what you want," the man at the memorial store said.

"Yes, it is."

I see smiles on the boys' faces when they read the words.

"Dad would like that," Matt says.

"Damn, eh?" Alex says. "They let you get away with that?"

76

"Yes, they did."

Ruth has already seen the stone. She came with me when it was being installed last month.

"Really, Mom," she said when she saw the writing on the headstone, but then she laughed. "Yeah, Dad would like it."

Sophie is awake in her arms. She's bundled up in a snowsuit and hat, so about all I can see are her blue eyes and pink, round cheeks. She smiles when I say her name.

Then we're quiet for a while. We're not the praying kind of family. The kids were raised without a religion, but I don't think it's hurt them any. We did teach them right from wrong, and to be nice to people. I can't say all churchgoers are that way.

The only sound around is a small animal moving through dried leaves, plus sniffling from the kids. Sam was proud of them. I am, too. Matt is a heavy equipment operator, a union guy, which shouldn't surprise anyone. As a boy, he was all-truck. He takes after my side of the family in looks. He's the only Portagee, I tell him. Alex is an engineer for an outfit in the valley. Smart kid. People find it easy to like him. Ruth, who works in finance, made a good marriage with Gregg. He's a physician's assistant with an open mind about alternative medicine. Sam and I approved. We had the wedding in our backyard.

I break the silence.

"Your Dad was one of the greats." I wipe away a tear. "I sure miss him, but when I look at you, I feel he's still here with me."

"I miss him, too," Matt says.

"Me, too," Alex says.

"I wish Sophie knew him," Ruth says.

Gregg pats his wife's shoulder, and I like him for it. Ruth was Sam's little princess all grown up. He would have done the same for Sophie.

"That would have been real nice," Gregg says.

The snow picks up although it hasn't started to stick. I'm guessing it's going to be a tough winter this year.

"Anybody wanna say something else?" I ask, but I only see

77

sad faces. "Okay, let's get back. Grandma's probably ready with the food."

We walk downhill to where we parked on the cemetery's semi-circular drive. On the way to my car, I pass a large stone for the Snow family. Smaller stones are placed around it. I didn't notice before that there's one for Adela Collins, but then again, I can't remember walking in this part of the cemetery. The last time I was here was when we buried Sam's urn in the ground. There's nothing in Adela's grave, but her family, likely her father, wanted people to remember her. Or maybe it's just holding a spot if her remains are ever found.

The kids are already in their vehicles and leaving. I stand in front of Adela's stone. There are no dates. It would have been odd to list the date she was declared officially dead, because it would have meant she lived seven more years than she probably did.

My eye catches something shiny on the headstone's pedestal. I stoop to take a closer look. It's a heart-shaped locket, gold or gold-plated, on a chain. Adela's name is engraved on one side. I remember Adela wearing it. Perhaps her son, Dale, or her father put it here. Maybe it was somebody else.

I get out my iPhone to snap a few shots of the necklace. I lift it by its chain to take a couple more before I return the locket to its spot. I pocket the phone.

Now I have another question to ask Andrew Snow. Was Adela wearing it the day she disappeared?

Then I think of something else. The town hires someone to mow the cemetery, actually it's the commissioner, who works as a landscaper but does this for the extra dough. He even uses a trimmer to get close to the stone. My guess at the length of the grass, he hasn't been back in a couple of months. I would think he would notice something like a locket beside Adela's headstone. Or maybe it wasn't there.

I get in my car. The kids must be wondering why I'm not right behind them. At the end of the road, Eleanor Smith stands on the corner with her three rangy mutts on leashes. I roll down the window on the passenger side. I'm trying to win her over.

"Out for a walk?" I ask Eleanor.

She shushes her dogs when they bark.

"Why you here?" she asks.

"The kids and I went to my husband, Sam's grave. It's the one-year anniversary today."

"Huh," she says before she walks along the side of my Subaru and up the road. I believe it connects with a dirt road that cuts over to the house she shares with Jack.

I can forgive Eleanor her odd manners. Part of it's her IQ. She also has lived a pretty isolated life, first working alongside her parents when they farmed. I hear she only went as far as eighth grade, and even then it was a struggle. She can read, but Jack told me to print the orders as neatly as possible. The Rooster is a busy place, but she's holed up there in the kitchen, where she likes it, I've discovered.

I watch Eleanor through the review mirror. She lets her mutts off their leash, and they bound up the road toward the cemetery. They know where they're going. I'm going to ask her the dogs' names the next time. Maybe that'll break the ice between us.

I'm the last one home.

"Gee, Ma, what were you looking at up there?" Alex asks me.

"Someone left a necklace on Adela Collins' stone. It had her name on it. Curious, don't you think?"

He chuckles.

"Yeah, Ruth told me about your snooping around."

"Snooping? I think of it as research. Besides, it's all for a good cause. Besides, your grandmother is helping me."

The kids and Gregg stare at Ma.

"Really?" Matt says for all of them.

Ma smiles.

"Somebody left a necklace?" she asks.

"Yeah, I put it back. I wouldn't want to upset her son or father if they left it there although I don't think Andrew would do something like that. I did take photos with my phone. What do you think, Ma?"

"I think we should eat," she says.

Now that the seriousness is over, we get into the food and kidding each other, a Long family pastime. Ma, who sits at the opposite end of the table, is in her glory. Sam built the table out of some black walnut boards he salvaged from a job. The woman said to toss them out, but Sam saw their worth. Didn't I tell you he was a damn good carpenter?

We're having roasted chicken with the fixings. Ma knows how to cook a bird better than anybody I know. She even made stuffing and mashed potatoes. I took care of the salad and the dessert, carrot cake, Sam's favorite. The guys have beer. Ruth and I drink wine, and we even manage to talk my mother into a small glass. The baby, Sophie, is taking a nap upstairs.

The conversation begins with the food, how good my mother made it, then onto Sam, but what more can we say, except we miss him. The boys, they'll always be boys to me, laugh again about what I put on their father's headstone. I catch Gregg grinning. No wonder Sam liked him. Ruth rolls her eyes. She's supposed to do that. Ruth is the most conservative of the family although she'd never vote Republican. My daughter is smarter than that. When I look across the table at my kids talking with my mother, making her laugh, I am happier. Sam and I did all right with them.

We are into dessert when I make an announcement.

"I want to hike the logging road where they found Adela's car. But I don't want to walk alone. Would one of you boys go with me?"

"When?" Matt says.

"Well, you all have to work, so how about next weekend? Let's make it Sunday. It's only bow season still, but I don't wanna get nailed by some yahoo's arrow."

"I can," Matt nods at his brother. "You have something better to do?"

"I'll go, too, if you want," Alex says.

"I should warn you, I'm gonna cross the river. That's about three miles in."

"What's there?" Alex says.

"Maybe nothing, but I want to see what's on the other side.

Dad didn't want to go that far. Bring your boots."

Later, after the kids leave, I think as I wash the pans. Of course, that locket's on my mind. I am debating with myself, not much of a contest there, about whether I should've taken the necklace with me. I did only handle the chain, but maybe there would be fingerprints on the medallion. I shake my head. Who would check the prints? I'm not a cop. Besides, suppose it came from someone who didn't have a record? Crimes are never solved as easily as the ones I see on the television shows or movies.

The last pan is in its proper place. I dry my hands. I get the phone from my bag.

Ma is watching the Patriots, of course. The kitten has found her lap.

"Hey, Ma, wanna see the locket?"

"I thought you said you didn't take it."

"No, I shot pictures with my phone." I bring up the image and show it to her. "Here."

My mother studies the screen.

"I see the necklace belonged to her. Who could have left it there?"

"That's what I want to figure out."

More of the Old Farts

I'm supposed to meet Andrew at the store although I was vague over the phone last night because I don't want to get his hopes up.

Once again, I'm doing the Sophie exchange. It's early as usual, but Ruth is running late, so there's only enough time to grab the baby and her things. I eye Ruth's car as it turns the corner then the store. Andrew's car isn't here.

"Come on, kiddo, let's give those old, uh, men another scare," I say.

I don't believe the Old Farts are scared one bit when I appear in the backroom. I see a few jabbing elbows and amused smiles.

"Well, well, well, look who the cat dragged in," the Serious Old Fart announces. "Can't get enough of us, eh, Isabel?"

"Guess not."

I squeeze in next to the Fattest Old Fart. Sophie is wide-eyed as she studies the men. It's a full house this morning with every type of Old Fart present, including the Visiting Old Farts.

"I heard you did okay on your first weekend at the Rooster and managed not to spill any beer," the Skinniest Old Fart says.

Of course, there is a chorus of chuckles. These Old Farts think they're the funniest men in the world, well, except for the Silent Old Fart who never says anything.

"Hmm, sounds like you have a spy at the Rooster. You fellows seem to be paying a lot of attention to what I've been up to lately."

"Lately," the Bald Old Fart says with a chuckle. "You've always been on our radar."

I smile, thinking that's probably true, first when Sam and I moved here, and then when I started working for the paper and when I stopped.

"Heard you and Andrew had a sit-down." The Fattest Old Fart beams at his cronies as if he's breaking the news.

"Yes, we did, but I'd rather keep what we said between us," I say.

"Fair enough," he says. "So, what was in the box he gave you?"

Shoot, those guys must've been watching Andrew and me through the window that morning.

"Wouldn't you all like to know?"

"Sure do," a Visiting Old Fart says.

All of their heads bounce as if they're rigged with string.

I laugh.

"Well, that ain't gonna happen."

I stand when I hear the side door open and Andrew steps inside. Everyone quiets down when he stands beside me. He smiles at Sophie.

"Hmmm, you fellows talking about me?" he asks.

"What do you think?" I answer for them. "I'll tell you outside. See ya, uh, fellows."

From the back, the Old Fart with Glasses, says, "Heard you were all up at Sam's grave yesterday. Hard to believe it's been a year."

Their faces have lost all merriment.

"Thanks for remembering."

Andrew follows Sophie and me to the car. While I wrestle her into her car seat, Andrew admits he told the Old Farts about meeting with me.

"Uh-huh, they brought it up. They also saw you giving me the box," I say. "Don't worry. I didn't tell them a thing although they were dying for something. We have to watch those guys."

Andrew nods.

"So, why did you want to see me?"

"I have something I wanna show you."

He's got a wondering look on his face.

"Yes?"

"When the kids and I were up at the cemetery yesterday, I saw the headstone for Adela in the family plot."

"Well... "

"I thought it was a lovely gesture." I keep pausing like an old Yankee lawn mower. "I also saw a gold necklace someone left on its pedestal. It had her name engraved on it."

"Her mother gave her one like that for Christmas."

"Here. I took some photos." I remove the phone from my bag. "Did you or one of the family leave it? It doesn't look like it's been there too long."

Andrew shakes his head as he studies the screen. I flip slowly through the shots I took.

"No, that's impossible," he whispers. "Adela was wearing it the last time I saw her. She never took it off. She loved that necklace. She used to joke she'd be buried in it."

Now this is unexpected. Andrew's eyes are wet with tears. He chokes on half the words he says. I don't know how much harder to push, but I get the feeling this is an important discovery.

"You're sure?"

"Positive. The ring holding the necklace's clasp opened up that day, and I fixed it for her in the backroom with a pair of pliers." His voice breaks when he says, "Adela told me, 'it's as good as new, Pa,' after she put it on. We didn't find it in her bedroom. We looked because Irma asked."

"Andrew, I'm so sorry."

His chin was up.

"No, this is good news in a way," he says. "Somebody might have a guilty conscience. Keep up the good detective work."

84

A Phone Call from Andrew

Ma says, "I think Sophie's awake. Hear her?"

I head upstairs. Sophie's babbling away and kicking her feet loose from her blankets.

"Hey, there, sweetie. Time for a change."

I'm just finished getting the baby clean when the phone rings. I let Ma get it.

"It's for you," she calls from downstairs.

I hold onto Sophie as I take the phone upstairs.

"Thanks, I've got it, Ma," I say into the receiver. "Hello."

"Isabel, this is Andrew Snow." His voice is shaky. "I went up to the cemetery." He takes a stuttering breath. "The necklace wasn't there."

"It wasn't?"

"I looked all around the stone. It's definitely gone." He pauses. "I called the cemetery commissioner. He says he saw the necklace when he was getting a grave ready. That was in late September. He figured one of us left it on her anniversary. I did ask if he took it, and he said no. He says he doesn't touch anything anyone leaves."

"Shoot, I'm real glad I shot those photos. Now I wish I'd taken that necklace."

"You didn't know."

"Next time, if there's something like that, I'm snagging it."

Sophie starts squirming in my arms and making noise she wants to eat.

"Andrew, I've gotta go. I'll call you when I'm done," I say. "I'm sorry about the necklace. Maybe some kids hanging around there took it."

"Maybe, but I doubt it. At least we have those photos. That's something, right?"

Chief Ben Hendricks

I have my list of people to interview. Benjamin Hendricks, who was police chief when Adela disappeared, is the first. He was the chief before Sam and I moved here, and for at least a decade later.

Being chief is a part-time job for token pay in Conwell and the hilltowns around it. Chief Ben, as he is still called, and the other officers on the force, all part-timers, went to traffic accidents, the occasional break-in, and the more frequent wife beaters and drunk drivers, after the law made cops in general take those cases more seriously. When he wasn't a cop, Chief Ben worked at a plant in one of the nearby cities. He was a decent guy, who would take my phone calls when I was a reporter and an editor although I suspected like everyone else, he wasn't all there toward the end. It took some persuading to get him to step down. The town even held a big party for him, with the usual plaques, certificates, and gag gifts. I came off the bench and wrote a story about him. That and the photo I took ran low on the front page after I did a little arm-twisting with the then-managing editor.

So, who else is on my list? For family members, I have Jamie, and his ex-wife, Clara. His current wife didn't live in Conwell then. There's Adela's son, Dale. That might be tricky, but if he's a regular at the Rooster, I might have a better shot after I've worked there a little while. I should talk with her ex, Bobby Collins, but that will be even trickier. Maybe I'll try the Floozy. I can find her at the Rooster, too.

But the old chief is first. I'm seeing him in an hour. His wife says he's at his best during the day. She is sympathetic when I call. I tell her why I want to see him. She sighs and says, "Oh, that. I heard. You do know my Ben isn't the same.

But it looks like today might be an okay day."

"Just so you know, I spoke to Andrew first and he gave his blessing," I tell her.

I feel sorry for his wife. Sadie's what I'd call a real nice lady, rather old-fashioned, wears an apron and slippers when she works around the house. I don't know if I've ever seen her in pants. She's a native. Her family was one of the originals in Conwell. My in with her is that I covered the 4-H when I was a reporter and the time I did a story about her brother's truck farm. She told me she liked my farewell piece for her Ben.

"You going now to see the old chief?" my mother asks me when I get my coat from the front closet.

The kitten, Roxanne, is on her lap as she works on the crossword puzzle from yesterday's paper. Ma's not coming along for this one. We both agree it might confuse the chief.

"Yeah, it shouldn't take too long." I zip my jacket. "Hey, I saw you finished all of those novels. How about we go to the library to get more? The library's open today. It's easy to remember. The days the dump is open, so's the library. You can drive this time. The roads are clear."

"Thanks, I'd like that."

Chief Ben sits in an easy chair in the living room. I am guessing it's his chair. My Dad had one, too. He squints when his wife, Sadie, introduces me. There is a bit of recognition in his eyes when she tells him my name. Maybe he remembers the Isabel Long who used to have dark brown hair.

"You," he says.

I take a spot on the couch closest to him. Sadie sits in her chair, but on the edge as if she's on the verge of doing something else. She's wearing an apron.

"I won't take up a lot of your time, but I wanted to ask you about Adela Collins," I say.

His head falls back against the chair.

"Adela," he says. "That was real sad."

"Yes, it was. I know it was a while ago, but I was wondering if you had any ideas about what happened to her."

"She's gone."

"That's right."

"It was real sudden like."

"Uh-huh."

"Andrew Snow called you to the house when he couldn't find her."

The man drifts off a bit. I saw it with my late uncle, my mother's brother, who had dementia. His was alcohol-related. Then he had a stroke. Anyways, we visited him at the rest home. Sometimes I just had to wait for him to make a circle back to my question. I wait for the chief to do the same.

His wife helps me out.

"Remember what you told me about that day?" Sadie says.

"It was a sad day. We couldn't find her."

I can see I'm not going to get anywhere with the old chief. He's too far gone or maybe it's just a bad day. He stares out the window as if he's forgotten I'm here, and he probably has. He watches the chickadees peck at the feeder.

I turn toward Sadie. She has one hand in the other. I am sure they have done their share of wringing these days.

"I think I'll go now," I say softly. Sadie nods before I turn toward her husband. "Chief, it was nice seeing you."

He doesn't look my way.

Sadie apologizes as she walks with me to the kitchen.

"He's just not the same anymore," she says.

"I understand."

"I do remember that day well. Like my Ben says, it was a sad day. He talked about it when he came home later, after he called the state police. Ben never talked about police business, but he did this time. What concerned him were all the smashed dishes on the kitchen floor. It seemed somebody was really angry to do that." She presses her lips together. "I wish I remembered more about what he said."

This is the second time I've heard about the dishes. The first was from Andrew. But the chief thought the person who threw them to the floor was angry about something. It wasn't just an accident.

"That was helpful," I tell Sadie. "If you or the chief recall anything else, please give me a call. I'm in the book."

"I will."

I'm walking toward the door when I think of something else. The Hendricks' home was the ersatz police station for many years.

"Do you think the chief could have written down anything? Maybe he held onto it," I say.

"No one's touched his desk for a long, long time," she says. "I could look."

"Thank you. I agree with the chief. It was a sad day because Adela was a really nice person. That's why I'm doing this."

Sadie Hendricks nods.

The Library

The Conwell Public Library is small, one room to be exact. It has a second floor and basement, but they stopped using them because of the state's handicapped-accessible laws. The town couldn't afford to put in an elevator, so it was easier just to jam all the stacks into the one room. No one needs cards, just a number, although now there is a computer to record what people take out. Ma was surprised at the arrangement. Since she lives with me, I vouched for her.

Mira Clark, the librarian, is good about stocking books the regulars want. For a while, I was into Hollywood bios, a particular weakness of mine, until I had enough. Ma likes her mysteries and steamy romance novels. There are plenty of those, and Mira vowed last time we were here, on Saturday, to get more.

"Back so soon?" Mira greets us.

I place a stack of books on the counter.

"My mother's a fast reader," I tell her.

Ma smiles as she goes to the stacks.

"I hear you're looking into Adela's case," Mira says, and then I remember they were close friends going way back, likely to their childhood.

"News travels fast," I say, glad I have Andrew's blessing.

Her head twists around as if she doesn't want anyone to hear what she's going to say next. The library has a few people perusing the stacks. I noticed their cars outside.

"I bet there are some in town who won't like it," she says. "You know, leave well enough alone and all of that. But this is different. We used to be real close, and I just know something bad happened to her."

I nod. I want to know Mira's theory, but like her, I don't

want anyone else to overhear us.

"I'll do my best. By the way, where do you keep the old town reports?"

She thinks a bit.

"They're in that back corner," she says.

"Thanks. It's just for my research."

I head to the corner. The reports fill the bottom two shelves. Every year, Conwell, like other towns and cities in Massachusetts, issues a formal report about the past one. It details the budget, what articles passed or didn't pass at the official town meetings, and reports from each department. For the past ten years, I've written the dedication on the front, typically for someone of note who died that year. Sometimes there's been more than one person to honor. I tried to make the tributes as sweet as possible even for the sons-of-bitches who gave me a hard time when I was a reporter or were a general pain in the ass to everyone else in town. I make them almost walk on water in those dedications. It might have been fun writing about them as they really were, but I wouldn't want to be run out of town.

But I'm not interested in any of those. I am looking for the town report for the year before Adela disappeared, specifically the list of building and septic system permits issued. I'm remembering that deep throat phone call someone made to me a few weeks after Adela was gone telling me to check who was putting in a foundation or septic system around that time. After all, it would take a mighty big hole to dump a body. Either a cellar hole or septic system would work. Plus there was no way of finding that body once that hole had a foundation or a septic system's holding tanks.

I find the report I need. I don't have time to read it and I can't take it out, so I use my cell phone to snap photos of each page, and then replace the book. What I would have given as a reporter to be able to take a photo of what I wanted to use later. In those days, I had to write everything down longhand or use the copy machine.

I search for another town report. It was for the year after Adela was declared officially dead. That year's report was dedicated in her memory. Someone other than me wrote a bare-bones piece about her. It didn't even mention the date of her death, except "her family, friends, and town lost her seven years ago," which was a rather nice way to put it. What the heck, I snap a shot of that one, too.

I find Ma at the stack with the sign: NEW BOOKS. She clutches three. That will likely hold her until Saturday, when the library is open again, the same as the dump, although we won't need to go there for a couple of weeks. Two women don't generate much trash or recyclables. Besides, I've got a compost heap brewing in the backyard.

Mira logs the books Ma is borrowing into the computer.

"Did you find what you wanted back there?" Mira asks without looking up from her work.

"Uh-huh, the town reports were just where you said they'd be."

"You find some clues?"

"Too soon to tell. I took photos of the pages. I'm just following a lead someone gave me a long time ago."

Mira hands the books to my mother.

"Here you go, Mrs. Ferreira," she says smiling, and then she turns to me. "Isabel, let me know if you want to talk."

I get the feeling she wants to tell me something but not here in the library.

"Be glad to," I say. "I'll give you a call soon."

"You do that."

Outside, I slow my pace to match my mother's. I'm a fast walker. Snow has started to fall since we were inside.

"The weather guy says the hilltowns might get a couple of inches," Ma tells me.

I smile. As I said, I stopped paying attention to the weather because I no longer have to drive into the city, but I'm glad my mother does. Maybe now that I'll be working nights, I should do it again, but I've got my Subaru, and it's a helluva short ride.

"You sure you have enough books?" I joke.

By the time we get home, the snow is coming down at a good clip. I get a fire going in the woodstove and head upstairs to my office to print out what I found in the town report. Ma tells me she's in the mood for chicken stew, Portuguese-style, of course, so I'll help her with that later.

As I watch the paper chug through the printer, I think back to the late eighties. I was still a reporter then for the Daily Fart. Truthfully, I've grown fond of the name my buddies in the store's backroom call it. The economy was beginning to recover although bad times take their sweet time getting to and leaving the hilltowns. Still, there was some construction happening back then.

We had lived here long enough that Sam had work. When we first moved to Conwell, we struggled. People tend to circle the wagons when it comes to jobs during tough times. But Sam had skills a lot of the guys here don't have. They're more of your slam-bam-thank-you-ma'am breed of carpenters. Those guys could get a building up all right, but if you wanted a sweet staircase or cabinetry, you called Sam. He was a perfectionist, and one who always undercharged his customers. Anyone who hired Sam got 150 percent from the guy.

Among the building permits, I see renovations, additions, and a couple of new homes, including ours. We never owned a house until we moved here. We didn't have a pot to piss in for many years. But we managed to buy a small piece of land, which the bank let us use as collateral for a construction loan. The bank didn't give us much money, but lots of guys, who had worked alongside Sam and knew our situation, volunteered their labor on the weekends. I did a coffee run in the morning and made lunch. I also bought a case of beer for after work. I think it kept them coming back.

I see newcomers pulled most of the permits. They were the only ones with money then. Bobby Collins didn't get a permit. I see Jack Smith's sister, Eleanor, had an addition built on her side of their house. Her brother pulled the permit for her, it seems. It must be for the sun porch, which has lots of glass. When I drive that way, I frequently see her walking beside the road with her big mutts. She's got them on leashes, so they look as if they are towing her along. They're the usual hilltown mutts with a lot of German shepherd in them, so they bark like crazy whenever something or somebody upsets their peace.

As for septic permits, I see we got one. There was a slew of permits in one part of town, where a bunch of systems failed.

But nothing stands out.

Deep Throat

The home phone rings when I'm halfway through my second cup of coffee. Ma and I are going into the city this morning, and I will need extra fortification. We are looking for a dog at the shelter, the same place we got the kitten, Roxanne. Marigold, our cat of a dozen years, hasn't been in the grave a month, and we will have two new pets. Ma told me last night she would like a dog after all. I know I'd feel better when I leave her home at night while I tend bar at the Rooster. We both agree we want a female, a likable breed, and she must not have any puppy left in her.

"Isabel?"

The voice is gruff on the other end of the line. It's definitely a man, but he's clearly trying to disguise his voice. His ploy works. He could be anybody who knows me.

"This is Isabel."

"Did you look into those permits like I told you before?"

Now I know it's the same guy who called me after Adela went missing twenty-eight years ago. No one else has brought up that topic. Besides, he's calling me on my landline. The number is in the phone book. I don't give out my cell phone number to just anybody.

"I am. I found them in the town reports and made a map. I'm going to check each one."

"Okay."

He hangs up.

News travels awfully fast in Conwell. Surely, lots of people have heard what I'm doing, but then again, I did ask the Old Farts in the backroom of the store to give me a call if they had something worth telling. I bet one of them is my anonymous caller.

Ma glances up from her crossword puzzle.

"That was quick. Who was it?"

"Just somebody with an anonymous tip. You know that map I have upstairs where I marked who got a building or a septic system permit around the time Adela disappeared?"

"Yes, somebody thinks it could have something to do with her?"

"I suppose this man, whoever he is, thinks she could be buried under somebody's house or septic tank."

"Would that be hard to do?"

"It would have to be somebody who has access to heavy equipment and did it himself."

"I see."

"But it would be hard to get anyone to dig up under their house or tank to prove me wrong. I'd need evidence."

"Or a confession."

"Confession, right. You might like to know that's about the time Sam and I built this house."

"So, you could be a suspect?"

"Very funny, Ma. We put in the cellar hole in June and the septic system sometime in the middle of summer. That's before Adela disappeared. Besides, we didn't have any motivation." I carry my mug to the kitchen sink. "You ready to go anytime soon?"

"Let me get my things."

Mira the Librarian

We didn't find a mutt we like at the shelter, a bit of a disappointment, but then when I ask around, I hear Mira Clark, the town's librarian, has a dog that belonged to her aunt, who moved into a rest home. The place doesn't allow dogs although, personally, I think it would be a great idea to allow the seniors to bring their pets with them. It'd make them feel more restful, but, hey, I don't make the rules.

I figure I can kill three birds with one stone if my aim is true. I'm bringing Ma with me to see if she likes the dog. I hear she's mostly a black Lab, a people-pleasing breed from my experience, and about three, so she definitely has no puppy left in her, but she'd have a long life with us. She's spayed and housebroken. And she's used to being around old people, kids, and cats. Her name is Maggie, which I can live with. I'm hoping she's a winner.

Then, two, I'm thinking Mira and I can have our talk about Adela, who was her best friend way back then, and Ma can listen. Maybe my sharp-eared ninety-two-year-old mother will hear something I miss. That's three.

Mira and her schoolteacher hubby, Bruce, live on the south end of town, in a village beside the river. Long ago, the river's waters powered a sawmill here. The village has its own church, but it's only used once a year in the summer, more of a tradition than a religious thing, and for weddings and funerals. A couple of buildings look like they might have had businesses at one time when people didn't leave the village very often, and if they did, probably by a horse-pulled carriage.

"Come in, come in," Mira greets us at the side door. "How are you, Mrs. Ferreira?"

We follow her into the living room. Have a seat, she tells us, while she gets the dog.

I like Maggie right away. I can tell my mother feels the same. The dog comes right up to her for a pat. Ma gives me a nod.

"Looks like you're going to have a lot of company," I tell her.

"So, you'll take her?" Mira asks.

"I think she'll do just fine at our house," I say. "Right, Ma?"

The dog hasn't left her side. Maggie's not interested in me, which seems to be the story of my life with the animals that live with us.

"Uh-huh, I like her. Could we have her?" Ma asks.

Mira sits back in her easy chair. A good host, she asks if she can get us something besides the dog and her things, but Ma and I say we're just fine. I can tell Mira is relieved this is one problem solved. She told me on the phone she and her husband, Bruce, already have two dogs. Three would be too much. And her aunt, who I know, of course, will feel better Maggie is going to a local home. She didn't want her dumped at a shelter.

"How's your investigation going?" Mira asks.

"I'm still gathering bits and pieces. Didn't you say you and Adela used to be tight?"

"Yeah, at one time. Long ago. We used to be best friends since kindergarten. Course, we didn't spend too much time together after we both got married. I mean Adela's second marriage. Bruce couldn't stand Bobby Collins. Neither could I. He's such an asshole." She glances toward my mother. "Sorry, Mrs. Ferreira."

"In what way?" I ask.

"He was usually drunk for one and had a hard time holding onto a job. I know he hit her. I saw the bruises."

"Why did she marry him?"

"The usual reason. She got pregnant. Course, when they were going out, he was a lot nicer. But he turned out to be one lousy husband. She supported them mostly working at the store."

"How many years were they married?"

"Five, maybe six years. She really tried to make it work for Dale's sake."

I'm weighing my next question. Oh, what the hell.

"Do you think Bobby could be responsible for Adela's death?"

Mira's mouth puckers as she mulls over that question.

"Most everybody thought he had something to do with Adela's disappearance. They even thought he might've killed her then dumped her body somewhere. Leaving her car in the middle of that logging road was something he would've done. But… "

"He had an alibi that night."

"Some alibi." Mira glances at my mother. "Marsha. You know her right?"

"My mother doesn't, but she was in the Rooster the other night. She gave me the evil eye."

Mira laughs.

"I can imagine."

I have my next topic.

"Did Adela have any serious relationships?"

Her lips pucker again.

"She swore to me she'd never marry again after she divorced Bobby. Course, that didn't stop her from dating married men."

What? This was news to me. But then again, the pickings are slim for available men in the hilltowns. Maybe it was worse then, or it was easier to hide, except for the gossipers in the store's backroom, yes, an earlier version of the Old Farts although I bet they kept any comments about Adela Collins to a minimum in case her father or brother caught them. I've never heard of people being banned from the store, like Jack does at the Rooster, but the possibility of that happening would be a deterrent.

Every winter, Conwell has a noticeable purge of a few marriages and hookups. I guess the darkness and cold drive them to it, or like my mother would say, the hanky-panky.

99

"I didn't hear that one before," I tell Mira.

Mira snorts.

"Adela seemed so sweet and innocent at the store. But there was another side to her."

"Did she have an affair with Bruce?"

Crap, the words are out of my mouth before my good sense catches up with me. I expect Mira will ask us to leave. Maybe she won't let us take Maggie, who now has her head in my mother's lap. But I could tell Mira was dancing around something.

"Yeah." She pauses. "It didn't last too long. It happened at a rocky point in our marriage, but Bruce came clean. I was really hurt. I forgave him but not her. It meant I couldn't be friends with Adela anymore."

"That must've been hard."

"Yeah, it was, and I'd appreciate you not telling anybody about this. It happened a long time ago. I know what you're going to ask next. It was two years before Adela was gone."

"I promise," I say. "Can you think of anyone she could've been seeing that summer?"

"Like I say, we lost touch."

I nod. "Now, I'm going to tell you something I want you to keep a secret. Andrew gave me the box of stuff that had been in Adela's car. Inside there was a receipt to the Shady Grove Motel not long before she disappeared."

"The Shady Grope, eh?" Her head tips back, so it rests on the chair. "I wish I could tell you. But after she pulled that stunt with Bruce, I didn't have much to do with her. Course, I had to see her at the store. We never talked about Bruce."

"Thanks, Mira. You've been a help."

"I have?"

"Yes, I'm getting a better picture of Adela." I nod at Ma. "And we got ourselves a dog."

Later, the dog curls in the back seat as I drive my mother home.

"That was quite a story she told us," she says.

"It was. Do you think it was enough for her to kill Adela?"

"Maybe there was more to the story than she told."

"Like Adela got pregnant then had an abortion or a miscarriage?"

"It could've happened that way."

"Or maybe Mira was exaggerating. Maybe Bruce was the only one."

"That, too."

I hit the turn signal for our driveway and make the turn.

"So, I think I'm going to move Mira from the source list to the suspect list although she's a big maybe. She might have a motive, but I'm wondering how she could have hidden the body. There were no permits at her house."

"What about that husband of hers?"

"Hmmm, I hadn't thought of that. He's a schoolteacher, kinda soft and quiet, but who knows? See? That's why I wanted you to come." I park the car. "Did you see the new chart I've got going in my office?"

Ma smiles as she nods.

"And we got a good dog out of it."

Bar Keep

I carry a tray of beers to a table at the Rooster while trying to stay clear of the drunken dancers. I have a close call one time, but dodge out of the way before we have a catastrophe. This band is called the Potholes. What did I say about all the best names being taken?

Even Jack makes a comment.

"It's gonna be a bumpy night," he tells me with a grin.

"Maybe they mean the other kind of pot," I say.

He takes a look at the musicians, strictly redneck, and chuckles.

"Could be."

The band's repertoire is a crowd favorite at the Rooster: Country and Western, a bit of rock, and less blues. Yes, they know the local anthems, "Sweet Home Alabama" and "Free Bird." Yup, Lynyrd Skynyrd is big here at the Rooster. The Potholes' lead singer has a voice that carries decently across the crowded room. She's hitting the high notes well. It's not often the bands that play here have a woman singer. I'm a little concerned though about the drummer, who's been tossing back shots. He might not make it through the night.

I get the beers to the table unscathed. The drinkers are fans of the band, which is making its Rooster debut. The fans chose the table closest to the side door, which shows they've never been here before because they get a blast of cold air each time somebody steps outside for a smoke or back inside after they're done. The weather has been mostly dry and cold lately although that's going to change Sunday night when a Nor'easter is supposed to hit. The prediction is up to a foot here in the hilltowns. The storm is the main topic of conversation tonight at the Rooster. I bet the rednecks in

Conwell and beyond have their snowmobiles tuned up and ready to ride. I think about the hike the boys and I plan Sunday morning. Our timing is good.

We're past serving food tonight. Eleanor has finished cleaning the kitchen. She stands in the doorway between her domain and the bar. She's got a pouty lower lip as she searches for her brother, who's at a corner table trying to head off some potential trouble with a guy celebrating his twenty-first birthday. Jack is quizzing his buddies about who's driving tonight and assessing how drunk they could be.

I fetch beers, mostly the King, of course, for those who prefer to get their own. Besides, the stools at the counter and the tables are all taken, so it's standing room only tonight.

Eleanor watches me flip caps and take money.

"I like your dogs," I tell her. "What are their names?"

She blinks.

"Shirley, Pete, and Suzie."

"Those are good names."

That's enough socializing for Eleanor, who holds her jacket in the crook of her arm. She doesn't make small talk with the customers. No one attempts to do the same with her. They all know better. It's not just that Eleanor is slow. She's also unfriendly.

Jack hustles back.

"All set," he tells me, and then he's looking at Eleanor. "Ready, Sis?"

She answers by putting on her coat and cap, a knitted thing she pulls down almost to her eyes. She shuffles behind me.

"See you tomorrow, Eleanor," I say.

I hear a grunt before she follows Jack out the door.

Now I'm in charge, at least for the ten minutes it will take Jack to drive his sister home. The band is on a break. So are the smokers who are clustered outside. They don't even bother with their jackets. It was 2004 when the state banned smoking finally in bars and restaurants. I remember the date because we did a spread on it in the Daily Star.

It was a big deal for the customers at the Rooster. Personally, I was glad. Drinkers aren't the most considerate smokers. The worst was New Year's Eve. All the smokers who were planning to quit cigarettes for a New Year's resolution smoked their brains out that night. The air was so thick with cigarette smoke I was smoking along with them. Course, if any of the heavy smokers did quit, it didn't last very long, oh, maybe until they woke up sometime January 1 and started getting the urge really hard. They might as well have given up breathing for the new year.

With the crowd thinned out momentarily, it's easier for me to get a handle on who's inside. Mostly they're the Rooster regulars who don't smoke or who already have stepped outside. They're yakking up a storm, probably about the snowstorm.

The front door opens. Dale Collins steps inside. I bite my lip. Surely, he's heard about what I'm doing. He takes a free stool at the bar. I grab an empty weighing down a buck tip and swipe the spot with a rag.

"Hey, Dale, what can I get you?"

"Bud."

As I slide open the cooler and reach inside, I'm wondering where this exchange will take me. I flip the cap.

"Here, you go."

He knows how much a Bud costs, so he's got the cash out of his wallet. He's wearing the standard Rooster issue: a Carhartt vest over a flannel shirt and jeans. He's growing a scraggly beard and has curly hair, brown with a bit of gray, that's short in the front and long in the back, uh-huh, a mullet. About half the guys here have mullets. The rest either let them grow all the way long, some tied back in ponytails, or cropped tightly into a crew cut.

"Keep the change," Dale says, and after I thank him, he adds, "I heard what you're doin'. My grandpa told me."

"I hope you're okay with it. He is."

"That's what he told me." He nods. "I'm okay with it, too. I sure want to know what happened to my mother. And if somebody's responsible, I want 'em caught and punished."

"I know you were pretty young then, but would you mind meeting some time? I'd like to ask you some questions."

"Questions?"

"Maybe there's something you saw or heard leading up to that day that could help me solve this case."

"I told everything I know to the cops. I was only ten."

"I might ask some questions they didn't. Besides, it's not like they did a very good job trying to find your mom."

"You're right about that." He peels at the beer's label. "Sure, I'll meet with you."

"I'd like to do it soon if that's all right with you. Maybe your grandpa could join us. Would you like that?"

He nods. Even before this awkward business, I suspected Dale was a quiet guy. I wouldn't say he's on one of those roads to success. I don't know if he's happy. Sam and I would see him a lot at the Rooster. He was always alone, no woman or girl on his arm, although he'd yuck it up with some of the guys. He was the most animated ever the time Ma and I saw Dale argue with his father at the Rooster.

"You gonna talk with Bobby?"

I make a mental note he doesn't call him Dad.

"I'm working up to it," I say.

"I wish you luck there. You might want to meet with him in some place public like here if he hasn't already been kicked out."

I quickly eye the lists hanging behind the counter.

"Seems he's in good standing at least for now. But thanks for the advice. Oh, one more thing. The kids and I were up at Sam's grave on Sunday. When I passed your mother's stone, I saw a necklace."

"Yeah, my grandpa told me about that." He shook his head. "I remember the necklace. She wore it every day. But, no, I didn't put it there. I wonder who did."

I don't feel comfortable speculating who might be responsible in front of Adela's son. I can see his pain is real still. Hopefully, closure or justice will help.

"Me, too. I'll see you soon."

The smokers are filing inside. The band is back in place. We get busy again. Jack's return is well timed, and then I realize he planned on taking Eleanor home just then on purpose.

"Any bar fights while I was gone?" he jokes when he hustles behind the bar to hang up his jacket.

"Nope, everybody behaved themselves, even the birthday boy."

"I told that group I'd ban them from comin' in here for six months if they let him drive home."

"You handled that well, Jack."

He gives me a knowing grin. He tips his head.

"I've got a bit of experience there."

The rest of the night is a breeze. I check in with Ma, who says the dog went out once to do her business and came right back inside. Maggie made herself at home fast, which is a relief. She, the cat, and Ma are hunkered down in front of the TV.

Before I know it, the place has thinned to the usual late night regulars, the desperados who don't want to go to an empty house or an unhappy spouse. The band is packing up. The drummer did make it through the last set although he was a bit off on some of the fast numbers and one time he fell off his stool. Jack says he'll likely have the Potholes back.

Dale left around ten after a few beers and a cordial "good night" to me.

I help Jack clean up, and then I'll head home before last call. He doesn't need my help for the few drinkers left. Besides, I told him about the new dog, and this being her first night alone with Ma, I don't want to linger. I'll even pass up my free drink for the night.

I carry a tray of glasses into the kitchen and place them exactly where Eleanor wants them next to the sink. Jack stops me in the doorway. He checks over his shoulder.

"Isabel, my sister told me you were up at the cemetery on Sunday," he says quietly.

"Uh-huh, it was Sam's anniversary. The kids and I were at his grave."

"That's what she said."

"I saw Eleanor and her dogs as I was leaving. I stopped to say hi, but your sister isn't much of a talker."

He chuckles.

"That's Eleanor all right. She let her mutts run in the cemetery before she took 'em the back way home. I'm guessing they probably smelled you and got curious. That's why she went near Adela's grave."

I smile.

"I see."

He reaches into his pocket.

"Eleanor told me she found this on Adela's stone. I know for sure it's hers. She wore it all the time." The necklace rests in the palm of his hand. "I thought you might be interested in it. Sorry, it's got her and my fingerprints all over it."

If this was a crime show, I'd be ticked I couldn't run the locket for fingerprints or DNA. According to Andrew, his daughter wore it the last time he saw her. Even if the killer did take it from her, if he or she were smart, they would have wiped their fingerprints off the surface. Too much time has passed, and like I say, I'm not with some crime unit.

"Don't worry about the prints. I saw the necklace when I passed Adela's stone that day. I told Andrew about it. I thought maybe he or Dale left it there, like maybe they found it in her house after she took it off. Andrew said he didn't. When he went to see for himself, the necklace was gone. Dale told me tonight he didn't know anything about it being there." I smile. "So, Eleanor took it for safekeeping. Good thinking."

"I thought so."

"Eleanor didn't say a word about it," I say.

"You know my sister." Jack rolls his eyes. "Why don't you give this to Andrew when you're done with it?"

He drops the necklace in my hand. The chain's not broken and still clasped.

"Be glad to. Andrew said the necklace was a gift from Irma. Thanks."

"How's your investigation going?"

"Slow."

He grins.

"A big snow's comin' Sunday."

"So I heard all night."

Of course, Ma is up when I get home. The dog at least greets me at the door. The cat doesn't give a hoot. She's got my mother's lap and steady hand.

"How'd it go?" I ask her.

"No problems."

I can tell Ma is more at ease than last weekend when I worked at the Rooster. The dog makes a difference.

"You'll never guess what I got tonight." I reach into my bag for the necklace and dangle it. "Adela's necklace."

Ma hums when I hand it to her.

"You found this in the bar?"

"No, Jack gave it to me. He says his sister saw it on Adela's stone. He wanted me to give it to Andrew. Funny, Dale was at the Rooster. He could've given the necklace to him."

"That's odd," Ma says.

I sigh.

"Everything's odd about this case. But Eleanor told him I was up there that day. They both know what I'm doing about Adela's case. She's only trying to help in her way." The light catches on the locket's surface when I dangle the chain near the lamp. "But it'll make Andrew glad to have it."

I glance at the kitchen clock. It's too late to call, but I will first thing tomorrow morning.

Adela's Necklace

The next morning, Andrew Snow comes over to the house minutes after I call him about his daughter's necklace. He greets my mother politely and pats our friendly mutt, Maggie, but clearly he has one thing on his mind.

"Come into the kitchen," I tell him. "Would you like a cup of coffee or tea?"

"I'm fine, thank you. Already had two."

He doesn't even unbutton his red plaid jacket when he follows me to the kitchen table. Neither of us sits. I hand him the small box that once held a pair of earrings Sam gave me. I decided it would be better than just handing him the necklace. He lifts the top. He sighs.

"Yes, this is definitely hers."

I note the present tense. Adela was declared officially dead twenty-one years ago, but there hasn't been a finale for her father without her remains found or her mystery solved.

"Jack Smith says his sister picked it up Sunday. Eleanor found it after her dogs took off in the cemetery. She gave it to Jack to give me."

Andrew lifts the necklace by its chain. He points to the clasp.

"This is the part I repaired that day for her." He partially unzips his jacket and retrieves eyeglasses from his shirt pocket. He hums. "It looks like it came undone again. Someone did a lousy job fixing it though. I know how to do it so there's not a gap. See here how one end passes the other?"

I bend forward. It is a sloppy fix. Adela could have lost the necklace in a tussle or when her body was moved. I think back to my theories. Although suicide is still a possibility, murder or manslaughter has taken the lead in this case. If that's indeed

109

the situation, I wonder why the necklace wasn't buried with her. Maybe her killer discovered it afterward. And then, there's the sick thought that maybe the necklace was a souvenir. If so, why give it up now?

"Jack says his and his sister's fingerprints are all over the necklace."

"So, we couldn't take it to the police," he says.

"Andrew, the cops wouldn't open a case that old without more evidence." I pause. "Besides, if the killer was smart, he or she would have wiped it clean."

"She?"

I'm not about to share my suspicions about Mira Clark, who was wronged by her once best friend Adela. It would be too heavy a burden to make Andrew swear to secrecy. Besides, I have no evidence other than her being a wounded wife.

"It's probably far-fetched, but I'm not ruling out a woman could have done this. I'm trying to keep an open mind."

"I suppose."

"Would you like to keep the necklace?" I ask.

"Could I?"

"Sure. I've taken photos and made notes. It's yours."

He drops the necklace into the jewelers box.

"Thank you," he whispers. "Please tell Jack and Eleanor I'm grateful to have it."

"I'll do that when I see them tonight." I watch Andrew flip open the box then snap it shut softly. "I want to say something and I'm afraid it isn't easy."

Andrew's lips press into a line.

"Go ahead."

"I wanted you to know I might find out things about your daughter that are not very nice."

He sighs.

"I saw the receipt for that motel. I know what went on there."

I take my time.

"Did you know about her... relationship with Bruce Clark?"

"I think many people did. Well, afterwards... Mira wasn't

110

quiet about her hurt feelings. It was embarrassing there for a while."

"Was it enough of a motive?"

"It never crossed my mind. Why? What do you think?"

"Could it have been more than a fling?" Now I feel I'm stepping into an uncertain place. "Could Adela have gotten pregnant by Bruce?"

Andrew's head wags back and forth.

"That's impossible. She had her tubes tied a couple of years after Dale was born. She told her mother and me she didn't want to take a chance having another child with Bobby."

"That's good to know." I nod. "One more thing. Mira claimed Adela had lots of affairs with married men."

"Yes, I believe she spread that story around," he said. "Look. My daughter was a grown woman. I know she saw men, but whether they were married, I don't know. She kept that part of her life private to spare Irma and me."

"I understand." I pause. "I saw Dale last night at the Rooster. He's willing to meet with me. It might be easier for him if you were there, too. Would you mind?"

"That's a good idea. I'll call you soon."

Funny Ways

Eleanor's hands are deep in a bowl of ground beef. She likes to make the hamburger patties ahead of time and stick them on a plate in the fridge. From the looks of it, Saturday is a big burger night. Jack says his sister almost has a sixth sense of how many burgers to make. Eleanor's not wearing gloves, but I suppose if I don't rat her out, the customers and the board of health won't know. At least she's got her hair bound up in a red bandana.

She's reaching for the bottle of steak sauce when I say her name. She's already seen me hang up my jacket and ignored my hello. Now she ignores my presence as I stand in the doorway. I don't dare get closer. She doesn't like to be crowded I found out the first day. She's a strange one, all right. I don't know if I've worked here long enough to ask Jack what's really up with his sister and her funny ways.

"Eleanor, you made Andrew Snow very happy finding that necklace," I tell her.

She dumps some of the steak sauce into the hamburger. I wonder if she'll clean the hamburger gunk off the bottle when she's done.

Grunt.

"It meant a lot to him to have it back. He says Adela wore it everyday."

She adds powdered garlic, then salt and pepper. Her eyes stay on the bowl although I detect a slight nod.

"Anyways, thanks for asking Jack to give it to me."

Grunt.

Field Trip

It's almost noon when Matt, Alex, and I hit the logging road where Adela's car was found. I had hoped to leave earlier, but there's no rushing my boys. They wanted to play with the new dog, talk with their grandmother, and, of course, eat.

As we hike in, Matt and Alex tell me about their jobs and what they've been doing since I saw them last Sunday. They want to know about the Rooster and ask if I'd mind if they came in when I'm working. I tell them just don't embarrass me, and they know I'm joking. Then they want an update on my snooping, as Alex calls it.

"I prefer to think of it as investigating," I tell him. "It's all for a good cause. You were just little kids when this happened. It brought a lot of grief to her family and this town."

We shuffle in our boots through the downed leaves, now brittle and brown. Sometimes the boys get ahead of me, joking and poking each other in fun. They forget about their mother for a while until I use my two fingers to whistle, so they wait for me to catch up. Yes, whistling is one of my talents. It came in handy, too, when the kids were little. They could find me in a crowd or hear me in the woods behind our house.

The last time I was here was twenty-eight years ago, when I hiked in with Sam after Adela's car was found, although we did pass near it on snowshoes when we took the trail that crosses it. I check the sky. It's still blue although clouds are beginning their eastward creep.

"What's that? Hey, wait. It's a cross." Matt's head swings back. "This the spot?"

Someone has stuck a wooden cross on the ground, as if this is the place Adela died. But like the stone on the empty grave, it's likely just another way to remember her. I'll ask Andrew about it. The cross doesn't have her name, but we know it's for her. I wonder how long it's been here. I kneel to give it an inspection. The cross is definitely homemade, a bit crude I'd say with a nail holding the two pieces together. If it had paint, that was long gone. I take my phone from my jacket pocket and snap a few photos.

"Let's keep going," I tell my boys.

About a mile later and past the snowmobile trail, we reach the Brookfield River, which is rather low because of the lack of rain this fall. I point toward the flat stones we can take across. The boys go ahead, and Matt stretches to offer me his hand until we're on the other side. I snap photos of the river and woods from this angle.

"What are we looking for?" Matt asks.

"Something that doesn't belong here," I answer.

There's no road on the other side largely because it is heavy with ledge, and I don't see a wide enough opening for a skidder. We split up along the thin, rocky beach. All we find are beer cans, fishing line, and a faded Red Sox ball cap, which I stick in the shoulder bag I brought.

I point toward a wide break in the rocks.

"We might as well walk a bit more," I say. "We've come this far."

The woods, mostly pine, grow straight and tall on this side of the river. There's little underbrush but a thick layer of pine needles. I suspect it's been untouched by loggers for decades, if ever, because of the ledge. They'd have to find another way here. We walk straight ahead with the river at our backs until we reach barbed wire. The woods on the other side are heavy with maple trees, likely planted in the 1800s when making syrup got popular as a livelihood, so people didn't have to rely on sugar from the South. In the distance, smoke rises in a neat column.

I have my bearings. We're at the property line for the Maple Tree Farm. The Bernard family who lives there still does maple sugaring but also raises cattle. They grow corn and hay. But the generations are thinning out. I wonder how long they'll stick with what has to be a hard though honest way of

114

life.

"Boys, we've reached a dead end. Let's head back."

We return to the river and sit on flat rocks to eat the sandwiches I brought.

"What are you thinking, Mom?" Alex asks.

"Well, we can rule out a couple of things. I seriously doubt Adela left her house at night, dumped her car two miles in, waited until daylight, and then walked on this side of the river to do herself in. That's an awfully long time to change your mind. I also have to believe somebody would have stumbled on her remains."

The boys nod.

"The police reports say there was no sign of blood in her car. So, she wasn't dead inside unless her killer was super careful sealing her body in plastic, but that's a lot of effort. It would be a haul carrying her all the way here. She wasn't fat, but she had some heft to her. Plus, he would have to bring a shovel to dig a grave. The root system of the pines on this side of the river is pretty dense. And I don't think there's any way someone could drag her kicking and screaming over that river."

"You're saying it didn't happen here," Alex says.

"Uh-huh, but I'm still wondering about the car. Why leave it here? What would you do after? Walk or hitch home? Or were two people involved? And we have no way of knowing how long it was parked here before it was found." I stand. "Thanks for coming with me. I wouldn't want to do this alone. Maybe if I had a dog, but Maggie hasn't been with us long enough."

"You taking that trash we found?"

"Sure. Just because people are a bunch of slobs, we don't have to be."

Snow Day

Usually the storms the weathermen go gaga about don't amount to anything. Then there are the ones that get by them. I remember one late March watching the snow falling during a staff meeting at the Star and realizing I better get the hell outta there fast. We were only supposed to get a dusting that day. The road crews couldn't keep up with the snow.

The storm that started late yesterday does live up to its billing. I wake up in the middle of the night to hear snow slamming against the windowpanes. By the time I'm up for the day, the driveway is socked in with eight inches or more. I smile, thinking I don't have to drive into the city in this ungodly weather. Instead, I get on my boots and other winter crap to dig a path for the dog, so she can do her business in the woods. Even before I have coffee.

"Big storm," Ma greets me in the kitchen.

"Yeah, we get a lot more snow than where you lived. Well, we're set for it. We should get plowed out after the storm's done."

"What are you doing today?"

"I'm gonna organize all that paperwork I have. I'll call you up when I'm done."

It takes me two hours to finish. I step back from the wall. I tacked a photo of Adela in the center. To the far left, I placed the maps and a calendar, the ones I've held onto and those I downloaded from the internet. The Google maps even give me terrain without snow. I have a list with the header "possible suspects." So far, I only have Bobby Collins and Adela's ex-pal Mira Clark. Bobby has an alleged alibi for that night. I put Mira up there for the heck of it. I doubt if she had it in her, affair or not, unless, of course, it didn't end two years before like she said. What about her husband, Bruce, the schoolteacher? What the hell, I put his name up there with a question mark beside it. Now that would make a wild story: mild-mannered schoolteacher kills his lover.

More lists. One contains new tips about Adela like she allegedly slept with married men and went at least once to the Shady Grope. Of course, there's the list of septic systems and building permits. I'll cross our names off those lists. I pin up photos and my notes. The box containing the stuff from Adela's sits on the floor.

Ma walks upstairs. Her feet scuff the treads.

"I don't think I've made much progress," I tell her.

I roll over my desk chair. Ma sits and studies each piece of paper. Some of it she's seen before. Some of it she hasn't.

"Well, you've made some. You figured out things on that walk yesterday." She nods at the box. "I think that cap in that box may be a clue. Course, there's the necklace. You've found a few other things."

"I need to meet more people who knew her. I'm going to try her son, Dale, next. He says he'll talk with me." I glance toward the window. "But today I'm going nowhere."

Dale Collins

Andrew Snow agrees to meet Wednesday morning at his grandson's house. I'm a little surprised when he calls to set up the day, but then again Dale doesn't seem to have a steady job. He worked for the town once, but that didn't last. Sometimes he cuts firewood or does construction. Or he'll help out maple sugaring. From the plow on the front of Dale's pickup, I'm guessing he's clearing driveways this winter. Those who don't have a steady line of work have to do the hilltown shuffle.

Andrew did say it's okay to bring Ma along.

I park the Subaru behind Andrew's car, and then guide Ma along the driveway. I make the introductions when Dale lets us in the side door.

"Nice to meet you, Mrs. Ferreira," he says as we follow him to the kitchen. "Grandpa's in the kitchen making coffee. Would you like a cup?"

I'm impressed with Dale's good country manners, but, then again, except for a few Neanderthals, hilltown folks are a courteous group. I like that about them. They wave in their vehicles. The men hold doors for those coming behind them. They apologize when they curse, which can be a lot.

Dale also seems a little jumpy. He doesn't seem to know where to focus his eyes. Part of that is, of course, due to my mission today.

The house is filled with an embarrassing amount of bachelor clutter. But beneath the cartons of motor oil, assorted trash, and discarded clothes, I recognize a woman's furnishings. I'm guessing the house is pretty much how Adela left it before her son moved his junk in here. Now I have another question to ask: what happened to the house after she went missing.

Andrew turns from the stove.

"Coffee anyone?" he asks.

Ma and I politely decline. I watch Dale eye the table and its four chairs.

"This looks like a good place to sit," I say, and Ma nods. We remove our coats and hang them over the backs of the chairs.

Andrew brings coffee cups for him and Dale to the table.

"You sure?" he says. "It's no trouble at all."

I smile.

"Thanks. We're done for the day."

I'm thinking about how to get this conversation rolling. Remember what I said about those Yankee lawn mowers? But Andrew beats me to it.

"Isabel is doing a fine job trying to solve this mystery," he tells Dale in a pep talk kind of voice. "I was surprised when she told me what she was up to. She's only doing it out of the goodness of her heart. I'm so grateful."

Dale says, "Yeah."

I continue to smile. I note Andrew leaves out the part about paying me.

"When did you move into your mother's house?"

The heels of Dale's boots drag across the linoleum beneath the table.

"I was only ten when it happened. So, I lived at my grandparents' house until I was old enough to be on my own. You know, after I dropped out of high school. The house was empty until then. Well, it still had Mom's things. We kept hoping… "

Andrew nods.

"Now it belongs to Dale."

"Makes sense." I pause before I launch my next question. "Dale, what can you tell me about the last time you saw your mother?"

He picks up a matchbook lying beside the pack of Camels on the tabletop. I expect he wants to smoke, but he won't with Ma and me here unless he asks first.

"It was after school. The bus dropped me off at the store.

119

Mom and I talked a little. Grandma was picking me up at the house, and I was spending the night."

"Wasn't it a school night?" I ask.

"Uh-huh, I slept over a lot. Grandma used to be a teacher, so she helped me with my school stuff." He plays with the matchbook. "School was hard for me. I had to go to special classes. Anyway, I had a history report to finish."

"What did you and your Mom talk about?"

His fingers keep moving.

"The usual stuff. She gave me lunch money and told me to pick up clean clothes. We talked about going to the movies at the mall on Saturday after she bought me new boots and jeans. We were gonna eat pizza."

I glance at Andrew.

"It sure doesn't sound like she was planning to go anywhere."

"That's what I've said all along," Dale tells me.

"Can you think of anything else she said?" I ask.

"When I called her that night, she asked how the history report was going. She asked what we ate for dinner."

"Wait a minute. You talked with your mother that night? I didn't see that in the police reports. What time was that?"

Dale's head bounces hard.

"I don't know. Early. I told the cops that."

"You're doing great. Did you call her or did she call you?"

"She called me."

"What were you doing?"

"Helping Grandma wash dishes."

"So, it was right after dinner?"

"Yeah, Grandma didn't like the dirty dishes to sit too long. Right, Grandpa?"

"That's right." He takes a stuttering breath. "The store closed at six. Irma would always have dinner on the table when I got home."

"So, I'm figuring this was around 7:30 when your mother called."

"Must've been."

Ma hasn't said a word. In fact, she's so quiet it's like she's not even sitting there. But she gives me an encouraging nod. The next line of questioning is going to be tougher, but after rehearsing with Ma in the car, I believe I found a smooth way to handle it.

"Dale, I wanted to ask you about the relationships your mother had with men. Did she have any special friends?"

He tosses the matchbook onto the table. It's too twisted to use.

"I know Mom went out with men. But she didn't bring any of 'em home for me to meet. She didn't talk about 'em. Well, that's not true. There was one guy a while ago she really liked. But I guess it didn't work out. He doesn't live here anymore."

"What's his name?" I ask.

He turns toward his grandfather.

"You remember Roger, don't ya?"

"He was an okay guy," Andrew says. "But that was years before it happened. I think he moved out west somewhere."

"Nobody else?" I ask.

Dale makes a painful grimace.

"I was only a kid then. I suppose when she wanted to go out I stayed over at my grandparents' house."

"How often?"

"Once or twice a week at least."

"Do you think she was seeing someone steady before she went missing?"

Dale makes a hard swallow.

"I think so. Sometimes I'd see a shirt in the wash that didn't belong to me. There'd be dishes in the sink. Other things."

I bend forward.

"What other things?"

"She'd get calls late at night. Around her birthday she got flowers, but it wasn't from any of us. She acted kinda funny about it."

"And you had no idea who it was?"

Dale shakes his head emphatically.

We all get quiet for a while. The only sound is the tick of the kitchen clock. It's one of those silly cat clocks with the tail

121

moving back and forth.

I speak first.

"When I visited the old chief, he wasn't helpful at all. It wasn't a good day. But his wife remembered something he told her. The chief said there were broken dishes on the kitchen floor."

"I saw them, too," Andrew said.

I feel myself squinting.

"Did your mother own a gun? Your grandfather wasn't so sure."

"Nah," Dale said. "She wouldn't allow them in the house. But I own guns now, for hunting."

"I have another question. When my boys and I walked to where they found Adela's car, we saw someone placed a cross on the spot. Was that one of you?"

Dale nods.

"I did that long ago. I made it myself. I… "

I smile to ease his discomfort.

"That's a sweet gesture," I tell Dale.

"Yes, it is," his grandfather says.

Silence again.

I say to Ma, "Maybe we should go."

"Would you like to see her room?" Andrew asks.

I'm surprised. Even though so many years have passed, this conversation couldn't be easy for these two men. I know it wasn't for me. But I answer quickly.

"Yes, I would. Ma?"

"That would be nice," she says.

We follow the two men upstairs. They take the steps slowly for Ma's sake, I suppose. One door is open and the contents are a messy guy's room. Dale goes to the door beside it. Cold air rushes toward us when it's open. This is definitely a woman's room, neat as Adela left it. The shades are drawn halfway. The curtains and chenille bedspread are faded from sunlight. There's an upholstered chair with a floor lamp, a braided rug on the floor, handmade, and an antique dresser with an oval mirror.

"The drawers and closets?" I ask.

Andrew tips his head.

"We held onto everything until the seven-year mark. We saw no reason to anymore after that. We gave them away to the church mission."

"Do you mind if I look?"

"Go ahead," Andrew says.

I open each drawer, which is lined with floral paper. I pull each out one at a time and peek inside.

"What's this?"

I reach for a small card stuck to the back of the dresser. It's the kind of card you get with flowers. The writing says: "Happy birthday my love." There's no signature. I hold it for Andrew, Dale, and Ma to see. Andrew keeps it while I return each drawer to its place.

"Well, I'll be," Andrew says.

"Anybody recognize the handwriting?"

While the three of them study the card, I examine the empty closet. Even the hangers are gone. I use my hand to sweep the top shelf and only come away with dust. I swipe my hands clean and close the door. Andrew still stares at the card.

"When's Adela's birthday?" I ask.

"August 21," Andrew and Dale say at the same time.

"Was that the birthday she got flowers?" I ask Dale.

"Yeah," he says. "I asked who sent 'em, but she wouldn't say. She called him 'Mr. X' and laughed."

"That was during summer vacation. Wouldn't you have been home if the bouquet was dropped off?"

Dale shrugs.

"I don't remember. I could've been riding my bike somewhere with my friends or visiting Mom at the store or helping grandma in her garden. All I know the flowers were on the kitchen table when she came home."

"What was her reaction?" I ask Dale.

"She was really happy. I asked if Grandma and Grandpa gave them. She said no."

I turn toward Andrew.

"Would a city florist deliver all the way out here?"

Andrew shakes his head.

"Sometimes they do if you spend enough money," he said. "But they would've left it on the doorstep if nobody was home. They wouldn't have gone inside the house."

"That makes sense. Did your mother lock her doors?"

"No," Dale says.

"So, it looks like whoever gave her those flowers just helped himself inside."

Andrew hands me back the card.

"Why don't you hold onto this for safekeeping?" he says.

"Sure."

We're about to leave the room. Dale has his hand on the door and moves to close it. That's when I see a calendar on the back of the door. It's for the year Adela disappeared.

"Hold on a sec," I say.

"Huh?" Dale says.

We all stare at the calendar.

"Do you mind?" I ask.

"Go ahead," Andrew says, as he hands me the calendar

I flip quickly through its pages, which have notations throughout.

"Could I borrow this?" I ask.

"Take it," Andrew says.

"Do you want to see it first?" I ask Andrew and Dale.

Both shake their head no.

"Just let us know what you find."

I stop at the bottom of the stairs. I glance around the living room at the cabinets and bookcases.

"Did you clean those out, too?"

Andrew and Dale glance at each other.

"I didn't touch 'em," Dale says.

"Hmm, maybe you could go through them sometime," I say. "Or if you want, I can help you."

"I'll let you know," Andrew tells me.

Calendar

Adela's calendar is a freebie given out by a local hardware store that's no longer around, a victim of a later downturn in the economy. I have the calendar open on my kitchen table. Ma sits beside me. The pages feature idyllic photos of country living, heavy on maple trees, dirt roads, red barns, and rivers, plus puppies and deer. But I don't care about any of that. I'm interested in what Adela wrote on its pages.

The first four months are filled with notations about bills and appointments at the Conwell Medical Center. Of course, there are birthdays. Her father's is January 15. Her mother's a week later. She marks off February and April vacations for Dale.

"Nothing unusual here," I tell Ma, and she hums in agreement. I turn the page to April and May. "Same stuff here."

But in June she starts writing X's on certain days, Mondays the most, some Tuesdays, and weekends. I flip through the pages. In early August, she blocks off an entire week, the second. She wrote VACATION. I need to ask Andrew and Dale about that. Did she go away that week? If so, did she take her son?

She drew a red heart on her birthday, August 21.

"Looks like it was a good birthday for her," Ma says.

"I bet those are the days she hooked up with her guy friend," I say, avoiding the term boyfriend since women Adela's age, or mine for that matter, don't date boys unless they're cougars. "Funny, it's almost like she's keeping score."

The Twirl

The snowmobilers are out in force Friday at the Rooster. The tables are piled with helmets. Suits are draped over chairs or hanging from the hooks Jack placed strategically along one wall. A few of the guys just walk around with their suits unzipped to their waists and the top half hanging off their butts. Heavy boots thud across the floor.

Jack's grinning big. The riders bring big appetites for food and booze. Eleanor is one busy cook tonight turning out meals. But that's winding down as the band begins to set up. Tonight we have the Slim Jims, named that, I hear, because three of the four musicians — the lead guitar, keyboardist, and drummer — are named Jim. None of them are slim, but what the heck. The last guy, who plays rhythm guitar, is named Fred. I've heard them before. They'll rock the Rooster with the usual covers plus a couple of originals.

I'm stationed behind the bar with Jack. The kitchen is closed. Jack clears the tables. I smile and fill drink orders. I ask to see drivers' licenses when the drinkers look a bit young or I don't know them. Jack told me he's not about to get in trouble because some young punk can't wait until he's 21.

"Want a glass with that?" I ask a woman who orders a Bud.

Behind her I see a familiar face. The Floozy is here. I don't see anyone else with her. She steps forward.

"What can I get you, Marsha?" I ask.

"Bud."

"Coming right up," I say, reaching into the cooler and snapping it shut fast when I have the bottle in my hand. "Here you go."

Her hand digs into the front pocket of her jeans for the money.

"You see Bobby yet?"

"No, have you?" I say loudly because the guys in the crowd hoot and holler as the Jim at the keyboard bangs out the opening chords to "Truck Drivin' Son of a Gun." Now, if there were ever a redneck play list, this would be high on it. The trucker in the song is supposed to be this big stud with women everywhere on the road, plus one waiting at home. That's a lot more than a lot of the guys in this room could handle, except maybe in their wet and wild dreams.

The lead singer, one of the Jims, bends toward the microphone and says, "This is for all you mother truckers." Yeah, the guys holler their approval.

The Floozy raises her voice, "Yeah, I did. He was pissed you're gonna dig up all that old stuff."

"What's he worried about? He's got an alibi. That's you, right?"

"Hell, right."

"If he has nothing to do with Adela's disappearance, wouldn't he want to know what happened to her? She was the mother of his son."

She glares at me as she mulls what I just said.

"I suppose. He just don't want no trouble."

"I'd just really like to talk with Bobby." I tip my head, thinking about what Dale said about his father. "Here might be a good place but not on a busy night. You have his number… never mind. Here's mine." I grab an empty meal ticket and write my landline on the back. "If you talk with him, you can give him this."

I pick up the wrinkled bills, exact change, of course. She stares at my phone number before she shoves it in her pocket.

"Enjoy the beer," I say as brightly as I can make it. "Next."

Jack waltzes through the crowd with a tray filled with bottles and glasses. I tell him to leave it on the counter and give him a clean one to make another sweep. I drop the empties in a carton at my feet and bring the glasses into the kitchen where Eleanor washes dishes. She's got a real mess tonight. She'll be heading home later than usual for sure.

I set the glasses at the exact spot she likes on the counter.

There's no kidding around with Eleanor.

"Jack might have more."

She grunts.

"Really busy tonight, eh?"

Grunt.

"It's supposed to snow on Monday everybody's saying."

Grunt.

"Okay, I'll leave you alone."

No grunt.

Yes, it's supposed to snow again. The storms tend to come in a steady pattern, hitting the hilltowns on certain days of the week. So, maybe we will get snow on Mondays from now on, at least until a really huge storm hits and disrupts the flow. Remember what I said about watching the weather? I'm sure as hell glad not to start my workweek navigating bad roads.

I look out from my spot at the bar. The place is in motion with dancers. I hear happy voices and the clunk of boots. Over my shoulder, Eleanor's still working in the kitchen. I'd offer to help, but this is my post for the night. Besides, she'd tell me to get lost in her Eleanor sort of way; that is, she'd ignore me or maybe grunt. If she could manage a growl, I bet she would.

On the other side of the room, the Slim Jims gulp down beers before their next song. One of the Jims leans into the mike. "This is for all you bad hombres lucky enough to have a woman like this." Then the crowd goes a bit nuts when the Slim Jims play the familiar opening to Waylon Jennings' "Good Hearted Woman." Yeah, I bet all the bad hombres in this room would like one of those gals.

Jack drops a full tray on the counter and before I take anything, he grabs my wrist. He tips his head toward the direction of the band.

"Come on, Isabel, let's dance," he says, and then he announces loudly, "The bar's closed. No beer until this song's over."

I let him drag me onto the floor. I haven't danced in well over a year. Jack's a bigger man than Sam, but I'm surprised by his moves. I can't recall seeing him dance before, but then I might have just been having too good a night out with Sam

128

that I didn't pay attention. I let him have the lead, and he's got me twisting and twirling on the dance floor. I hear myself laugh. Jack laughs, too. The other dancers move aside for us. He's got that big Jack Smith grin going. He's spinning me this way and that, and even ends the tune with a corny little dip. We get a cheer from the customers when he pulls me upright at the end.

I'm a little breathless, but I manage, "Thanks. That was really fun, Jack."

He chuckles.

"We'll have to do it again soon," he says, and then he jokes, giving me a loud but friendly, "Now, woman, git back behind the bar."

I giggle to myself, yes, giggle, as I make my way back. If Sam were here, he'd think it was funny, too. Eleanor stands behind the bar with her knit hat pulled past her ears. Her coat is half open. Her pouty lips form a deep frown.

Jack is right behind me.

"Hey, Sis, ready for a ride home? Sorry to make you wait," he says before he turns toward me. "Isabel, think you can handle this rowdy bunch?"

He's joking, of course. People are having too good a time to do something stupid that would get them kicked out.

"Course, I can. Night, Eleanor."

Eleanor doesn't answer, but she does give me a brief, hard stare before she follows her brother. Man, when she's ready to go, she's ready to go.

Ma's Plans

Ma announces Saturday morning she'd like to go back home for a couple of weeks. She wants to spend Thanksgiving with my brother's family. I figure she must've been talking to Danny about it on the phone beforehand, but I'm not hurt. She's been celebrating the holiday for years at his house, with his kids and grandkids, and besides she has other business back there. Maybe she needs a break from me, I joke, but she assures me she likes living with the animals and me. I make a mental note she mentions the animals first.

So, here it is the next morning, Sunday. The plan is for me to drive her halfway. We even skip church. My brother will meet me off the turnpike. Ma won't have her car there, but my brother or one of his kids will chauffeur her around. I've got her suitcases in the cargo hold of the Subaru. The dog, Maggie, is in the back seat. I'm at the top of our driveway and thankful the storm won't start until after midnight.

"Good timing, Ma," I tell her.

"You sure you don't mind my going?"

"I'll miss you. But, nah, Ruth wants to have the dinner at her house," I say. "Gregg's folks are coming. Last year's Thanksgiving was just awful. Sam hadn't been gone that long, and it's the one holiday he actually enjoyed."

"Anyway, we'll have Christmas together."

"That's right."

The car seems to know its way through the hilltowns to the valley, where I pick up the pike. I will admit I'm not a fan of highway driving, but traffic is light, and it's all for a good cause: Ma's happiness. Along the way we talk, mostly about the case, naturally. I'm hoping to meet Jamie this week, and maybe his ex-wife although that will have to be on the phone since she high-tailed it out of the hilltowns after they got divorced. Maybe the Floozy will give Bobby my number. I'm also going to give the police chief's wife a call to see if she turned up anything. I might spend some time going through the drawers at Dale's house, if he lets me.

"You going to get all that done while I'm gone?" Ma asks.

"It sounds like a lot, but really I haven't made much headway. I don't want to let Andrew down, especially now that he's paying me," I say. "I keep thinking about that card I found in Adela's bedroom. It definitely looked like a man's handwriting. What if I showed it to a few people to see if they recognize it?"

"That might be asking for trouble."

"Why?"

"Suppose you show it to the person who wrote it."

"Good point. Maybe I'll just pay more attention to people's handwriting."

My brother, Danny, waits just where he is supposed to be at a fast food joint. We're going to have lunch. Fortunately, the place serves an okay salad. I love my mother, but I've got to draw the line somewhere although I do buy a burger for the dog waiting in the car.

Danny is clearly pleased to be bringing Ma back. He's a big guy with a big sense of humor, as we in Massachusetts like to say. He's the perfect baby brother, and the only boy in our family. My sisters and I teased the hell out of him when he was a kid. It's still fun to do.

I give Ma a hug.

"I'll let you know if there are any developments."

"You do that. And take good care of Roxanne and Maggie."

"Don't you worry about that."

Sunday at the Rooster

The house is quiet when I get home hours later. If she were here, Ma would have the television's volume turned up as she watches the Patriots or one of her shows, because she's a little hard of hearing, although like Sam she'd never admit it. While I'm a fan of the team, I'm not that much of one I'd sit alone in my living room with a beer and my feet up. Besides, I'm out of beer.

I head down to the cellar for firewood. The dog follows me. I've already got a fire going in the woodstove, but I'll bring up a pile of logs for the night. Burning wood to keep our house warm requires a lot of carrying and moving. Here's the process. I get green wood from Charlie because it's cheaper, but I've got to let it season a year. I carry the logs I stacked the previous year into the cellar, as much as I can fit, and the rest goes under the deck, which I haul inside sometime mid-winter. Are you still with me? Then I stack the green logs just delivered in a long, neat stack outside to dry for next year. We burn four cords a year, so essentially I touch eight during the fall. Oh, then I carry them upstairs.

Don't get me wrong. I do love stacking wood. My piles are neat and sturdy. I feel it's a bit of an art. The kids sure didn't. Sam and I would get them out here, and before we knew it, they had disappeared. Sam always worked beside me, of course, unless he had a paying job. There's nothing romantic about stacking wood together. It was a chore that needed to get done, and it was better with four hands than two. We didn't sing or talk a lot because Sam couldn't hear me anyways. The job took us several weekends. Of course, this fall I did it all by myself. I had plenty of time. If the weather was good, I brought a chair out for Ma to keep me company. If she wasn't up for it, I cranked music up loud.

Local wisdom has it that you should only burn half of your firewood by Christmas. I have burned more than the usual amount because of my mother, but we're okay. I believe in a few weeks, I'll bring in more. Maybe I can guilt the boys into helping me.

The dog sniffs around Sam's woodshop.

"Yeah, you would've liked him," I tell her. "Come on, Maggie, back upstairs."

Damn, it's too quiet up here. I glance at the clock on the kitchen stove. I tell myself, "What the hell." I don't feel like spending the evening alone or on Adela's case, so I'll do what most everybody else in Conwell does. I'll head to the Rooster and have a beer. But I'll feed the animals first.

When I arrive, Jack is behind the bar, with both hands stretched flat on the counter as if it's holding him up. He revs up that Jack Smith grin when he sees me.

"Hey, Isabel, can't get enough of the place?" he asks.

I take a stool.

"No, I need a beer, and I'm fresh out at home," I joke.

He goes for the beer on tap I like and pours me a glass with minimal foam.

"Here ya go," he says.

I glance back. The drinkers have thinned to the True Blue Regulars. For them, the Rooster is their second home, likely because their first one isn't as much fun. If Jack put in showers and beds, they wouldn't have a reason to leave, except to work and gas their trucks.

That's when I see the Floozy in the corner of the room. She's with another of the Rooster Floozies, but the next generation. Marsha's mouth is open when she laughs. The poor woman really could use a trip to the dentist.

I have a decision to make about food. I'm hungrier than I thought, but then I only had a salad at the fast food joint. It's burger night. I can smell the grill's hot fat from my stool. I can't imagine Eleanor agreeing to fix me a salad. But there are always French fries.

"Could I get an order of fries?" I ask Jack.

"Sure, I'll go tell the cook."

He dutifully writes down the order in a neat block print.

"You have nice handwriting," I say.

"I've had to work on it for Eleanor's sake. I used to have lousy handwriting like most guys. She complained a lot she couldn't read it." He sticks the pencil behind his ear. "Be right back."

I turn when I hear footsteps behind me. The Floozy makes her approach.

"Hey, Marsha."

She stops less than a foot from me. I smell beer, cigarette smoke, and BO, not an appealing combination for a woman. Her dry, gray hair sticks out like a sloppy halo around her head. Her mouth twists into a sneer.

"Just so ya know, I gave Bobby your number. He says he's gonna call and straighten you out."

"Straighten me out?"

"Uh-huh, he didn't do anything to her. I told the cops and everybody else he was with me that night."

"That's fine, Marsha. I'm not planning to make any trouble for him. I just want to hear what he has to say. Like I said, he might know something that could help."

Jack is back in his spot. His brow has a heavy edge. He tosses the pencil next to the pad of order slips.

"Can I get you somethin' else, Marsha?"

Her head tips back like suddenly she's damn proud of herself. She jerks her chin side to side a bit.

"Nah. Just wanted to have a talk with Isabel. I'm headin' out."

Jack wipes the counter with a rag, which I am learning is a good bartender distraction.

"Sure enough. See ya soon."

"Thanks for letting me know about Bobby," I say.

Jack waits until the Floozy wobbles back to her seat and pulls on her jacket. She's already got a cigarette stuck between her lips although she knows she can't light it until she goes outside.

"What's that all about?"

"Bobby Collins. I gave her my number, so he'd call me. I want to set up a meeting."

He nods.

"Wow, you're really taking this serious."

"Yes, I am."

Eleanor slams the kitchen bell.

"Be right back."

A minute later, Jack sets the red plastic basket of hot fries and a bottle of ketchup in front of me. He grabs a Bud from the cooler and twists off the cap as he takes the seat beside mine. He takes a gulp.

I salt and pepper the fries then slide the basket his way.

"Help yourself."

He slaps his gut.

"No, thanks. I'm fat enough already."

I give his belly an appraising look.

"Ha, Jack, you don't look so fat. Besides, a couple of fries aren't going to hurt."

He shoves a fry in his mouth. I swear he's blushing.

"You talked me into it." He chuckles. "Bobby Collins, eh? I'd be careful with him."

"That's what I've heard. Even his son said as much."

"There's no love lost between those two." He takes a gulp. "So, how's your investigation going?"

"Slow so far." I am not about to tell Jack about my arrangement with Andrew or the stuff I've found. It's not that I don't trust Jack. I'm just keeping it to myself for now. "I've been going through a bunch of paperwork and meeting people who were close to her like Andrew and Dale. I went to see Mira Clark. I did try talking with the chief, but it wasn't a good day."

Jack nods.

"Yeah, he's in a bad way. Real shame he ended up like that."

"You must've known Adela well. You grew up in the same town."

"She's a bit younger than me. She and Eleanor were the same age."

"Close enough. So, what can you tell me about her?"

He takes a drink.

"How much time you got?"

I glance at the clock.

"Hmm, I'm guessing a lot. Maybe we can do this another time real soon."

"Your mother waiting for you?"

"No, she went back home for a couple of weeks. Ma wanted to spend Thanksgiving with my brother's family. My brother and I met halfway off the pike. I've been on the road a few hours today."

"What are you gonna do while she's gone?"

I laugh.

"I'll work on the case. I have a list. I may go snowshoeing after the storm's over although I hate to do it by myself."

"I remember you and Sam coming in here after snowshoeing."

"Yeah, we'd park here, take one of the snowmobile trails for a while and then come back for a beer." I sigh. "You ever try it?"

"Drink beer?"

"No, wise guy, snowshoeing."

He shakes his head.

"Never have. My mode of transportation is a snowmobile. You ever try it?"

"Only once, for a story. The guy showed off a bit. You know Ted, right?"

Jack's chuckle echoes in his beer bottle as he holds it near his mouth.

"He's a show-off all right."

It's easy talking with Jack. Sure, I've had long conversations with men before, but usually it was for a story or some business in the newsroom. This is different. Our tone is casual and friendly. There's no off-the-record bullshit. Once in a while, Jack has to get somebody a beer, but he has nothing pressing to do tonight.

Jack fetches us two more beers, and I'm glad we're taking our time drinking because I don't want to drive home buzzed.

We gab about the weather and, of course, the coming storm. There's town stuff, including the latest Rooster hookups and breakups, which we both agree is early in the season for that. It's not even officially winter. He brings up shotgun season, which begins Monday after the Thanksgiving holiday. Jack says he gave up hunting a while back since he got too busy with his bar. But this year he got a license. He says he's planning to go out on his days off with a few of the regulars. He hasn't bagged a deer in years, but he looks forward to tromping around in the woods. I offer to lend him a pair of snowshoes. He says his boots will do him just fine.

He and Eleanor will be cooking the traditional deer supper at the Conwell Rod and Gun Club on the Sunday night after the season closes. Steak instead of venison will be on the menu, as if the hunters would have been living it up on freshly killed deer meat in the woods and wanted a change of pace. The Rooster will be closed that night since most of his best customers will be at the supper instead.

One by one the True Blue Regulars leave with a big "see ya" before they head out the door. Cold air washes over our backs each time the door opens, but no snow is falling yet. The only ones left are Jack, Eleanor, who's slamming pots and pans around in the kitchen, and me. The noise sounds a lot louder than just cleaning.

I check the clock. I'm surprised how long Jack and I've been talking.

"Your sister okay in there?"

"Yeah. She makes a lot of noise in the kitchen when she cleans. She always does it on Sunday night. This week we won't serve food until Friday cause of Thanksgiving. Wanna work Wednesday night? We usually get a big crowd that night, mostly guys. I guess the women are all home cooking."

"Sure, I can be here."

"And get ready for Friday night. Everybody and their cousin will be here. The newcomers like to show up with whoever's at their house to take in the local color."

"I'll remember that."

"The Cowlicks are playing. Maybe I'll ask you to dance

another fast number."

"Oh, are you going to ask me this time?" I joke.

"Yeah, I kinda dragged you onto the floor."

"I'm only teasing you. It was a lot of fun. You're a great dancer."

Jack sets his empty down. He points toward my glass to see if I want another. I shake my head no. Two's enough.

"How are you doin'? I mean about Sam. I hope you don't mind my askin'."

I think for a moment. It's a question I ask myself a lot.

"I'm okay. It was really tough after he died, but I gave myself a full year to grieve for him properly. I decided I wouldn't do anything foolish for a year. Now it's time to… "

"Do somethin' foolish?"

"Maybe. Or at least have some fun." I smile. "Can I ask you a personal question?"

"Shoot. Go ahead."

"Have you ever been married?"

"Once, when I was a kid until she came to her senses." He shrugs. "I've had women friends, but nothing serious enough that led us to the altar. No kids either, well, none that I know of."

Suddenly, it's dark and quiet in the kitchen. Eleanor stands fully dressed in her winter coat and knit hat behind the bar. She clutches a paper bag with grease stains, filled I suppose with meat scraps for her mutts.

Eleanor glances at the clock then her brother. The clock's face says ten although it's really 9:50, an old barroom trick to move the time ahead ten minutes to fool the lingerers.

"Ready to shut the place down, Sis?" He stands. "Hold on a sec. I need to make sure the back door is locked and a few other things."

"Hey, how much do I owe you for the beer and fries?" I ask.

"Nothin'," he says. "It's on the house."

Bobby's Call

The red light is blinking on the landline's phone when I get home. I have two messages. The first is from Ma. She got to my brother's just fine. "Where are you?" she asks. I glance at the clock on the stove. I know she's up, but likely my brother and his family would think it odd if I called this late. Too bad Ma doesn't believe in cell phones. I could send her a text. It could say: "Got back okay and went to the Rooster where I got a little bit sloshed. The dog and cat say hello." But I'd leave out the sloshed part.

The second message just has a number, so I know the caller's not a regular.

The raspy voice says, "This is Bobby. Marsha says you wanna talk about Adela. Sure, I'll talk, but you're wastin' your time." Then he rattles off the number I see on the phone's window.

I wonder where Bobby is staying. It couldn't be with Marsha because the time he called, which was 8:53, is after she left. Or maybe, he is, and he thought I'd be home by now. I'll call him sometime tomorrow.

After the Storm

We did get a good dump, about eighteen inches by my estimation, sloppy, wet stuff so the roads must be a mess. I'm drinking coffee and waiting for the driveway to get plowed. I'm one of the last on Mary, the plow lady's list of customers, especially now that I don't work in the city. The dog has already been out once to do her business and bounce around in the snow. I kept watching from the front porch to make sure she doesn't take off. My mother would have a hard time forgiving me. But Maggie comes when I call. She knows there's food in the house.

Here's my list of people to call today although not necessarily in this order: Bobby, of course, although that will be one of those deep-breath phone calls; Clara, Jamie Snow's ex, which is set for nine; Sadie Hendricks, to see if she found anything in the chief's old papers; Andrew Snow to ask if he and Dale have gone through the drawers downstairs; and, yes, Ma.

That's a lot of phone calls, but except for shoveling snow, I have no business outside the house.

I call Ma first. She's out with my brother. She'll call me back, my sister-in-law tells me.

Sadie Hendricks is up already, of course.

"How's the chief today?" I ask.

She sounds almost hopeful when she says, "He's got his birds to keep him company. They're at the feeder because of the snow."

I pause, thinking about how small things like that matter to her. Everybody still calls Ben Hendricks the chief, out of reverence, I suppose. Besides his son, Ben Jr., is now the official chief. He's called Chief Ben Jr.

"That's good," I say. "Sadie, I was wondering if you happened to find anything useful in the chief's office."

"I'm glad you called. I've been meaning to get back to you, but I wanted to ask Ben Jr. first if it was okay."

I wait on her words. Even Yankee women have a hard time getting to the point right away.

"You found something?"

"Yes, I have a box of papers," she says. "They're my Ben's notes. Ben Jr. said to go ahead and give them to you since the case is so old. He said to tell you 'good luck.'"

"I don't know when I'll get plowed out. Could I come by tomorrow for the papers? What's a good time?"

"Do you mind coming early, say 7:30?" Her voice drops for the next part. "I need to take Ben to the VA for a checkup."

"That time works, Sadie. I'm up early."

I fix myself another cup of coffee and feed a log into the wood stove before I call Clara Snow, now Clara Moreau, because she's remarried. Clara lives in Florida, and according to a few folks in town, she doesn't have to work since her husband's retired and loaded. The Old Farts in the store's backroom would likely say she married some rich, old guy with a bad cough. I called her once before, but she was too busy to talk then. Now I'm in my office upstairs, with a pad of paper and a pen.

Clara answers right away.

"Hear you got a bit of snow," she says.

"I'm guessing a foot and a half. Bet you don't miss that."

She laughs softly.

"I sure don't."

"As I told you before, I'm looking into Adela's case. I know it was a long time ago, but I was hoping you could answer a couple of questions to help me."

"I'll try."

"How close were you two?"

"Close enough for sisters-in-law. I mean we didn't hang out, but we were friendly enough at family get-togethers. My kids were around Dale's age."

This conversation would be better face-to-face, but a

141

telephone call to Florida is the best I can do.

"I'm trying to learn what Adela was doing in the months up to her disappearance. Does anything stick out in your mind?"

"I can't think of anything unusual," she says. "Adela liked to keep things to herself."

"So I've heard from Andrew."

"Those two were close. If anyone knew, it would be her father."

"Was she seeing anybody?"

"A man? I wondered about that. Some days she had a real shine to her. You know how women can get when… She was sure happy when she got flowers for her birthday. She talked about it a lot."

I fill in the blank mentally for Clara. Adela was happy when she had sex.

"But she wouldn't say who sent them?"

Clara laughs softly.

"She'd say things like, 'I'm not telling' or 'Wouldn't you like to know?'"

Yes, I would.

"Do you think it was somebody in town?" I ask.

"Conwell or one of the towns around it. We didn't have dating sites on the internet then. And as far as I could see, she didn't leave town much. It could've been one of the delivery guys, too."

"Delivery guys, I hadn't thought of that," I say.

"A couple of them were always being extra-friendly. Maybe Andrew will remember."

I scribble notes as we talk.

"What do you think happened to her?"

"Personally, I never believed she'd take off. She was a real good mom to Dale. Or commit suicide." Clara pauses. "I believe someone killed her. It could have been an accident. But whoever did it, sure hid her body well. Maybe the guy had help."

"I've heard that theory before," I say. "If you were to guess who could have done it, who would it be?"

There isn't even a pause when she blurts, "Bobby Collins."

"Yeah, he's high on almost everyone's list. But what would be his motive?"

"They could have had an argument about money. Or Dale. She wouldn't let him see his son much. She was worried he'd drive drunk. Like I said, it could have been an accident. But he would have needed help."

"He says he was with Marsha that night."

"Maybe she was his helper."

"I hadn't thought of that angle. She sure is ticked off whenever I see her now that she knows I'm involved in this case."

"Marsha's a tough woman, but she has good reasons to be. I wouldn't have wanted to grow up the way she did."

"Terrible parents?"

"The worst. There was no love in that home. It explains a lot."

"That's too bad," I say, now feeling more sympathy for the Floozy. "Thanks for your help. If you think of anything, please give me a call. You have my number."

"Will do."

I study my notes. I underline the part about delivery guys. Clara's right. I'll have to ask Andrew about that. Of course, if it were somebody like the guy who brought beer or groceries, there would be no way of tracking them down. Too much time had passed although it was worth a shot. It definitely appeared Adela was in love with somebody.

Andrew is next on my list. He sounds glad to hear from me.

"I've got a question for you. Were any of the delivery guys extra friendly with Adela?"

"Delivery guys? I hadn't thought of them."

"Neither did I, but I just got off the phone with Clara. She brought it up as a possibility."

Andrew is silent for a moment.

"I can think of a couple. Let me get back to you on that."

"That's fine. By the way, have you or Dale found anything interesting in those drawers downstairs?"

"Not yet. There's so much stuff to look through."

"I could help."

"That's a thought. Let me talk with Dale."

I hear the rumble of the snowplow's blade. Mary is here. I need to get outside to move our cars out of her way. I say good-bye to Andrew.

A Curious Visitor

The driveway is now a straight white shot up to the road. It's going to be tricky getting my mother's car out of here. This is strictly a four-wheel-drive way now, but I think I can manage it if I dump some sand. I'll bring a shovel and a few compound buckets to the highway yard, which is okay with the town. Right now, I am shoveling walkways and paths into the woods for the dog. Maggie leaps through the deep snow. She's one happy mutt.

The sky is bluebird blue, which is typical after a storm's cleared. Much of the winter, the sky here is cast a gloomy gray that can drive people nuts. I know Sam would get a bit down in the middle of the winter. I hear New Mexico has 300 days of sunshine a year. Maybe Sam would have liked it there. He talked about it a few times. He wanted to see Taos and Santa Fe. Maybe I'll bring some of the ashes I didn't bury, so a part of him is there, at least, symbolically.

I am done shoveling the last walkway, the one that extends between two large flowerbeds. It's the easiest way in and out of the house for Ma because the front porch only has three steps and sturdy handrails Sam built. I hoist the shovel handle over my shoulder to bring it into the cellar where it belongs, but I get distracted when I hear the distinctive whine of a snowmobile on the road. There isn't a trail close by. Someone is riding alongside the snow-covered road. I believe it isn't legal to ride on the road, but the part-time cops aren't going to be bothered patrolling for snowmobilers, especially during the day when they're all at work. Note to myself: If I ever do something criminal, I'll choose daytime.

Maggie darts from the woods and goes a little nuts barking when the snowmobile makes a turn into our driveway. I march into the snow to grab her by the collar.

"It's all right, girl," I say although I'm curious about my visitor.

The driver waves as he slows the machine and stops a few yards from the end of this path. He takes off his helmet.

"Jack, what are you doing here?"

He chuckles as he dismounts the machine.

"I was in the neighborhood and decided to stop by." Maggie leaps through the snow toward Jack, who stoops to pat her head. "Nice dog. Didn't know you had one."

"I got her for my mother. Maggie belonged to Mira Clark's aunt. She's in a home now and can't have her." I squint in the sunlight bouncing brightly off the snow. "What brings you here?"

"I came by to see if you wanna go for a ride."

I push the shovel's blade into the snow.

"On that?"

"Uh-huh. I've got an extra helmet with me."

I laugh.

"That's thoughtful of you, but I don't think I have anything warm enough to wear."

"Too bad," he says. "Let me see what I've got around the house. What size boot you take?"

"A man's 10 ½ or 11. I've got big feet."

He studies my boots.

"Didn't notice that before. Isn't that kinda unusual for a woman?"

"Yeah, don't rub it in. It's a bitch trying to find women's shoes that fit."

He steps closer. I don't believe I've seen Jack outside very often, except briefly at the dump or outside the store. I like his eyes, and the lines around their corners make him look wise and friendly like he laughs a lot, which he does, usually a low chuckle. The gray in his dark hair stands out in the daylight. He's a foot taller than me. I'd rank him as a good-looking older man.

"I bet it is. I think I'd have some boots at home that can fit those big feet of yours." He grins. "I guess I'll have to be

146

careful the next time I dance with you. I wouldn't want to trip over them."

"Very funny." I tip my head toward the house. "Want to come in for something hot to drink? Sorry, I'm still outta beer."

"Thanks for the offer, but I better head home. I've got some chores to do or I'll catch hell from Eleanor. She took care of the plowing at the farm. Mary does the Rooster for us."

"Eleanor plows? I thought she didn't drive."

"Well, she's real handy with the tractor and just about any piece of equipment. She just doesn't drive on the road. She gets spooked too easily. She never got her license." He rubs his jaw. "What are you doin' tomorrow?"

"I was going to go snowshoeing, but I'm not sure I want to do it alone."

"I could go with you. I'd like to try it. Never have. The ones we have at the house are antiques on the wall. Probably my grandfather used them at one time when he was working the farm. Now they're decorations."

"Well, I have an extra pair. They belonged to Sam."

"Sure, if you don't mind."

I shake my head.

"They're just hanging up downstairs. How about I meet you at the Rooster at one?"

"That works."

"Uh, don't overdress. Work boots, jeans, and a jacket will do it. Wear gloves and a hat. You're gonna build up a sweat."

"I believe I can manage. I'll see ya tomorrow, Isabel."

Jack flashes me one of his grins, and then his helmet is back on his head. He moves the machine in a slow curve on the driveway, and then he's gone.

I lean on the snow shovel and tell myself, "Isabel, what the hell are you up to now?" I'm a bit surprised by the playful exchange with Jack. Maybe he just wants to do something with somebody, too. I know I'm getting tired of being alone, except for when I'm with Ma. And Ma's not here.

It's been a while since I've been in this situation, a man who's not my husband paying attention to me. This doesn't have to be true love, I remind myself, just having fun with a man and maybe being a little foolish again.

Bobby Collins

I call the number Bobby Collins left me. He answers after the fourth ring.

"Yeah," he says when I say his name and tell him who I am.

"I was wondering if you have any time to meet with me this week? You know, to talk about Adela."

He blows smoke in one noisy exhale near the phone.

"How about tomorrow?"

I have an early exchange with Sadie Hendricks, and then I'll be snowshoeing with Jack.

"I could do it anytime between eight and eleven."

"At night?"

"No, no, morning."

"Morning, eh. Yeah, I can do that. Make it ten. I have things to do." He makes one of those smoker coughs. "Where?"

"How about the Town Hall parking lot? I bet we could talk in the big room inside."

He's silent for a bit.

"All right," he says.

There's not much more to the conversation, but afterward I go upstairs to add Marsha to the suspect list. Maybe she wasn't an alibi but an accomplice after all. I add one more name: Deliveryman with a question mark.

Ma Calls Back

I tell Ma all about my conversations with Clara and Bobby.

"Hmmm, I didn't think about it being a deliveryman," she says. "It's a possibility, but he would still need help. I mean unless he loaded Adela and her car in the back of his truck."

"That's a good point. It would have to have been one mighty big truck, and I think that snoopy neighbor would've heard something like that even in the middle of the night." I pause. "What about the Floozy helping Bobby?"

"I could see that. When are you meeting him?"

"Tomorrow around ten at Town Hall. I figure it would be safe there. I suppose he knows where I live, but I don't want him coming here. Jack said the same thing."

"Jack, your boss?"

"Yeah, that Jack." I've decided to keep Ma out of the loop concerning Jack. Anyway I'm a grown woman and not some teenager living under her roof. "Oh, I almost forgot to tell you about Sadie, Chief Hendricks' wife. She's got a box of papers for me. I'm picking them up tomorrow."

"I'm gone one day, and you get all of that done."

"How's it going there?"

"Just fine. Danny took me shopping and I got to go to Wendy's."

"Did you get any snow?"

"Only rain."

"Well, you missed a big snowstorm here."

"No, I didn't miss it."

Old Farts Again

Just for jollies, and to follow up on a clue, I stop at the store to visit the Old Farts the next morning. I have plenty of time before I pick up that box from Sadie. The Skinniest Old Fart bends over from his bench when he hears my unmanly footstep between the stocked shelves.

"Oh, oh, here comes trouble," he announces to the rest of the group as if he's the lookout.

All the Old Farts stare my way. They wear heavy jackets unzipped and large snow-crunching boots.

"Howdy, fellows? What's the news today?" I ask.

"Don't ya watch the news and read the Daily Fart?" the Old Fart with Glasses says.

"Nah, not that kind of news. I'm talking about the dirt in town."

The Fattest Old Fart chuckles. He knows what I'm up to.

"Are you trying to say we're a bunch of gossiping roosters?"

I laugh.

"Yeah, something like that. So, what's new? Come on, you must've been talking about somebody before I came in."

The Bald Old Fart nods.

"Speaking of roosters, we were talking about the new bartender at the Rooster," he says. "A woman. Heard she and Jack put on quite a show dancing the other night."

I smile.

"Yeah, I heard about that, too," I say, deadpan.

The Serious Old Fart elbows the Silent Old Fart beside him.

"Funny, I saw him riding his snowmobile down her way yesterday."

"Really?" I say, feeling a little hot around the neck. "Are you following Jack around town?"

"I just happened to be driving into town with the missus," the Serious Old Fart says.

The other Old Farts laugh in a low chorus.

Then I remember the Serious Old Fart has a rep as one of the snoopiest men in town. Malcolm Woodbury is known for driving around to make sure people pulled permits for the work they did on their house. Bingo. I believe I have my deep throat. But I want to make sure.

"Malcolm, you're on the zoning commission." I keep my voice casual. "If I decide to build a garage at my place, would I need to get a permit? Sam usually took care of those things."

He grimaces like I should know better.

"Of course, you'd need a permit, Isabel," Malcolm aka the Serious Old Fart says.

Got him. It's the voice although a little lower on the phone as if he was trying to disguise it, but he's not fooling me. I add the name Malcolm Woodbury aka Serious Old Fart to my contact list.

"Just checking," I say.

Now the Fattest Old Fart asks if I want coffee, and when I decline, he jokes, "I bet you like that fancy, schmancy stuff, eh, Isabel. There are no baristas here. You should know that if you're gonna keep showing up."

"I'm fine, really. I was in the neighborhood, so I decided to stop by and give you guys a hard time again. I may make it my hobby."

There's another low chorus of laughs.

Jamie Snow walks into the backroom with a wrench in his hand.

"Hey, Isabel," he greets me, and then he raises the wrench and announces to the group, "I think I fixed it."

The Bald Old Fart turns toward Jamie.

"Maybe you should get one of those espresso machines back here for Isabel," he says.

Of course, there's another rumble of laughter.

"I'm glad to be the source of your amusement," I tell them.

152

"How's the case coming?" the Fattest Old Fart asks.

Now everyone has a serious mug. They wait for my answer. There are no jokes or light banter about Adela. I give Jamie a slight nod.

"Slow but sure," I say. "I have a bunch of leads. Some guy called to say I should check out the building and septic permits for that time. He didn't give his name." I avoid looking at Malcolm. "It'd be helpful if he called again and helped me narrow down the list."

I check Jamie's stone-faced reaction. He's put off meeting with me a couple of times. I honestly believe it's a matter of his being busy and his only sister's disappearance too painful a subject rather than a case of the guilts. Getting him to talk is another of my motivations for coming here this morning.

"What else?" the Fattest Old Fart asks.

"I don't want to give anything away. It's too soon." For that reason, I decide to withhold my questions about a deliveryman. I could see that spreading fast around town. "I've been talking with people and going through stuff. The clues are piling up."

"I hope you nail the bastard," the Skinniest Old Fart growls.

The Old Farts' heads bounce in solidarity. The Silent Old Fart gives me a thumbs-up.

"Well, you know how to find me if you have something useful," I say, and despite their protests, I say good-bye and head out the door.

The Chief's Box

Minutes later, Sadie Hendricks doesn't answer right away when I ring the doorbell, but then her son, Chief Ben Jr., who's a younger version of his father, does. He lets me into the kitchen. From another part of the house, a man moans and protests loudly. The old chief is having a bad day, and I feel guilty bothering his family.

After the typical pleasantries, Chief Ben Jr. says, "I have what you need." He stoops for a box on the floor. "Let me carry this out to your car."

"Sure."

He follows me to the Subaru and places the cardboard box on the back seat. Someone printed "Adela Collins Missing" on the top. It's a man's handwriting, probably by the old chief. And, no, it's nothing like the writing on the gift card I found at Dale's.

"I stopped by to help Mom get Dad ready for the VA. He's not, uh, being cooperative today." His head twists toward the house. "I should get back inside."

"I understand. Give your mother my best and thank her. It looks like she went to a lot of effort to find this for me."

"She was happy to do it," he says. "And let me know if you find enough to pursue a case."

I eye the box before I shut the door.

"I sure will."

Bobby Collins

I only have enough time to go home, let the dog out, and give the contents of the boxes a cursory look. Some of the paperwork I already have, like the official police records from around the time Adela disappeared. I see pages of handwritten notes. I smile. Chief Ben drew up his own list of suspects. Of course, Bobby Collins' name is at the top.

I wait ten minutes for Bobby to show at the Town Hall parking lot. I've already been inside and asked the town clerk if we can meet in the big hall. She said okay. The newcomers' yoga class doesn't start for an hour.

Bobby drives up in a beater of a Chevy pickup with Nevada plates. He chucks his lit cigarette in the snow bank as he drops from the driver's seat. I walk across the parking lot to greet him. No handshakes or smiles, just a curt, "Hey, there," from Bobby, but I'm grateful he's willing to meet me. I tell him that. He's a short guy with a semi-mullet and the standard country issue of flannel, denim, and Carhartt canvas. He squints at me like he's got a pain in his gut but doesn't want to let on.

"Why don't we meet inside? It's a lot warmer."

He frowns.

"In there?"

"The big hall's empty. I already checked. It's okay. Nobody'll bother us."

Bobby silently follows me inside to the big hall, where town meetings are held. I covered them when I was a reporter. Now I just go as a resident, raising my hand and saying "aye" or "nay" to the articles of business. The folding chairs are stacked away in one of the closets because the rest of the time, the hall's used for pickup basketball games and classes.

Sometimes there's a performance or a school play since it's the only building in town that has a stage.

I choose a spot to sit on the edge of the stage and beneath the basketball hoop. Bobby takes a place several feet away. He unzips his jacket as he looks around.

"Haven't been here in a long time," he says.

I figure maybe the last time was during the reception at Adela's so-called funeral. I recall people avoided him as if he had something contagious. He didn't even stand with the family in the receiving line.

I know enough about Bobby's background, like where he grew up and his line of work, construction. I'm not going to waste any time on that stuff because I don't know how long I can hold him. I need to get down to business, but I do have a softball question ready.

"How long were you and Adela married?"

"Four years, I think. Yeah, four."

"How did it go?"

"We got divorced, so you tell me." His voice has a don't-ask-me-stupid-questions-edge. "Me and her only got married cause she got knocked up. You did that sort of thing then. Don't get me wrong. It's not that she and I didn't like each other. But I wonder if we would've stayed together if she wasn't going to have my kid."

He glances down at his work boots, scuffed at the toes, before he continues.

"We tried, but her family made it clear from the get-go they didn't like me one bit. I guess I don't blame 'em. I was drinkin' heavy then. Drugs, too. You could say I was a real asshole. I did some stupid stuff." He makes a squinty smile. "I've cleaned up my act. I'm doin' the AA thing now."

I think back to when I saw Bobby and Dale at the Rooster. As I recall, Bobby didn't have a beer in his hand but a glass of something dark, probably Coke.

"What kind of stupid stuff?"

"Not stupid enough to kill my ex-wife." His voice is a low growl. "I know everybody thinks I did it. They still do. I can see it on their faces. But I was with Marsha that night."

156

"That's what you told the cops," I say. "When was the last time you saw Adela?"

"Actually that afternoon."

"That afternoon?"

"That's what I said. I went to the store to give her a check for my kid. Child support. I wasn't too regular about it, but I just got paid. I thought it'd mean she'd let me see my boy more."

"A check? Was it ever cashed?"

"No."

So, his check was never cashed, and Adela didn't touch her bank account before or after she disappeared. I believe it's safe to surmise she didn't take off unless she had some rich sugar daddy.

"I was looking at my old notes from back then. One woman said she saw you and Adela arguing outside the store a couple of weeks before she went missing."

He works his jaw as if he's trying to loosen it.

"It was probably about money and my kid. She said she didn't trust me takin' him cause I drank too much," he said. "She was right. I see that now. I didn't then. Like I said, I was an asshole those days."

When I look at Bobby, I see a man filled with regrets. He was too busy having fun to see the consequences. Now I wonder what he was telling Dale that night at the Rooster. Maybe he was giving him a warning. Maybe he just wants to be his father after all.

"Can you think of anything that might help me solve this case?"

"All I know is that Adela wasn't the angel everybody thinks she was."

"I've heard that from a couple of people."

"Mira Clark?" He chuckles. "From what I understand Bruce wasn't the only one."

"I get the feeling Adela was having a serious relationship the months before. Do you have any idea who it could have been?"

"Nah, I wasn't interested in her business anymore."

157

I feel I need to wind this up. I don't know how much longer I can keep Bobby.

"Here's a question I'm asking everybody. What do you think happened to Adela?"

He shuffles his boots.

"Nobody disappears like that. Somebody did somethin', and they ain't tellin'. I'm just sick and tired of people thinkin' it's me. So, hurry the fuck up and find out who, will ya?"

"You staying at Marsha's?"

"Uh-huh, until I get back on my feet. I'm tryin' to find some work. I did save some dough, but that's not gonna last long."

"Anything else you want to add?"

"Nah."

Snowshoeing with Jack

Jack hovers, watching, as I crouch in the snow to adjust the lacings on his snowshoes, so they're taut around his boots.

"Okay, that should work," I tell him, rising. "Why don't you try them out while I put on mine?"

"Is there a trick to it?"

"It's pretty flat here. Just walk straight ahead like you normally do. But if you're gonna turn around, walk in a semi-circle, so you don't step on the backs of your shoes and fall down. And if you do fall down, you'll have to roll yourself up as if you're a really fat guy."

"I think I'll avoid that last part."

"Good thinking."

I grab my snowshoes from the back of my Subaru while Jack makes deliberate steps over the Rooster's parking lot. I smile to myself as he moves forward and around his pickup truck and my car, which is parked beside it. I bend over to fix my laces.

"How am I doin'?" he asks me.

"You're a fast learner." I am upright and slipping on my gloves. "Which trail should we take?"

Four snowmobile trailheads lead from the parking lot. One even continues across the road. The Conwell Snowmobile Club sent its groomer out after the storm, so the snow on the trails will be smooth and hard beneath our shoes. Walking on them will be a piece of cake compared to breaking freshly fallen snow. Sam and I found that out fast. All we had to do on the trails was step aside when we heard a machine coming and give a wave.

Jack doesn't answer. He stares at the black, woolen leggings I usually wear when I snowshoe or hike.

"Nice legs," he tells me.

"They go with my feet, long and skinny," I joke.

He chuckles as he gestures toward the trailhead farthest to right in the parking lot.

"How about that one?"

"Sure."

Jack bucks forward, a little awkward at first, but then he gets into a rhythm. I'm right beside him. It doesn't take long before his gloves are off, and he's unzipped his jacket. He stuffs his cap into a pocket. He's huffing and puffing a little.

"Phew. You're right about working up a sweat. Next time, I won't wear this heavy jacket." I note he says next time. "Maybe I should get me some leggings like you have. Think they make 'em in my size?"

I giggle thinking of Jack in leggings.

"I bet they do."

"What's so funny?"

"I can hear the boys at the Rooster calling you one of those men in tights."

"Well, I'll set them straight I'm snowshoeing and not cross-country skiing." He scoffs. "Men in tights."

I slap his arm. I can't stop laughing.

"Maybe they won't believe you. They'll think you've gone soft on them."

"Well, they'd better or I'll put them on the six-month list." He chuckles. "It seems to me you're having a lot of fun at my expense."

"Yup." He stops walking when I stop. "Hey, look how far we've come."

We've reached the old logging road where Adela's car was found. We are already in Wilmot.

Jack points toward the right.

"That's where they found her car."

"My boys and I walked this way a couple of weeks ago. We found a wooden cross near the spot. Turns out Dale put it there for his mother."

"Yeah, the kid took it pretty hard. A lot of people did. Me included."

160

"Were you two close?"

"Knew her all my life," he says. "I know what you're gonna ask me next. Did we ever, uh, go out?"

"Yeah, did you?"

"We hooked up a couple of times, once when we were kids, and then later on. We had a lot of fun. Yeah, we slept together. But I guess it wasn't meant to be. Shame what happened to her."

"I met up with Bobby Collins this morning. Did you know he's on the wagon?"

"Hmm, makes sense now that he hasn't been comin' into the Rooster," he says. "How'd it go with him?"

"Oh, fine. He's pretty insistent he had nothing to do with it. He wants me to find the person who did."

"That's what he keeps sayin'."

"You're not convinced?"

"I hate to pin the blame on somebody who's innocent, but Bobby is sure tops on everybody's list."

"If that's true, what did he do with her body?"

Jack smiles.

"Well, detective, that's for you to find out."

I nod in the direction from where we came.

"This was good for the first outing, probably almost two miles. Maybe, we should head back." I giggle. "I wouldn't want to tucker you out."

"Silly woman. But, okay, we can take a different trail next time. I have the map memorized in my head."

Jack and I keep up a lively banter as we step our way back. We talk about the holiday. His sister will cook a bird with all the trimmings. It'll just be him and her. He could invite a couple of the loners from the Rooster, but Eleanor wouldn't like the intrusion. Besides, they see them enough times already.

I tell him Ruth wants to do the holiday up big. She doesn't even want my help. I'm just bringing the wine. I'll have to make a trip to the city tomorrow morning. "Last year's Thanksgiving was pretty miserable. Sam was only gone two weeks. There was a lot of crying that day. This should be a much happier time. Besides, we've got Sophie."

"I saw her in the store with your daughter. Ruth sure looks a lot like you did when you first moved to town."

"Some people say that," I say. "I didn't know you were paying attention to me back then."

"Ha, we all were. You and Sam were newcomers. We natives had to keep a close watch to see if you passed the test."

"What test?"

"The hilltown test."

"What's that?"

"Like if you move to town and want to shut the gate behind you, so nobody else new can come here. That's a bad mark. Or you think the natives are a bunch of stupid hicks. That's another. Or you think this is supposed to be some goddamn paradise. You flunk out on that one."

I nod. I've seen and heard it all.

"So, did we pass?"

"I'd say. We didn't run you out of town, did we?"

"No, you didn't."

Probably, at the start it was Sam who won over the natives. They saw how hard he worked for his family, taking any crappy carpentry job that came his way until he could establish himself. We were renting a shit box of house on the other side of town. I helped our cause when I became a reporter. I wrote about the stuff a lot of the natives wanted to read.

We're back at the Rooster's parking lot. Jack lowers the tailgate on his pickup, so we have a place to sit while we take off our snowshoes. He keeps looking my way as I unsnap the snowshoes' laces and clap them together to shake off the snow. Jack copies me.

I jump to the ground and open the back of the Subaru. Jack is beside me, standing awfully close.

"Here, let me have those," I tell him.

Instead, Jack tosses the shoes in the back over mine. But before I can shut the hatch, he grips my upper arms and pulls me toward him. My mouth drops open. I mean it's been a while, but I recognize the signs he wants to get close. We kiss, gently, a good first kiss, not too sloppy, though I'm nervous as hell, stop briefly, and after I give him the go-ahead smile, he kisses me again, really kissing me, tongue and all, and I'm kissing him back. His hands slide down my lower back as he brings me closer. I wrap my arms around him. He kisses me again. He means business. This is clearly an invitation for something more.

Congratulations, Isabel, you were looking for trouble, and here you've got it. Alleluia, God, and thank you very much.

Jack drops his hands when a car pulls into the lot. I do the same, and when I turn, I see a SUV with New York plates. I step to Jack's side as casually as I can muster.

A man rolls down the window. A woman in the front seat bends forward to get a better view. They know what we were doing.

"Are you open?" he asks.

Jack shakes his head.

"Sorry, we're closed Mondays and Tuesdays. We were just checking on the place. Hope you come another time. We always have a band on Fridays."

The man nods and rolls up his window before he pulls the car onto the main road.

"Ha, that was close." Jack chuckles. "Makes me feel like a kid getting caught like that. At least, they weren't local, not that I mind anybody seeing us. But you know what I mean."

I laugh, too.

"When I was in the backroom of the store this morning, one of the Old Farts said he heard we danced together at the Rooster. Then another one announced he saw you riding your snowmobile toward my house. I asked him if he was following you around town."

Jack shakes his head.

"Nosy old bastards. Guess they have nothing better to do." He chuckles. "Did I hear you call them the Old Farts?"

"Uh-huh, with a capital O and a capital F."

Jack presses his lips.

"Good one." He chuckles. "I had a great time with you today, Isabel. Too bad I promised Eleanor I'd take her grocery shopping, uh, for Thanksgiving. She's already ticked off she couldn't go earlier. I didn't dare tell her I was going snowshoeing with you."

"It was fun, wasn't it?"

"Yeah, it was. We'll have to do something else fun real soon."

And then he kisses me again.

What's in the Box?

Hours later, I'm upstairs in my office. I brought up a bowl of soup, kale, of course, to eat while I go through the contents of the box from the old chief's house. The dog, Maggie, is at my feet. The kitten wanders over my desk.

I've already called Ma to give her a report about the box and my meeting with Bobby. She told me I sounded sympathetic. I admit I am. I can appreciate he's trying to stay clean and sober, that he's remorseful for the things he's done. Ma says, "Maybe he has a reason for that." So, I keep Bobby on the suspect list but with a question mark beside his name. The same goes for his friend, Marsha.

I didn't tell Ma about Jack, even after she asked me what I've been up to since she left. I was vague. I said I went snowshoeing, which is a foreign concept for Ma, so she didn't ask if I went alone or with somebody. She probably figured I did it in the backyard. Like I said, most snow turns to rain on an ocean-facing town like where she lived. If it does get a snowstorm, it's usually a whopper. But no one snowshoes in my old town.

I've already seen most of the paperwork in the old chief's box, mostly police records and news clippings, mainly the stories I wrote when I was the town reporter. Chief Ben Sr. drew his own map and created a very short list of suspects. Like I said, Bobby Collins is first. Number two is a name I don't recognize: Walter Bartol. Bruce Clark is number three, but there is a line through that one, as if he was eliminated. The last name, a man who used to be one of Adela's neighbors, has been dead for at least ten years. I knew the guy well. I can't imagine his motivation. The old chief was fishing on that one.

Who the hell is Walter Bartol? I can't recall anyone with that name living in Conwell. I find out who he is at the bottom of the pile when I see the paperwork for a restraining order Adela took out against him six months before she disappeared. He wasn't allowed to come near her, including her home and workplace, which would be her folks' general store.

Adela writes on the order's form Walter Bartol was real friendly to her at the store, so she agreed to go out on a date with him. It appeared he expected a lot more from her that night than she wanted to give. She says he tried to rape her, but she fought him off. The trouble continued. He made lewd and rude comments when he saw her at the store. Then he started parking outside her house. Once in the city, he scared her badly when she was shopping with her son, Dale.

I glance at the time on my computer. It's only seven, and still early enough to call Andrew Snow. I tap the numbers on my phone.

"You find anything?" Andrew asks me.

"I sure did. I was going through the old chief's paperwork from that time and found something really interesting. It's a restraining order Adela took out against a Walter Bartol."

Andrew curses softly. "Walter Bartol. I forgot all about him."

"Who is he?"

"He drove a beer truck. From what Adela told me, he was making a real pest of himself. I don't know if they ever went out, but something must've happened that scared her bad enough to do that. As I recall, he stopped delivering to the store. His replacement didn't give me much of an explanation."

"So, Walter Bartol was a delivery man?"

"Yes, he was," Andrew whispers. "What are you going to do now?"

"I've got more to go through. But I plan to find this Walter Bartol and ask him some questions. There's an address on this order, but that was twenty-eight years ago. I might have to do a little digging. Course, it'll be easier with the internet. I'll just Google his name."

"You'll Google?"

"It's a way to search," I say. "Do you have any idea how old he was at the time."

There's a pause at the other end of the line.

"Let me see. He was middle-aged. I believe he was divorced cause once in a while he complained about an ex-wife. He was tall and with a full head of hair. He was strong from carrying all those cases of beer. My Irma thought he was kind of handsome. He'd been coming to the store for years."

"Did he hang around Adela when he came in?"

"Uh-huh, the guys in the backroom sure noticed. They were careful not to talk about my family back there, but sometimes I overheard them."

"That helps. I'll let you know what I find. By the way, I met Bobby Collins today."

"I heard," he says. "The town clerk's my cousin's daughter."

I laugh. I don't need the internet in Conwell. The local family network is alive and well. So is the Old Farts network in the backroom.

"I forgot. Anyway, Bobby insists he didn't do it. It looks like he's trying to clean up his act."

"That's what I hear. I still don't trust the guy."

I get to work on my computer. Roxanne, the kitten, has jumped in my lap. Maggie is curled near my feet.

"Well, look at what I found," I tell them.

Two Walter Bartols live in the valley, one the right age, if my math is correct, and miraculously at the same address. I figure the other Walter Bartol must be a junior. I print out the page, which I tape to the wall of crime along with the restraining order. I write Walter Bartol at the top of the suspects' list and shoot an arrow from deliveryman to his name. Maybe I'm getting somewhere.

My cell phone rings. It's not Andrew calling me back, and not Ma, although I can't wait to tell her about the restraining order, but Jack.

"Hey, Jack, what's going on?"

"I just wanted you to know I had a swell time today."

Jack would see me blushing a little around the neck if he were telling me this in person. Snap out of it, Isabel. You just went snowshoeing. You only kissed a little.

"I had a swell time, too."

"I hope you didn't mind my kissing you like that."

I giggle. Oh, no, I'm giggling.

"As I recall, Jack, I was kissing you back."

He makes one of those explosive laughs, like he's been holding it inside.

"You're right. I'll see you tomorrow then."

"Yes, you will."

I get up and walk across the hall to my bedroom. I give it a close study before I go to my bureau, where I keep a framed photo of Sam. I took it when we were on vacation, the time we camped at Mount Monadnock in Southern New Hampshire and climbed it twice. He's got a nice smile as he sits on the mountain's very top. I hold the photo close to my heart as I carry it into my office and place it on the tall bookcase he built for me. I can keep an eye on him there from now on.

Thanksgiving

Dinner is over. We've cleared the table and put the food away. The dishwasher chugs away in the kitchen. We continue to drink wine while our bellies make room for dessert, as my mother would say. I called Ma already, and let the kids take turns talking with her until I brought the phone to the other room to tell her about Walter Bartol and the restraining order.

"Good work, Isabel," she tells me.

Matt and Alex are here, without girlfriends, plus Gregg's parents, who drove here from Connecticut. Nice folks, already retired, but busy with traveling and volunteer work. I get along just fine with Anne and Phil. Our politics are similar, on the liberal side, but we avoid talking too much about that topic. They're just back from China, so they have a lot to share about the trip.

"Hey, Mom, it was funny seeing you at the Rooster," Matt says.

I smile at him and Alex, who showed up last night.

"I was glad you two behaved yourselves. I'd hate to see you make one of Jack's lists."

The boys laugh. As Jack predicted, it was a busy night, heavy on local guys and kids of drinking age home from college or their new lives. The men outnumbered the women. Bud was King, naturally, although I did make a margarita, straight up and light on the salt, for one of the college girls. The Rooster didn't serve food, so we sold out of potato chips. Empty chip bags were everywhere when I went to fetch bottles from the tables. But at least Eleanor wasn't there, so Jack didn't leave me alone with the horde.

Jack was friendly, but not too, too friendly. We worked side by side filling orders behind the bar, joking, laughing, and taking turns to fetch empties. He walked me to my car when the bar was closing, but there were no good-night kisses because a couple of the snowmobilers were smoking dope in the parking lot before they took off. It was all right by me. It's kind of early to expect that sort of thing in whatever Jack and I are doing although he did stroke my upper arm.

"Is the Rooster that barroom in town?" Anne, Gregg's mother, asks me. "You're not going to work for another newspaper?"

I set down my glass and slide it toward Alex for a refill.

"No, I'm outta the newspaper business. I like tending bar. You should stop by tomorrow night. It's local color night."

"What's that?" Anne asks.

"Oh, it'll be a mix of natives whooping it up and the newcomers slumming it," I explain. "The Cowlicks will be playing. They have a solid redneck play list."

Anne looks at Phil, who gives her a "we'll see" kind of look. She may be interested in going for an anthropological trip to the Rooster although I seriously doubt Phil, who's a bit of a stiff, would. His son isn't a stiff, but he's a quiet kind of guy who goes along with our family's zany outbursts. Anne must have had a bit to drink because the Rooster is definitely not their style. She and Phil are more of the quiet cocktail set. Besides, the bar will be super-crowded. The Rooster may exceed its legal limit of people tomorrow night, if there is actually one.

"Mom's also a detective," Alex says.

Anne's eyebrow arches.

"Detective, really?"

"Tell them about your first case," Alex says.

At that, Ruth lifts Sophie from her high chair. It's time for the baby's nap, but then again, Ruth has heard enough about my new life as a detective. She doesn't want to hear a repeat performance for her in-laws although Gregg sits back with an amused look on his face. I give the baby a kiss when Ruth brings her to me.

"You have a case?" Anne says. "What's it about?"

I nod, planning to give her the very condensed version.

"Adela Collins, who lived all her life in our town, disappeared one night twenty-eight years ago. No one knows what happened to her. She was declared dead officially seven years later by her family."

"In this little town, really?" Anne says. "A woman disappeared? What do you think happened to her?"

I slide the half-full glass back toward me.

"I'm still gathering clues, but I'm leaning toward murder or an accidental killing rather than suicide. Her father hired me to find out what happened after I started snooping around. I was only doing it for myself then. I wrote about the case when I was a reporter, and it bugs me still."

The boys hoot.

"Hired? You didn't tell us that part," Matt said. "Now our mother is a real detective. Isabel Long, P.I."

"You know, Matt, that has a real nice ring," I say. "I think I'll use it."

Local Color

The Rooster is jumping and bumping tonight, and from my vantage point at the bar, I can tell a lot of the customers will be humping later on. Yeah, I'm being a bit crude, but I've seen more men and women getting felt up here tonight than by the TSA at the airport.

The kitchen is slammed. Jack smartly decided to serve only burgers and fries to keep it simple for Eleanor. When I arrived, she had plates of burgers, likely formed by her naked hands, in the fridge. The poor thing was slicing onions, and tearing up something awful, so I let her be, except for a "hi, ya," and I didn't expect even a grunt back.

The slips pile up and Jack warns folks that Eleanor is doing her best in the kitchen. But no one seems to mind. You would've thought nobody had stuffed themselves with turkey and pie the day before as they wolf down burgers and fries. I check the kitchen a couple of times, but frankly, I don't know what I could do to help Eleanor, if she'd let me. Besides, I'm busy chatting as I open bottles and pour beer from the tap. I even have mixed drinks to make, including a Manhattan for some newcomer. I ring up the orders. Jack's the runner tonight.

I know most of the newcomers. Their kids grew up and went to school with my kids. We watched them play soccer or baseball on the sidelines. We even socialized. They all came to Sam's funeral and told me how sad they were he died. Many tonight seem surprised by my new job. I guess they aren't part of the Conwell network although everyone in town knew I wasn't working at the Star.

"How's it working out for you here?" they say, as if they're trying to squeeze the real story out of me.

I joke back, "That Jack's a real slave-driver," and hopes he

172

hears me.

My customers include those kids who grew up with my kids, or younger, and I ask all of them to show me IDs. My standard reply is, "When did you get old enough to drink?" and then, "Okay, you're good to go. Now be careful."

The natives are out in full force. They outnumber the newcomers and their guests three-to-one. Dale Collins comes alone and orders at the bar. I don't have time to ask him if he's searched those drawers yet. By the way, his Uncle Jamie called me as I was leaving the house to set up an interview tomorrow afternoon, say around three, at the store. He said we could talk privately in the store's office, which I didn't know existed next to the walk-in cooler. I am guessing the discovery of the restraining order against Walter Bartol has something to do with Jamie finally agreeing to meet me.

Actually, a number of the people connected to this case are here tonight: Mira and Bruce, and Marsha, of course. Bobby Collins sips Cokes at a table with his Floozy friend. He gives me a gruff hello and neither tip when I bring them their drinks.

Some in the crowd give a welcoming holler when the Cowlicks carry their amps and instruments through the side door to the spot reserved for them. Jack greets the band, and then he's back at the bar with a full tray of empties and dirty dishes.

"Hey, who's that guy over there who looks a little like you?" I ask Jack. "I don't think I've seen him in here before."

Jack turns briefly.

"Sure you have. That's my cousin Fred Lewis. He's on my mother's side. Lives in Titus. He must've come by snowmobile. Yup. See his helmet?"

I check out Fred, who's sitting with a group of local guys, as I drop empties into the cardboard case at my feet. Jack gives his cousin a big family howdy-do as he strolls over. They grab each other's hands in a full-bodied shake that's close to arm wrestling. Jack and Fred appear to be about the same age. Both have full heads of dark hair with some gray.

Jack is back.

"My cousin says you're a pretty woman," he says.

"How much has he been drinking tonight?"

"Very funny, Isabel."

At 7:50, which is really 7:40, Jack rings a cowbell hard to announce the kitchen is closing in ten minutes. Then he sets the bell beside the cash register, so some drunken clown doesn't make off with it.

"Where'd you get the cowbell?" I ask him.

"I found it in one of the barns back home." He tips his head toward the full room. "I thought I'd need somethin' to get their attention besides my loud mouth."

The bar's level of excitement rises significantly when the Cowlicks begin their first tune, "Gimme Three Steps," an automatic crowd-pleaser by Lynyrd Skynyrd, of course, and as soon as they grind out those opening chords, guys holler in approval and race with their dates to the dance floor. Those newcomers unfamiliar with the Rooster's layout get jostled aside. Or a few brave ones join the stampede.

Maybe that'll hold them for a while. I haven't had a chance to sit all night.

Jack takes Eleanor home an hour later. She's really beat. She smirks when I tell her good night, and then she shuffles through the customers with her head down toward the closest door. She does stop when she sees her cousin, Fred. Her back's to me, so I can't see her reaction, but she lingers a bit as he talks with her. I swear she talks back before she continues on her way outside to her brother's pickup. Jack follows right behind her. He points to a couple of kid drinkers old enough to drink.

"Behave yourselves," he warns.

As soon as Jack's gone, Fred Lewis comes to the bar to order a Bud and a shot of whiskey, which he tosses back as soon as I set down the glass.

"Jack says your name's Isabel. I kinda remember you from before. You used to come dancing here a lot with a guy."

"Yeah, he was my husband."

"Was?"

"Yes, he died a year ago."

"So, you're available?"

174

"Available for what?" I ask him.

"Oh, now, I see why Jack hired you." He actually gives me a wink. "You're one of those sassy women."

"I suppose I am. Can I get you anything else?"

"Maybe I'll start comin' around here more often."

I nod. Cousin or not, this guy is giving me the creeps. I decide to get all business-like. I ignore his attempts at being too friendly. I don't know who the hell this guy is, and right now, I'd prefer Bobby Collins' attention to his.

"You ready to settle up? I could ring you up right now."

"Nah, I have a tab."

I fish through the stack of tickets.

"Oh, here it is." I scribble the amounts for the beer and shot. "You can settle up with Jack before you leave."

"Sure enough."

Fred returns to his table.

"Did I miss anything?" Jack asks when he returns.

"Not a thing," I say."

Jack and I dance a fast one in the Cowlicks' second set. He clangs that cowbell to announce the bar is closed, and then he's pulling and twirling me to Waylon Jennings' "Good Hearted Woman," what else, and I'm wondering if that's what Jack thinks I am. Certainly, Sam thought I was his "Brown-Eyed Girl."

The newcomers clear out faster than the natives. By the time it's close to eleven, only the True Blue Regulars are left. Even Jack's cousin is gone. The pace has slowed enough that I can begin cleaning behind the bar. Jack carries cases of empties to the storeroom. He slides open the coolers.

He whistles.

"We sure went through a lot of beer tonight," he says.

Jack shuts the cooler just as the Cowlicks' lead singer announces the next song is the last for the night. It's Patsy Cline's "I Fall to Pieces," and I hum along with the opening. I even begin to sing along. I know the words by heart because I'm a huge Patsy fan.

Jack takes the rag from my hand and tosses it in the sink.

"How about a slow one this time?" he asks.

175

My heart ticks a little faster as he tugs on my wrist and I go with him to the dance floor. He pulls me so close about all I can do is wrap my arms around him although I stop short of resting my head against his chest. I follow him around the floor. People must be staring. I would if I were in their place, but I don't care.

Jack smiles down at me.

He asks, "What do you say, Isabel?"

In Bed

Jack and I are going at it in my bedroom. I knew it was going to happen. Jack was hoping it would happen. Perhaps you were rooting for the guy.

We closed up the Rooster, jostling and teasing, laughing, and finally when the last drinker left, a bit of kissing and inappropriate touching. Jack followed me home, and as I let the dog out briefly and fed the cat, Jack sat and watched as if he were studying me for an exam. He was in Sam's old chair, the one he died in, but I can't bear to part with it because he built it.

But now Jack and I are upstairs in my bed with our clothes off and having a grand old time.

Jack whispers, "I may come awfully fast. It's been a while."

And I say, "That's okay. I'm a little nervous, too. It's been a while for me, too."

Then he says, "Aw, Isabel, I won't hurt ya."

Jack's doing his best to warm me up, and he succeeds. I'm panting and moaning. And, yes, when the moment does come, it's over quickly.

Afterward, I smile when I say, "I'll make sure it won't be a while before the next one."

Jack gives me a kiss before he rolls to his side.

"I'll hold ya to it."

The top sheet is down by our feet, so we get a look at each other. I lit candles on the bureau and the nightstand beside the bed. I believe there's just enough light for me to be firm and beautiful in Jack's eyes. Maybe. Jack, I see, has one of those square solid bodies, with a bit of a belly. He's not a hairy guy, I'm pleased to see, not even on his chest. He does have one nasty scar on his abdomen, and he shudders when I run a fingertip over its edge.

"Operation or knife fight?" I ask.

"Neither. Motorcycle accident. Actually, I was with my cousin you saw tonight. We were fooling around. And we weren't even kids then. We were a bit drunk and stupid that day."

"Sorry, but I don't care much for your cousin."

"Somethin' happen?"

"Not really, just a feeling. He came up to the bar while you were gone with Eleanor. It wasn't so much what he said but how he said it."

"Yeah, I can see that."

"Your sister actually stopped to talk with him," I say. "I was a bit surprised."

"Those two go way back. Fred lived with us for a while."

"I see. Well, the Rooster must've had a great night tonight."

"Oh, yeah. I haven't counted it up yet, but I bet it was quite a haul. I've got the money stashed under the front seat of my pickup. Don't worry, it's locked and has an alarm."

"What?"

"Hey, I don't want some yahoo breaking into the place."

"Don't you have a safe?"

"Yeah, at home, but I didn't make it there last night. Remember?"

I make one of those silly giggles.

"Yeah, you didn't."

"Thanks for all your help tonight," he says. "I couldn't have done it without you. Well, I have in the past, but it wasn't as much fun."

"You're talking about the Rooster, right?"

Jack chuckles.

"You naughty girl." He plays with the nipple of one breast. "Come here, Isabel, so you can drive me crazy again."

Morning After

I'm half-asleep when I hear the buzz of a vibrating cell phone and realize it belongs to Jack. The phone is in the pocket of the pants he discarded on the floor with the rest of his clothes and my clothes. Jack is asleep beside me, snoring lightly. Last night, after the second time we had sex, he mentioned going home but kept putting it off until I joked either he had to stop mentioning it or I was going to kick him out. And then we both drifted off to sleep. I'm glad he stayed. It's been over a year since I had a man beside me in this bed.

The phone buzzes again. I believe it's the fourth time. I check the clock. It's around nine. I shake Jack's shoulder.

"Somebody keeps calling you," I say.

He has one eye open, then the second. His chest rolls in a sigh.

"Morning, gorgeous."

"Morning, yourself."

The phone stops.

"I bet it's my sister. She's probably wondering where the hell I am."

"You two are awfully close."

He stretches over the side of the bed for his pants. He plops back down beside me and raises the phone, so he can check the screen.

"Yeah, we are. I'm all she's got," he says. "It's her all right. She called four times."

I lie beside Jack as he speaks in a jovial voice to Eleanor. He's sorry if he worried her, but he's just fine. He'll be home soon.

I note Jack doesn't offer his sister an explanation about why he's not home or who he's with. Maybe she thinks he slept at the Rooster although I doubt it.

And now I have a dilemma. What happens if this thing with Jack continues? Unless I'm reading Jack wrong, this isn't just a one-night stand. I can tell Jack has feelings for me. I have them for him although I'm not sure what they are.

But it's the sleeping arrangements that worry me. It's my house, but I don't know how comfortable Ma would be having Jack stay overnight or that we're having sex upstairs. How would it be going to Jack's place with his odd sister spying on us?

"See ya, Sis," Jack says.

"Eleanor okay?"

"She's fine." He sticks the phone in the pocket and drops his pants onto the floor. Then he's back in his place, lying beside me. "What are you doing today?"

"The usual Conwell triangle. First the dump, then the library, and the store," I joke. "I'm meeting Jamie Snow finally to talk about his sister."

"Has Jamie been avoiding you?"

"A little. It's probably too painful a subject."

Jack nods.

"I can see that."

"Do you remember a guy named Walter Bartol?"

"Bartol, Bartol," he repeats the name as the last name sounds familiar. "Yeah, he used to deliver beer up here. The Rooster was on his route. Why?"

"The old chief had him on his short list of suspects. I saw other paperwork about him."

"Another guy took his place, but I didn't think anything of it. Chief Ben had him down as a suspect? Hmm, never thought of that before." His eyebrows make a quick up and down. "Next, you'll be telling me I was on the chief's list of suspects."

I poke his side.

"No, silly, your name didn't come up," I say. "Hey, why don't you take a shower? I'll go downstairs and fix us some breakfast. What do you take in your coffee?"

"Just make it black for me, ma'am."

Jamie Snow

As I described to Jack earlier this morning, I hit the dump, the library, and then the Conwell General Store, in that order. The Old Farts have long deserted the backroom, so I can meet Jamie Snow without drawing too much notice although I'm sure word will get back to them. The store's office, tucked beside the walk-in cooler, is nothing more than a closet with a window facing the back of the store. It has enough room for a four-drawer filing cabinet, a desk with a computer, and a few chairs. The shelves built into the walls are filled with old loose-leaf binders.

"Please have a seat," Jamie tells me, and then he nods at the open doorway. "Hey, Dad."

Andrew Snow shuts the door behind him. He holds a manila envelope.

"Isabel, how are you?"

"I hope you don't mind my Dad joining us," Jamie says. "At Thanksgiving, he told me about some papers he found in my sister's home. They concern Walter Bartol. I believe you know about him now."

"Walter Bartol. Yes, I'm very interested in him."

Jamie raises a hand.

"Just so you know, I wasn't in favor of you looking into what happened to my sister. I didn't see the point. So much time has passed... but I'm all right with it now. Dad told me about the box of papers you got from the old chief."

"That's how I found out about Walter Bartol." I pause. "Your sister took out a restraining order against him. I saw the paperwork."

"What?" Jamie says.

Andrew's head bows. He lifts a fingertip to his right eye. "I honestly didn't know," he says hoarsely like he's working up to a cry. He turns toward his son. "Jamie, did you?"

"No, Dad, I didn't." Then he asks me, "What did she write about him?"

I reach into my bag.

"Here, I made copies for you both," I say as I hand them over. "Adela describes a bad experience on a date with Bartol, and then how he stalked her. She mentions another time she got scared when she was with Dale."

The men's heads are down as they read the forms.

The paper shakes in Andrew's hand.

"Why didn't she say something to one of us?" he says afterward.

Jamie drops the papers on his desk.

"Do you think he could have something to do with my sister going missing?" he asks.

"The old chief did have him on his list of suspects. I found that in the box. Of course, Bobby Collins' name is on it, too."

Andrew hands me the manila envelope.

"This is for you."

"What's inside?"

"Letters. They're from Walter Bartol. No wonder she was afraid of him." He swallows hard. "I found them in a hutch downstairs in her house. I started to read them, but I... I couldn't."

I take a peek inside the envelope but decide this is not the place or time to go through them.

"Just so you know I found out a Walter Bartol still lives at that address. I plan to talk with him. I think it would be better to meet him face to face."

Andrew shakes his head.

"Isabel, that could be dangerous," he says. "Especially if he's the one."

"Could be," I say. "Actually, I'm nervous about it. Maybe I'll find somebody to go with me, other than my mother."

"That would be the smart thing to do," Andrew says.

Jamie has been quiet during my exchange with his father.

I ask him, "Is there anything that you can think of that

would help my investigation?"

Jamie's head jerks side to side.

"Sorry, I'm still in shock about this," he says. "Like what?"

He's clearly shook, so I decide to go easy on him.

"When was the last time you saw your sister?" I ask.

"That day. Actually just before closing. We talked about the usual stuff."

"Okay. From the clues I found, she appears to be having a serious relationship with a man. Do you have any idea who he could be?"

"No." He raises both hands. "I don't think I'm being very helpful at all."

"That's all right. Maybe something will come to mind now that I've brought it up," I say. "I have one last question I'm asking everybody. What do you think happened to your sister?"

Jamie's brow hangs forward.

"I think we all know what happened to my sister. Please find out the person responsible."

"I'm trying."

Andrew pats my arm.

"Isabel is doing a great job... "

I check the wall clock. I need to get home and get things done before I head to the Rooster.

"Oh, Andrew, I almost forgot. On that calendar we found, Adela blocked off a week in August for a vacation. Do you know what her plans were?"

He shakes his head.

"I honestly don't remember. I'll have to ask Dale about it."

"Good enough."

A Dead Rooster

It's dead at the Rooster for a Saturday night. I am guessing people ran out of gas after last night's blowout. Still, the True Blue Regulars show up to drink. Some of them play pool now that the tables have been pushed back in their places on the dance floor. A few drinkers feed the jukebox. The television sets are tuned to sports games.

The big topic of conversation is the start of shotgun season Monday. As I do this time every year, I plan to keep out of the woods in case some yahoo thinks I'm a deer. I'll wrap orange cloth over the dog and stick close to her whenever she's outside. Right now, everybody's hopeful they'll bag a deer, especially since it'll be easier to track the animals in the snow. The weather has stayed consistently cold enough the snow hasn't melted except, thankfully, on the roads.

"You're lucky, Jack," one of the True Blues tells Jack. "You can just go out back of your house and into the woods."

Jack nods.

"That's what I'm planning to do."

Eleanor has an easy night of it. A couple of times, she stands in the kitchen entrance, her hands curled by her side. She watches her brother and even peeks at the room to check the crowd.

Jack keeps telling her, "Just take it easy, Sis. Last night was a doozy."

Around eight-thirty, Dale Collins rushes into the Rooster and hops onto a stool across from me.

"I remember," he gasps.

"You remember what?" I ask.

"The vacation. My grandfather said you asked about it."

I hand him a beer.

"Go ahead."

"I was at Boy Scout camp that whole week. She went away by herself to Cape Cod. At least, that's what she told me. But now I'm wonderin' if that was true. Maybe she went with the guy who sent her the flowers."

I nod.

"That's helpful, Dale."

Dale takes a gulp of beer.

"Hey, Eleanor," he says.

Jack's sister watches from the kitchen doorway. She grunts and gives me a long, hard stare before she returns to the kitchen.

I shrug.

Frankly, Dale's revelation is the highlight of my night, except for Jack's constant flirting. Even one of the Rooster regulars makes note and says, "What's up with you two?"

"Just having a grand ole time at the Rooster," Jack tells him. "What about you?"

Jack takes Eleanor home on the early side tonight. She doesn't respond to my, "See ya, Friday." Maybe Jack told her he spent the night with me and that it's probably going to happen again tonight. Or she's just the grumpiest co-worker I've ever had.

Back Upstairs

I'm home an hour before Jack shows up. I take a shower, and the God's honest truth, I wear a slinky, black nightgown that's been in the drawer for years. Oh, why not, and Jack is overtly appreciative when I greet him at the front door.

"Hey, there, handsome," I greet him.

He sets a bottle of red wine on the floor and says, "I guess we won't be needing this to get us started," and then he chases me upstairs. We're both laughing our heads off.

I let the robe fall to the floor and lay back in bed as I watch Jack undress.

Goddamn it, I'm still nervous as hell.

But I get over it fast.

Pillow Talk

The next morning, Jack and I face each other in bed. It's ten, later than any time I'm usually up. I'm an early morning person. It seems I never got over waking up at 5:30 to head to the newsroom.

We're both smiling. We don't have to say a thing.

But finally I do. I tell Jack something that's been on my mind since this thing between us started.

"My mother's coming back next Sunday. I'm going to meet my brother halfway again." I pause. "I'm thinking it might make her uncomfortable if we have sex here and sleep together. She's a bit old fashioned although she surprises me more and more all the time. Maybe she'd get used to the idea, but at first, I'm not so sure."

"I was wonderin' about that."

"I like having my mother here. She's good company. I don't… " I'm trying to read Jack's face. "That is if you want to still do this after she comes back."

He laughs.

"Are you kidding me?"

"No, just testing you."

He rubs his chin and jaw.

"We'll figure somethin' out." Now he's got a big Jack Smith grin on his face. "We could do it on one of the tables at the Rooster or in my pickup like real rednecks." He laughs because my mouth hangs open. "Nah, we can go to my place. Course, I'd have to clean it up. I'm afraid it's your typical bachelor pigsty. I'm not too bad of a slob, but things do pile up over the years."

"How would Eleanor take it if I came over?"

"What do you mean?"

"Sometimes I get the feeling your sister doesn't like having me around. I try to be friendly, but she mostly grunts or stares at me. You should've seen her last night when Dale and I were talking about his mother."

"Eleanor's real funny around people. That's why she sticks to the kitchen." He slips his arm under and around me, so I move closer. "Besides, she has her half of the house and I have mine. They're separate apartments although there is a door connecting the kitchens."

"Okay, I won't take it personally then."

He sighs.

"Shit, I wish I wasn't going hunting on my days off. I'll be really beat getting up way before dawn and tromping through the woods hunting for deer. I'm having a couple of buddies from the Rooster join me. My cousin, Fred, too."

I ruffle his hair.

"No, no, have a good time. You can tell me all about it."

"I won't see you for a couple of days."

"Hmm, I know how you can make it up to me."

His eyebrows shoot upward.

"Really?"

I laugh.

"Hold on, cowboy. I was wondering if you'd come with me to talk with Walter Bartol. Remember him? He was the beer truck driver from that time."

"Course I know who you're talking about."

"Andrew Snow doesn't want me to go alone. I'm kind of scared to do it, but I have some pretty damning evidence about him."

"Like what?"

"I told you about the restraining order. Yesterday, Andrew gave me an envelope filled with the hate mail he sent her. I only read a couple. They're pretty bad."

"So, it could be him."

"Maybe. Would you come with me? Please? I'm guessing it wouldn't take long."

"Sure, what day?

"Wednesday or Thursday."

188

"Let's get it over with. How about Wednesday morning? I'll pick you up at say nine."

"Thanks, Jack. I appreciate it."

Walter Bartol's Letters

Jack leaves in the early afternoon after we fool around some more and I make him breakfast. He tells me with a wolfish grin he hadn't eaten homemade pancakes in years. I used the syrup I bought from the Maple Tree Farm, the place the boys and I saw on the end of our fieldtrip earlier this month.

Now I'm upstairs in the company of the dog and cat, of course, although I know they'll desert me once Ma comes back, the little turncoats. I remove Walter Bartol's letters from the manila envelope. There are nine letters, and Adela kept them in their original envelopes, mailed to the Conwell General Store, so I can easily date them. I put them in order on my desk.

They're all written in a manly scrawl, but definitely not the one on the card that says "Happy Birthday my love."

The first one was mailed Jan. 7.

"Adela, I'm sorry about the other night. I was being a jerk. I don't blame you for kicking me out. Give me another chance and I'll make it up to you. I'll show you a good time. Walter."

The second came the following week.

"Adela, I said I was sorry. I really mean it. All I want is another chance to show you how I feel about you. Walter."

Here's the next one.

"Adela, Why won't you talk with me at the store? I tried to tell you the other day it wasn't my fault. You

shouldn't have led me on that night. I thought you wanted it like that. Call me. Walter."

The tone changes in the next letter.

"Adela, stop ignoring me. If you didn't, I wouldn't have to write you like this. Stop making me feel bad. It's not like I really raped you. Walter."

The letters get progressively more hostile. It's typical of a relationship gone bad in the mind of this man. In this case, at least reading between the lines, Walter Bartol tried to force himself on Adela. It must have been rough sex or even rape because I've gotten the impression Adela enjoyed a good romp in the sack. Walter starts being nice, apologetic, and then ends up blaming her for what happened.

"Adela, I saw you with that guy. I bet you let him do what he wants. You are just a tease like all the others. I thought you were different. Walter."

I pause at "that guy." Is this Adela's mystery lover?

In one letter, Walter Bartol accuses her of being a lousy mother. He could tell when he saw her and Dale together. He wrote the boy looked scared. She probably beat him. Actually, Dale was probably scared of Walter.

The last letter, dated April 10, is the worst.

"You bitch. I'll get you for this."

He didn't sign his name on that one, but the handwriting is the same. The restraining order is dated early the next week, presumably after she got the letter at the store. I reread the form Adela signed. Walter Bartol stalked her. He watched her house and followed her to the Rooster. She didn't dare go alone into the city, and the time she did with Dale, he scared her something awful.

I sit back in my chair. I wonder why the cops didn't

consider Walter Bartol a possible suspect. Or maybe they interviewed him but did nothing about it. After all, they treated Adela strictly as a missing person. In their minds, there was no foul play. Too bad I can't ask the old chief. It's unlikely he would remember even on a so-called good day. I feel sorry for him and his family. People shouldn't end up forgetting their way like that.

But these letters are pretty damning. Walter Bartol shoots to the top of the suspect list. That's what I tell Ma when I call her.

"You're really going to visit that man?" she asks.

"I'm not going alone. I asked Jack, and he said he would join me."

"Jack, your boss? You two getting chummy?"

I smile. Chummy is a funny word. I'd say it was more than that between Jack and me, but I'm not telling Ma over the phone. Once, she told me I should get remarried. I was too young to be a widow living alone. It's interesting the perspective on what is young by someone who is ninety-two.

"Yeah, we're getting chummy."

"I go away for a few days, and you get yourself a boyfriend," Ma jokes.

My mother would laugh even more if she saw my red face.

"Very funny, Ma. Anyways I'm glad he's coming with me. I read you those letters. He sounds really angry."

"Maybe you'll have this case solved before I get back," Ma tells me. "Then we'll have to find another mystery to solve."

"We'll see about that."

"So, how are my cat and dog doing?" Ma asks, and I laugh because she didn't ask the same question about me.

"They're just fine. Hunting season starts tomorrow. I'll have to stay close to Maggie when she goes outside, so some knucklehead doesn't shoot her by accident. Roxanne is not allowed out ever."

"I miss them. Your brother's animals aren't as nice."

"By the way, I'm watching Sophie for the next two days while Ruth works. I figure it'd be a good time to check out the addresses on those permits. I'll just strap her in the backseat

192

and take a drive. I'll drive around looking for a hole big enough to bury a body."

"Let me know what you find."

"Don't worry, Ma. I will."

A Question for the Old Farts

I meet Ruth at the store to make the Sophie transfer. It's early enough for the Old Farts to be inside the backroom gabbing about everybody's business but their own.

"Did Gregg's folks have a good time?" I ask Ruth.

"They left Sunday, so I guess they did," she says. "Did you have to tell them about Adela?"

"Hey, your brothers brought it up. I didn't. Why? Something wrong?"

She's loading Sophie into the backseat. Maggie jumps from the back of the car to check her out. Her tail wags as she sniffs the baby.

"I just don't want them to think we're… "

"Nuts?"

Ruth laughs. Sometimes I think she's torn between loving her family for all of our eccentricities and wanting us to be more, let's say, civilized.

"Hey, what's this I hear about you and Jack Smith dancing at the Rooster?"

"Who told you that?" I ask, and then I remember a couple of her school friends were there on Friday's blockbuster night. "Never mind. We're just having a good time."

"Hmm, I see."

Ruth pulls away in her car. I gaze down at my granddaughter.

"What'd ya say, kiddo? Wanna visit the Old Farts?"

She gets those pink boots going. I take that as a yes.

The Old Fart with the best view makes the formal announcement, "Here comes trouble and she's got her sidekick." It's the Skinniest Old Fart, who appears to be the group's lookout today.

I laugh as I approach their group.

"Very funny," I say. "Just so you know, this is a pit stop. I have a question."

I have their undivided attention.

"Go ahead, Isabel," the Bald Old Fart says.

"Do any of you remember Walter Bartol? He used to drive a beer truck, oh maybe twenty-eight, thirty years ago."

They all have long chins as they ponder.

The Fattest Old Fart snorts.

"I believe we were all too young to be sitting back here then. We all had jobs."

The Skinniest Old Fart bends forward.

"I kinda remember him. Loud guy. Why? Is he a suspect?"

Their heads turn my way.

"Maybe, maybe not. He's just somebody that's come under my radar."

"Aw, come on, Isabel, you can't leave us hanging like that," the Serious Old Fart says.

"Sure, I can." I adjust my hold on Sophie. "Well, it's been nice seeing you, guys."

Along for the Ride

I spend the rest of the morning amusing Sophie. I keep an eye on the clock for her first nap of the day. That would be the ideal time to make our field trip. I feed her a bottle, change her diaper, and get her dressed properly.

On the front seat I have my paperwork: the map of where each building or septic system permit was issued the year Adela disappeared, the list of who took them out, and a pad to take notes. On one sheet, I draw lines to create three columns. At the top I write: Yes, No, Maybe.

Here is my plan: I have mentally divided the town into north and south. I will take the south today, making notes about each property and taking photos. There are about forty-six permits total. Some are duplicates since the person took out a building and septic system permit for a new house. There are about eight of those. If I cross off ours, that leaves seven.

Snow on the ground does present a challenge, but so much time has passed that if Adela were buried somewhere, the excavated spot would be grassed over or beneath somebody's house. I'm just trying to get my bearings today and tomorrow. The next big step will be confronting Walter Bartol. Thank God, Jack will be with me for that.

I peer over my shoulder. Maggie has stationed herself beside the baby.

"Ready, kid?"

Sophie kicks her little boots.

I head to the village near the town's border with Hartsville, where Mira and Bruce Clark live. They aren't on the list of permits, but their neighbor is. Mrs. Hanover needed a new septic system. The houses in this village were built long before any zoning laws were passed, so they are close together, almost cheek to jowl, because it's likely they all belonged to the same family at one time. They are also near a rather large river. Mrs. Hanover had to get a fancy tight tank, which according to this map, fills up a rather tiny backyard. The house has since changed hands twice. Newcomers now have it.

Yes, Mira Clark made the suspects list, but at the bottom. So did Bruce, her schoolteacher hubby with the wandering eye, but I seriously doubt either of them dumped Adela's body in old lady Hannover's hole without the guy putting in the septic system noticing.

My guess it is unlikely Adela's body is here. These people aren't the type. But I dutifully make my notes, roll down the window, and take a shot of the house with my phone. I do the same for the two next-door neighbors, who also had to get new septic systems.

I recall the board of health, much to the displeasure of some of the skinflint old-timers, was cracking down then on septic systems near bodies of water. It was brave of the board members to take on this project, but they had real ammo when it was discovered somebody's septic system was draining shit into the river. I believe it was one of these three. I take notes and photos. I register them in the No column.

Three down, a bunch more to go.

I check the review mirror. Sophie gazes out the window. The dog does the same on her side of the car.

"Hey, Sophie, I don't want you ratting me out to your mother," I tell her.

She gets those little boots moving again.

The next house, a saltbox-style, is one of the eight with double permits. Sam built the staircase, one of his specialties, and all the trim for the newcomers. The couple still lives there. No kids, so I didn't have much contact with them outside of the open house they threw when the house was finished. They are his-and-her-lawyers, so I doubt they had a motive for killing and sticking Adela in their artfully landscaped backyard. Besides, they hired one of the contractors in town to handle everything. He's one of those upstanding types I know personally. I scribble and snap photos anyways.

I check behind me. Sophie is conked out already. So is the dog. Good girls.

Now I head to a back road, mercifully frozen and snow-covered, but not thawed and muddy. Pickup trucks are parked along the shoulders. If I drove by early this morning, I would have likely seen hunters in their cabs, drinking coffee, maybe smoking, while they waited for dawn to signal the start of shotgun season. I used to see them on my way to the newsroom.

At this time of day, the hunters are likely tromping through the woods. The better the hunter, the deeper they go, I hear. But then again, if you kill a deer, it's an awfully long walk back with something that heavy.

A lot of the guys have their spots staked out. This part of the forest is owned by the state, so they can hunt freely. Otherwise they need to get permission ahead of time from the landowner. Or the land belongs to them or their family, as in Jack's case. He and Eleanor own over a hundred acres they inherited from their folks, most of it wooded, but the farm has large fields somebody hays for them. The gardens their parents used for growing vegetables have long been abandoned. The farm stand fell apart in a windstorm about ten years ago. The barns and pens are empty.

I'm wondering how Jack and his buddies are doing. I called him last night at the Rooster to wish him luck. He said his cousin was there. He and Eleanor were yakking it up. Now that would have been something to see, silent Eleanor talking. But I was glad I stayed home. Fred Lewis gives me the willies.

The next house is a log cabin built by one of those solitary guys who never has much to do with the rest of the town. Victor Wilson doesn't like anyone coming near his property, so no-trespassing signs are nailed to the maple trees every hundred yards along the road. I bet he did the same along the entire border. I typically see him pumping gas outside the general store.

Once in a while, Victor comes to town meetings to bitch about something. He's a scrawny dude with a long hipster beard, from before they came into style, and naturally, a wild head of hair. I have no idea what he does for a living.

I can barely see his house through the trees, but the permit says he built a garage. I take a shot of his driveway.

Just my luck, Victor Wilson steers his pickup into his driveway. He stops and rolls down the window.

"What'd ya want?" he growls.

"Nothing, Mr. Wilson. I just stopped to check on my granddaughter. See her in the back seat?"

Now the dog is curious. I hope she doesn't start barking.

"Who are you?"

"I just live here in town. Name's Isabel Long."

"Yeah, I seen you at meetings. You used to be a reporter."

"That was a long time ago. Take care. Bye now."

In the mirror, I see he's waiting for me to really move on. Maybe he and Eleanor would make a good couple. Victor Wilson may be a nut, but I wonder about a motive. Did he want a woman so badly he kidnapped her and held her hostage as his sex slave in his log cabin?

Come on, Isabel, you're watching too many bad movies and TV shows with your mother.

Still, I add him to the maybe list.

It's afternoon when I finish the properties on the southern half of town. I find nothing remarkably suspicious, just newcomers doing the right thing when they built their houses or fixing bad septic systems for those delightfully antique homes that turn out to be money pits. There are a few do-it-yourselfers. They are all listed in the No column, except for Victor Wilson. I will have to ask Andrew Snow about him.

Sophie is awake. She blinks and smacks her lips. I better get home to feed and change her. I'll call Ma to give her a report on what I found today.

A Question for Andrew

I call Andrew later in the afternoon when I put Sophie down for her second nap.

"You go yet?"

"To Walter Bartol's? No, that's Wednesday. Jack Smith is coming with me."

"Good, good, that makes me feel better. Jack's a big, strong guy."

I smile thinking of him and Walter going at it.

"That's why I asked," I lie. "I have a question for you. What do you think of Victor Wilson?"

There's a pause on the other end of the line.

"Victor Wilson. Why do you bring up his name?"

"Well, he took out a building permit for a garage he put in that summer. I drove out there today. He's got an awful lot of land you can't see from the road. And he's not very friendly, I found out, when he saw me taking photos."

"What?"

"Nothing too serious. He just wanted to know why I stopped near his driveway. I told him I was checking on my granddaughter in the backseat. I didn't mind lying to him."

"Isabel, what are you doing?"

"I'm visiting every property that got a new septic system or building back then. I'm halfway done," I say. "Do you think Victor Wilson and Adela could have had any kind of relationship?"

"Other than paying for gas and groceries? I doubt it," he says. "But then again, I'm finding out things about my daughter that I didn't know before. Let me talk with Jamie and Dale."

"Thanks."

"Are you adding Victor to your suspect list?"

"I may have to," I answer.

Drive-by Shootings

The next morning, I time my second day of drive-by shootings, of the photography kind, of course, with Sophie's first nap of the day. I told my mother last night I'm hoping for more success today, but as she reminded me, that only works if Adela's killer lives in Conwell. Adela's killer, that's what Ma now calls the person responsible. She's ruled out suicide. I am leaning that way, too.

I turn in my seat. Sophie plays with one of her squeaky toys. The dog is attentive.

"Hey, kiddo, thanks for not squealing on me to your mother yesterday," I tell her.

Those little pink boots start moving.

I take a left at the driveway to check out a house that's been empty for years. The owner died years ago and the family still fights about what to do with it. It's another case of a small yard facing a river, actually the lower end of the Brookfield. This spot is wide open. Everybody would've seen what was going on. I give it a place on the No column and move on.

In a low spot across the river, I recognize hunters in orange and red making their way among the trees. Jack called last night. He didn't get a deer, but one of his buddies did. His cousin, Fred, shot one, too.

"The guys will be celebrating hard tonight at my place," he said. "Eleanor's making us supper."

"Sounds like a guys' night out. Good luck tomorrow."

Jack asked about my day. I mentioned Victor Wilson, and he answered, "That's one crazy dude. Didn't you see his name on my permanently banned list? Been on it for years. It would take an act of God to let him back inside."

"What did he do?"

"He'd come in and spout all this White Supremacist crap. He made a big deal about it, the loud mouth. I know he's always carrying a gun. Bet he has an arsenal up there. I don't need somebody like that at the Rooster."

"Do you think he could've done something to Adela?"

"Hmm, never thought about that." I heard a loud commotion in the background. Guys were shouting. "I gotta get goin'. The grub's on the table. Eleanor made pot roast with all the trimmings."

"Bon appetite," I joked.

The properties on my list are heavy with newcomers. I see a lot of nopes there although my mother wondered last night about the contractors in town. That's likely a stretch, I told her, but I won't discount it. It would require me to go to Town Hall and pull files. Course, I have an in with the town clerk because she's the daughter of Andrew's cousin.

Surprise, surprise, a septic permit was pulled at Marsha's trailer. I didn't realize it was her property because I didn't recognize the last name. I bet the place belonged to her parents, who left it to her, likely the only nice thing they ever did for their daughter. I recognize Bobby Collins' pickup in the driveway. Marsha is a maybe. Bobby is, too, although I'm convinced his attempt to straighten himself out is sincere. Ma says differently.

I pass Jack's place. He and his sister took out a building permit for a sunroom on Eleanor's side. I pull to the side of the road. Eleanor marches through the field with her mutts, all of them wearing orange construction vests. The dogs crisscross in front of her. I take a quick shot and hope she doesn't see me. Where should I put this one? Come on. Jack wouldn't do something like that.

So, when it comes down to it, I have a whole lotta nopes and two maybes.

Visiting Walter Bartol

Jack picks me up, as he said he would, at nine Wednesday morning. He looks beat. Too much drinking and hiking, he says, as he chats about his failed hunting trip, well, at least for him. But he had fun being one of the guys in the woods for two days. He says Eleanor was in her glory making them food, and frankly, I find his description of his sister amusing. I roll my eyes when he says his cousin Fred mentioned me a few times.

"Fred wants to know when he'll see you again."

Jack laughs when I say, "In his dreams."

"So, did you solve your case while I was gone?"

"Hardly. I drove around with my granddaughter, Sophie, checking out everyone who took out building and septic system permits. You and I are on the list by the way."

"So, we're suspects?" he jokes.

"No, but I do wonder about Victor Wilson. And I was ready to write off Bobby and Marsha, but she had a new septic tank put in her place around that time. Certainly, Bobby had access to heavy equipment in those days. Course, I would have to go to Town Hall to see who did what when."

"Let's see if you get that big break today."

It turns out Walter Bartol lives in an area of the city that was built up during the fifties, similar to the neighborhood where I grew up. Things were promising in post-war America. Couples could get a mortgage to buy a home. Mom stayed home with the kids. Businesses gave pensions.

When we turn off the main drag onto Maple Street, I point toward a red ranch-style house with a breezeway and a garage. A pickup truck is in the driveway. Of course, I didn't call ahead. That would have been nuts. I'm just relieved Jack came with me on this fact-finding mission.

"That's the one," I tell Jack.

"All right," he says as he steers to the side of the road. "He might remember me, so let me do the introductions. And if we get a bad feeling, we're not going inside. Okay?"

I blow out air.

"I'm with you on that, Jack."

We enter the carport. I ring the doorbell. I bite my lip wondering if we'll get a response, and after a while, I see movement through the kitchen door's window. A man is coming to see what we want. He opens the door partway.

"If you're Jehovah's Witnesses, I told you people already, I'm not interested."

Jack greets the man.

"Walter, remember me? Jack Smith. I own the Rooster in Conwell. You used to deliver beer to my place a long time ago."

"Jack Smith? Course, I remember. You one of those Jehovah's Witnesses now?"

"Hell, no. I want you to meet my friend, Isabel Long. She wants to ask you some questions."

Walter only has the door open about a foot. He looks like your average old white guy with a balding head and short whiskers, and a fat ring around the middle.

"What kinda questions?" he says with a bit of a snarl.

"Do you remember Adela Collins? She went missing twenty-eight years ago," I say with a shimmy to my voice. "Her father has hired me to find out what happened to her. I was hoping you could help out with some information."

"What kind of information?"

"The police chief gave me the restraining order Adela Collins took out against you a few months before she disappeared." I study the man's face as I talk. His features form sharp, hard folds. "Her family recently found letters you sent her. You seemed really angry about something."

Walter snorts.

"I sure as hell was." He stops for a moment. "Are you tryin' to say I could've done somethin' to her?"

"I didn't say that, but it doesn't look too good you sending her those letters and stalking her."

Walter Bartol flings open the door and charges forward a few steps. I'm ready to flee but instead I slide closer to Jack.

"Now how do you suppose I could have killed that bitch? Take a look at me."

Walter turns to make a point, but it isn't necessary. He's missing his left arm. The sleeve hangs in a flap. It certainly would be a hindrance trying to get rid of a body with only one arm.

"What happened to you?" Jack asks.

"I was in an accident. Drunk driver. Happened on Labor Day Weekend that year. I was in the hospital for months. The doctors tried saving my arm, but it was too mangled." He jabs the forefinger of his remaining hand my way. "So, it couldn't have been me. Got it?"

I nod. This man is such an ass, I would've liked that he was the one who killed Adela. But he isn't. Walter Bartol drops off the suspect list with a huge thud.

"Mr. Bartol, you cleared up things nicely," I say. "Thanks for your time."

"I don't wanna see you here again."

Walter slams the door hard.

Back in Jack's pickup, I am silent for a moment. Walter Bartol seemed like such a solid lead. But maybe his accident didn't happen like he said. I have an idea.

"Jack, do you mind going to the Daily Star?"

"The newspaper, what for?"

"I want to take a look at the bound volumes of the old papers. It's easier than going to the library and using the microfiche machine. We can find out if Walter is lying about when he lost his arm."

"Really?"

"Sure, you can wait outside if you want. It shouldn't take too long."

"No, no, I want to watch you in action."

I smile.

"You're a pretty good stand-in for my mother."

At the Daily Star

Jack, who's getting the hang of my wicked sense of humor, like we say in Massachusetts, chuckles when I say, "Stay close to me," as we enter the Daily Star. I give the place the once over and except for fewer desks in the editorial department, it isn't much different under the new regime.

Cindy, the newsroom's librarian, greets me from her big corral near the front door. That's where she tends to the bound volumes of editions and files of black-and-white photos dating from the pre-website era. The paper dates back to the early 1800s, so there are a lot of them.

Cindy is a tall woman, a little on the round side, with short gray hair. She began working at the Star about the time I was hired as a correspondent. She was always helpful, honoring my requests for assistance without giving me a hard time. I'm surprised she still has her job. I mean how many newspapers still have a librarian. I bet the new owners will eventually have everything loaded into an archival website to save paying someone to babysit.

She has a big smile for me.

"Hey, Isabel, coming back for your old job?" She glances around before she lowers her voice a little. "Did you know the guy who took your place already gave his notice?"

"No and no." I glance at Jack. "Hey, I want you to meet my friend, Jack."

She greets Jack a hello, and then says what she always said when I made an appearance in her part of the newsroom, "What can I do for you today?"

I step close to her counter.

"I was hoping you'd let me look at one of the old books."

"What's the year?"

I tell her.

"The last half, please."

"Be right back."

As Jack and I wait for Cindy's return, I give him the lay of the newsroom, which department is located where. I point toward the far end of the building.

"That used to be my office," I tell him.

"Pretty fancy with all the glass."

"Yes, I was a pretty fancy editor," I joke.

People are turned in their desks or their heads are up because I've been recognized. Several come over to say how much they miss me, including Lloyd, my former assistant editor who's become the regional editor under the new owner. They want to know if I'll be re-applying for my old job. I shake my head. They get to meet Jack. A few say they've stopped by the Rooster. I tell them I'm there Friday and Saturday nights. They should check out my bartending skills. I tell them about my mother.

"You look great," Lloyd tells me. "So relaxed."

"Lots of people say that. I must have looked like a heinous wench before." Of course, my smart-aleck remark draws a good laugh. "So, how's it going here?"

People eye each other as if they're not allowed to spill company secrets.

"Hanging in there," Lloyd says. "What are you doing here?"

"A little research for a mystery I might be writing." I nod at Jack, who chuckles at my lie. I'm not about to reveal too much about my new life. "Isn't that what all retired journalists do?"

Cindy is back with the book. She places it on the counter. My former co-workers split back to their desks with fond good-byes and a couple of hugs.

"They sure love you," Jack says after the last one leaves.

"I was their mom for a long time. I fed and burped them, and turned them into good little journalists."

Cindy spins the book, so it faces Jack and me.

"Take your time," she says.

I flip through the pages.

"You okay?" I ask Jack.

"Uh-huh."

I find the end of August. I keep flipping.

"He said Labor Day Weekend, right? I am guessing the accident would be in the paper that Tuesday. Yup, here it is on the third page."

Jack and I are shoulder to shoulder as we read. Walter Bartol was in a single-car accident. He was over twice the legal limit for being drunk when he missed a curve and hit a tree coming back from a party.

"Drunk driver? He didn't mention it was him," Jack says.

"Shoot, now I really wish the liar was still on my list."

Jack's head is up. He's done reading. He speaks softly.

"Isabel, are you ready to give up on this case yet?"

He is the first person to ask me this question. Except for people like the Floozy and Bobby Collins, who each had their own reasons, everybody seems to think I can get the job done. I know Jack's being honest and kind, but at this point in my investigation, especially with this dead end, it hits me that I may not succeed despite my best efforts. Damn, I hate to lose, and frankly, as a reporter, I never lost a story, or as an editor, a fight.

I had so convinced myself that Walter Bartol might be the one. Well, there was some pretty damning evidence, including his ass-ugly personality. Could he have killed Adela with one arm? Sure, the man had a paw the size of a giant. Since there was no blood found anywhere, I suspect she was either given an overdose or strangled. He could have wrapped his hand around her neck easily, but not if he was laid up in a hospital. And Adela went missing a week and a half later, on Sept. 16.

Maybe it was my mother joking that I would solve this case before she returned Sunday, and then we would find something else to investigate. Maybe this Isabel Long, P.I., thing has gone to my head. No one has solved this case in twenty-eight years. No one with a guilty conscience ever confessed, not even a deathbed confession. Why should I think I could figure it out?

I haven't taken any money from Andrew Snow yet, and I

sure as hell won't if I don't discover the culprit who killed his daughter.

Jack waits for my answer.

"Not yet. I'm beginning to believe there's a strong chance I might not solve it, but I really want to try a little bit more. Remember what I told you about my cousin?"

"Uh-huh, I do. Something like that sticks with you forever."

"I'm sure the Snows feel the same way about Adela."

I take photos of the stories with my phone. I keep turning pages. Now Adela is in the news, or rather her disappearance. I have these stories in a folder at home. I find the one about Walter facing charges after he was released from the hospital six weeks after the accident. The doctors tried to save his arm, but it was damaged too badly.

I shut the book.

"Done already?" Cindy asks from her desk.

"Yes, thanks for the peek," I say.

She raises a finger.

"Wait a second."

She gets up from her desk and pulls a cardboard box from a lower shelf. She sets it on top of the closed book.

"These were taken from your neck of the woods. They're probably going to chuck them out. I've already scanned most of them into the system, but a lot of them aren't newsworthy or they don't have cutlines. Maybe there's some you want."

I go through the top few photos. Jack points out people he knows.

"Look at that one. It's the Rod and Gun Club's annual pig roast." He lifts the photo. "Hey, I'm in this one."

Jack, who is twenty-eight years younger, is slicing up pig meat for a line of folks. I flip the photo over to read the back.

"It says Labor Day. Doesn't the club always hold the pig roast on that holiday?"

"Every year as long as I can remember. You really took this?"

"Uh-huh. I remember some of the guys were pretty crude that day, so it was hard getting a photo that wouldn't gross out our readers. Thanks for not holding your dick when I took that."

By now I have a sizable stack of photos. Cindy shoos me when I ask again if it's really okay we have them.

"Take the whole box if you want," she says.

I do as she says, and outside the newsroom, Jack gives me a fun-loving grin.

"Why don't we get some grub somewhere and then head back to the hills where we belong? I've got some time before I have to be at the Rooster."

"Don't forget I'm picking up my mother this Sunday. You start cleaning your place out yet?"

"Nah, don't you worry none, woman. I'm gonna start real soon."

Disappointment

I break the news about the dead end to Andrew Snow after Jack drops me off at home. I can hear the disappointment in his voice after I tell him about Walter Bartol, his accident, and missing arm. I leave out what the bastard said about his daughter.

"I was so sure you had something there," he says.

"Me, too. I can tell he's not a nice man, but it's impossible he's the one. I even found the news story when he went to court. It said he was in the hospital for over a month."

Andrew is silent for a moment.

On our way back to Conwell, I ponder Jack's question about whether I was ready to give up just yet. Yes, things were against me with twenty-eight years gone and lousy police work. Maybe I've been watching too many crime shows where everything wraps up neatly in an hour.

"Now what?" Andrew asks.

"Tomorrow I'm going to check the paperwork in Town Hall for the permits, to see who did the work."

"What about Bobby Collins?"

"He's still a possibility," I say. "One of the permits was taken out by his friend, Marsha."

"That's something, isn't it?"

"Yes, it is. I do want to find out more about Victor Wilson although, frankly, he's a long shot. I definitely won't go to his place alone."

"You sound discouraged, Isabel."

"I am, but I'm not quitting yet. I'll take this case as far as I can."

"That's all I ask, Isabel."

Old Blacks and Whites

I go through the black-and-white photos, one by one, at the kitchen table. The animals are with me. The cat is on my lap, the dog snores at my feet. Who are they trying to kid?

The photos date back to the late eighties when I was a correspondent for the Daily Star. Most were taken to go with the stories I wrote about Conwell and the other hilltowns. Others are standalones, as we call them in the news biz. As for who took them, it's a toss up between the staff photographers and myself. The staff photographers had the better equipment and got the quality shots. I took the lucky ones, mainly because I was up here and knew when things were happening. I used a point-and-shoot the paper gave me, plus rolls of film.

Who's in the box? A lot of people I know. Some of them are dead, like the old-timer who went house to house selling the vegetables he grew in his back yard. Once he came to ours, when we were renting this dump of a place on the other side of Conwell. We've lost sweet ladies that were nice to my kids at the church fair. There's a portrait of a woman, who had a rep as the nosiest person in town, yes, even nosier than the Old Farts at the store, but at least she turned it into a profession: reporting for a local weekly.

I find a nice shot of the old chief, who was the middle-aged chief then. He was speaking that day to a class at Conwell's elementary school. He wore his uniform. I shot him holding up a set of handcuffs. I wonder how many times he had to actually use them.

I'll give that photo to his wife.

I find photos of kids who are now young adults with kids of their own. They are performing at an assembly in school or showing off a project. They're hitting and kicking balls. My own, Matt, Alex, and Ruth managed to sneak into a few.

I shot lots of local events: the country fair in the town one over, parades, a contra dance, and town meetings.

There are photos of folks at work. I laugh when I find one of Jack at the Rooster I took for a feature. He's about twenty pounds slimmer and has a head of dark hair. Of course, he's smiling right into the camera. I had forgotten I wrote the story. I wonder if he remembers.

I believe I'll give this photo to him. I'll have it framed, so he can hang it behind the bar.

At the bottom of the box, I am surprised to find another photo of the Rod and Gun Club's pig roast. I shot this one at the picnic tables. Jack sits between two women on a bench.

His weirdo sister sits to his right. It's quite remarkable how little Eleanor has changed, but then again I imagine living such a simple life must be relatively stress free. She does whatever she does at home. She works a few nights at the Rooster. Her brother drives her wherever she needs to go. She has her mutts. I bet any money she's still a virgin unless her cousin, Fred, is even creepier than I think.

Eleanor has her eyes focused on her brother and the woman sitting on the other side. Her face is twisted in a familiar scowl. Hot damn, the woman is Adela. Jack's got a beer in his hand and an empty paper plate on the table in front of him. His attention is clearly on Adela. Her head is tipped back. She laughs. She is obviously enjoying herself.

I feel a small lurch.

Jack is definitely the source of her enjoyment. Could he be her mysterious lover? It seems a very real possibility. Adela may have kept her private life with men to herself but not in this photo. I don't know if it even ran in the paper. I used to drive the finished rolls of film to the newsroom for the photo editor to develop. Sometimes the photos got published in the paper, sometimes they didn't, especially if the subjects weren't timely. Maybe the photo editor didn't think a bunch of rednecks hanging out at a pig roast was newsworthy.

I study Jack's happy face. I feel another lurch. I get the feeling he hasn't told me everything about Adela. I think back to when we went snowshoeing. He said he and Adela went out off and on. Their relationship never went anywhere.

What did he say when I asked him about her? He answered, "How much time do you have?"

Jesus, Isabel, your interview skills are slipping. This sex with Jack is clouding your judgment, or what I used to call for my reporters, 'my spidey sense.'

It's about time Jack and I had a heart to heart about Adela. I'll tell him I have plenty of time to listen.

Bragging Rights

Later that night, around eight, I make an appearance at the Rooster. The bar is noisy with loud male voices bragging about their hunting exploits in the woods. They're drinking beer and shots. They're downing Eleanor's burgers. She's not usually here Wednesdays, but Jack doesn't want to pass up a good moneymaking opportunity. Eleanor moves around the kitchen, all business. I'm not even going to bother to say hello.

"What'll it be, Isabel?" Jack asks.

"Make it the usual."

"Sure enough."

Of course, Jack is in his typical, shit-eating grin mood thanks to a barroom filled with drinkers, and hopefully, my appearance.

"You go through that box yet?"

"Yeah, I did. Found lots of good memories in there. I bet there are a few photos you might want to hang up here. I'll show them to you when you come over."

He raises his eyebrows playfully.

"I'd like that."

A sheet of white poster board is on the upright post close enough to the bar. I can read it from my stool. At the top, Jack wrote ROOSTER DEER HUNTERS in a thick, black marker. Of course, I expect there'll be a number of jokes tonight about what actually is a ROOSTER DEER until Jack tells them to shut up. They know very well what he means.

Jack drew columns for the hunter's name, date, and size of the deer. Hunters were supposed to fill in their info. The one on the list who nabs the biggest deer by the end of the season gets a free dinner for two at the Rooster. Several names are already written down on the sheet, including the two guys who went hunting with Jack.

There's no line to use the women's room tonight, I should note, because I am one of four women in the Rooster. One is Eleanor who never seems to take a piss the entire night she works. She must have remarkable holding powers or she's doing something back there I don't want to know about. There are two other women customers, both wives of hunters. Actually, one gal is a damn good hunter herself. I see she got a buck. Hubby has come up empty so far, which has to be a source of some hard ribbing tonight.

Damn, everybody's in a great mood.

As for Jack, I think he enjoyed being part of the Adela Collins investigative team today. I told him, of course, as part of the team he couldn't tell anybody what we found. Everything is top secret. He agreed.

Of course, he's looking forward to spending the night at my house. We have four to go before Ma returns. He warns me he's pretty beat from hunting. "This just might be only a sleepover," he says, and I tell him okay. Jack's no young stud. I don't know if I could take it if he were. But it's nice having a man's body next to mine again. I froze the first winter after Sam was gone. I had to pile on the blankets. Jack's body, typically naked, gives off a solid, bone-soaking heat.

Jack's plan is to drop Eleanor at home first and make sure everything's okay inside before he heads to mine.

Now I'm wondering how I could convince Ma it would be all right for Jack to stay overnight. Sure, Jack supposedly is going to clear out his dump of a place, but I'd still have to drive home after we do the dirty deed. I'd feel funny leaving Ma alone at night.

I check to my right when somebody jostles my arm. Crap, Jack's cousin, Fred, is taking the empty stool beside mine.

"Hey, Isabel, nice to see you." He lifts a finger to Jack. "You know, cousin, what I drink by now."

"Fred." I lift my beer. I'd rather talk with any one of the yokels in this room than Jack's cousin. But there appears to be no escaping Fred. "Did you go hunting today?"

He shakes his head.

"Nah, I only got two days off. I tried to get the whole week, but no dice. My boss is a real asshole."

I smile at Jack.

"Not like my boss."

"Him? Oh, he can be a real asshole sometimes." Fred chuckles. "And I'm a better hunter. Did he tell you about the deer I shot?"

"Uh-huh, Fred. What do you do for work?"

"Construction. Heavy equipment. If you need a hole, I can dig it."

"You ever work in Conwell?"

"Sure. Lots of times, especially when the economy was booming, and those newcomers all wanted new homes. Things have slowed down here since the bottom fell out, but I still get jobs from time to time. Why? You interested? You got a hole that needs digging?"

I set down my beer. I ignore any double meaning in his question.

"No, I'm fine."

"Well, if you change your mind, Jack can give me a reference. Right, cousin? I did the excavation for that sun porch on Eleanor's side of the house. It's still standing, ain't it?"

"Yup," Jack says. "Eleanor and her dogs love that place."

So, Jack's cousin who gives me the royal creeps has been digging holes, as he says, in Conwell and the towns around it. I'm a little more interested in what he has to say.

"Fred, can I ask you a question?"

"Sure, honey, what is it?"

I have a thing about men who I don't like calling me honey, but I try to stay light and friendly.

"You might've heard I'm investigating Adela Collins' disappearance for her family."

"Yeah, I heard."

Fred's head bobs like one of those stupid bobble-head dolls. His could be the Redneck Fred doll. Good one, Isabel, I tell myself although I try not to laugh.

"I was wondering if you knew Adela."

218

"Sure, I did. We had some good times together." He tips his head toward Jack. "My cousin did, too. I bet half the guys in this barroom tonight did."

"Were you together for a long time?"

"Nah, on and off over the years. We'd go hot and heavy for a little while. Then she'd drop me for somebody else."

"Did that bother you?"

"Shit, I wasn't planning on marrying her. Nobody was. And after Bobby, Adela wasn't looking for Prince Charming."

I nod, thinking about the woman's image forming in my brain. Adela liked having a good time with men. There's nothing wrong with that. Men do it all the time. I just hope it didn't cost her.

"When's the last time you saw her?"

He hums while he eyes Jack.

"A couple of days before she was gone," he says.

"You were on a date?"

"Yeah, something like that," he says, turning briefly toward Jack. "Sorry, bro."

I'm trying to read the exchange between the two men. Jack is on the verge of frowning, an unnatural occurrence at the Rooster.

"What do you have to be sorry about?" I ask.

"I think I'll let Jack tell you himself. Right, Jackie boy?"

Jack doesn't respond. He just gives Fred a look that if it were any more powerful would have knocked him off the stool.

What the hell?

Something about Jack

At the top of the stairs to the second floor, Jack asks, "What's in this room?"

"That's my office."

"Office? Mind if I take a look?"

"Go ahead," I say. "Let me get the light."

Actually, what else could I say? Sorry, my office has private stuff. You can sleep with me and have sex, but you can't look at a bunch of papers I have about Adela. Besides, at this point my leads are fading. I haven't had Ma here to bounce off ideas. Maybe Jack will see something I'm missing.

Jack faces the wall of crime.

"Whoa," he says.

I make a half-laugh.

"Welcome to the CSI of Isabel Long, P.I."

"Isabel Long, P.I., eh?"

Jack steps closer. He studies the papers, photos, and maps. He bends nearer to read my handwriting, which journalism ruined into an almost illegible scrawl. It's like I'm signing checks to everything.

"I haven't updated the wall yet," I tell him.

He points to my suspect list.

"Yeah, Walter Bartol is still number one. I see Bobby and Marsha are here." He squints. "Oh, you have Victor Wilson. You really gonna visit that nut?"

"Might have to. You can see I crossed out Mira and Bruce Clark's name. That was a long shot anyway. Walter Bartol's a goner. Now, Victor seems a possibility. Would you be willing to come with me to see him?"

"And get shot? No, thanks, ma'am. We have a history. Why don't you try Chief Ben Jr.?"

220

Jack is more interested in what's on the wall right now than listening to my voice. He gives me a half-hearted "uh-huh" when I talk about my experience with Victor Wilson as he inspects each piece of paper. Would I have enough nerve to visit him alone? I guess if I told somebody where I was going and when to expect me back home.

"Can I ask you a question?"

Jack studies the map, where I marked scenes related to Adela's disappearance.

"Go ahead."

"What did your cousin mean when he said 'sorry, bro' at the Rooster tonight? Did you two have some argument about Adela?"

Jack has moved onto the list of old comments I collected after Adela disappeared and seven years later at her memorial service.

"Somethin' like that." Now he points toward the card that came with Adela's birthday flowers. He lets out a long stream of air. "Where'd you find this?"

"That card? It was in the back of Adela's bureau. I found it when I took out the drawers. It must have slipped back there. You recognize the handwriting?"

He turns toward me. His eyebrows shoot up.

"Yeah, it's mine."

"That's your handwriting? You're the one who sent those flowers to Adela?"

"I sure did."

"I thought they came from the man she was having a secret love affair with before she went missing."

"That's me all right."

My mouth hangs open because right now I feel a bit foolish or fooled. Did I actually tell Jack I was looking for this mystery lover? I honestly don't remember mentioning it. The only ones who've heard about any inner-circle revelations about this case have been Ma and Andrew Snow. But still, I'm annoyed. Jack knows what I've been doing, and he didn't think I would want to know he was her lover?

What's going on here? It's gotta be the sex.

Isabel, snap out of it.

I go to my desk, where I stashed the photos from the pig roast.

"I want you to see something. This was in the bottom of the box." I hand him the picnic table photo. "You two look pretty cozy in that photo. This was what, a couple of weeks before she disappeared. How come you didn't tell me that before?"

Jack studies the photo.

"Isabel, I told you when we went snowshoeing that she and I had a relationship a couple of times, but it didn't work out."

"Like her disappearing? Come on, Jack. I'm gonna be honest with you. This is bullshit you didn't tell me."

Jack touches my shoulder.

"Isabel, do you really think I could hurt or kill somebody? Tell me straight."

I study his face. There are no happy grins this time from the Rooster's owner, just big questioning eyes.

"No," I say quietly. "Now tell me straight about what happened between you two. Don't leave anything out."

His cheeks puff a bit before he exhales.

"I guess we were in love for maybe four months. Maybe less."

"You guess?"

He shrugs.

"I really thought it might go somewhere this time. Adela had other ideas."

"More, please."

I let Jack ramble on about his feelings for the woman, how she liked keeping their relationship a secret. At first, he found it exciting, their sneaking around, but then he wondered why she couldn't be open about it. Mondays and Tuesdays, when the Rooster was closed, was their time to get together, which explains why the newspapers in her car were from those days. He slept over at her house whenever Dale wasn't there. He admits, when I ask, they did it one time at the Shady Grope, just for kicks.

Course, Adela came to the Rooster, but in those days there

222

was no music or food, and they kept things so casual nobody suspected.

Jack talked about his grief when everyone decided Adela wasn't coming back.

"It broke my heart," he says with a knot in his voice.

I remember that photo some newcomer took of Adela in the store, and how Jack was in the background, staring at her. I believe I would describe his expression as affectionate. Maybe Jack was there to talk with Adela.

"I know it's not the same as you and Sam. You two were married a long time. But I knew Adela all my life, and like I'm sure you've heard over and over, no one goes missing in a town this small."

I make a deep, long sigh.

"Okay, Jack, but if this relationship is going to continue, you can't hold important stuff back like that. I feel real funny you did. Like you didn't trust me."

He bends, so his eyes are on my eyes.

"You want me to leave?"

My lips form a small smile. I'm still a bit annoyed, but then I realize it was my fault, too. I let my personal feelings get in the way of this investigation.

"No, stay. I didn't pay close enough attention to what you said. I should've asked you a follow-up question."

"Follow-up, what's that?"

"Oh, it's when you get an answer, but there's a lot more you want to know. So, you follow up with another question. It's a reporter's tool. Lawyers use it in court. I should've asked you when you had relationships with Adela. If I did, would you have told me?"

"Course, I would've. I'm sorry, real sorry. It won't happen again."

"Anyways, I'll know better next time. Have you seen enough in here?"

Jack nods.

"Yeah, I'm beat. Let's go to bed."

Ma's Call

My mother's call wakes me at eight. I look over. Jack is gone. The bathroom door is open, and I don't hear the shower running. None of his clothes are here. I didn't hear him leave.

"Hey, Ma, what's going on?"

"Would you mind if I came home early? Danny's working nights this week, so he says he could meet you at the same place."

"How early?"

"Tomorrow?"

"Friday? It would have to be early since I work at the Rooster that night."

I shake my head although Ma can't see me. That complicates things. But how could I refuse her? Besides, I don't know what's happening with Jack. That's when I smell coffee from downstairs. He's still here, and I will admit I'm relieved. Damn him if he'd split this morning without saying good-bye at least. That would have been cowardly, but not Jack's style it seems.

"Of course, Ma. So, you miss Maggie and Roxanne, huh?"

"And you a little."

I laugh.

"Thanks. Hey, I have a dangerous assignment for you and me."

"Really?"

"Really."

I'm thinking now my best shot is to visit Victor Wilson. I bet it would catch him off guard if I bring my ninety-two-year-old mother. I was more afraid of Walter Bartol. Victor's just one of those guys who lives alone and mad at the world. Nobody understands him and that's the way he wants it.

"Hey, put Danny on the phone so I can arrange a time."

I pull on a nightgown, a flannel number, as I speak with Danny. We're meeting at the same place, same time, and same crappy restaurant.

Then I am downstairs. Jack sits at the kitchen table. He looks like he's made himself at home, drinking coffee and reading the paper. He probably let the dog out when he walked up the driveway to get the paper. I dutifully kept up my subscription, for Ma's sake, but to me all the paper is good for is starting the fire at night.

"What's going on in the world?" I ask Jack.

He folds the paper.

"Not much," he says. "Good morning, by the way."

"Morning to you, too. I thought for a moment you deserted me."

"Why would I do that?"

"Because of our conversation last night."

He raises a mug.

"It would take a lot more than that to scare me off, Isabel."

"Glad to know." I take the chair beside his. "I've got some news. I just got a call from my mother. She's coming home tomorrow."

"Shoot."

"Shoot all right." I eye Ma's coffee machine. "I'm glad you made yourself at home."

"I didn't know how strong you like your coffee," he says.

I get milk from the fridge.

"Oh, somewhere in the middle." I sit down. His attention is on me as I pour the milk. "I need to ask you a serious question."

He stretches back in his chair. He looks ready for anything.

"Go ahead. We might as well get everything out of the way."

I blow a little air first.

"I believe you had nothing to do with Adela's disappearance. But where were you when it all came down?"

Jack's head rocks a bit.

"Fair enough. I was on a fishing trip to the Florida Keys

225

with an old buddy when it happened. I can give you his name if you wanna check." He pauses again, but I don't respond. "I closed the Rooster for a few extra days. I hadn't had a vacation in years. I found out about Adela being gone when I called home from the airport. Eleanor told me." His head swung back and forth. "Like everybody else, I couldn't understand what the hell happened to her. Until that hunter found her car, I thought maybe she ran off with some guy she met. She was flighty enough to do that even though I know she loved her son. She was a real good mother."

"You didn't have a vacation in years? Adela took one that August. You didn't go with her?"

He shakes his head.

"She told me she went with a girlfriend to the Cape."

"You didn't believe her?"

"Before she went, I did. But I heard differently later on. Let's just say she went to have a fun time. Ask my cousin. He was there."

"Oh, Jack."

He shrugs.

"I didn't find out until months later, but I had my suspicions." He lifts his mug. "I kinda went on the fishing trip to clear my head."

"And?"

"It was great being out on the ocean. I could see for miles. That big sky. Don't get me wrong. I love our woods, but sometimes they just hem you in. I was glad to be away from it all. I did a lot of thinkin'."

"About what?"

"Adela and me. I was gonna go back and tell her I wanted her to cut out all the games. I loved her and didn't want to hide it." He takes a drink. "I told her as much before I left. Course, it was before I knew about her messin' around with Fred."

"How did she take it?"

"She said it was good I was goin'."

"Ouch."

Behind us the kettle begins a soft whistle.

"There's one more thing. I did call her the night she

226

disappeared. It was around eight. First the line was busy, but then I got a hold of her. I was heading home the next day. I wanted her to hear how I felt." His voice breaks a bit. "For the first goddamned time she told me she loved me. Do you believe it?"

"Oh, Jack, I'm so sorry."

"Me, too."

Back with the Old Farts

I'm up early Friday morning to meet my brother halfway back east, and damn, I am out of coffee. Jack used the last of it yesterday. I haven't bought any groceries since Ma left. I just lived on what I have in the house.

It's not even seven. Jack left in the middle of the night because he knew I was heading out early. Oh, why not have coffee with the Old Farts? The store's coffee only resembles what I drink, but it does give a buzz. Besides, it's been a while since I tormented those guys.

Naturally, they are amused to see me make my way through the backroom.

"She's back," the Skinniest Old Fart announces.

They bend forward on their benches as they watch my approach.

"Morning, fellows," I say as I walk past them to the coffee station. I pour myself the largest cup the store has and drop in some milk. I fish through my jeans pocket for fifty cents. Such a deal for coffee even if it's bad. I can feel them all studying me from the back of my head.

I choose the bench with the Fattest Old Fart. He likes his space, but I'm not about to stand or squeeze between the others.

"What brings you here today?" he asks.

I raise the white Styrofoam cup.

"Coffee. I'm all out at home." I cringe a bit when I take the first swallow. "What's the latest gossip?"

The Serious Old Fart beats his buddies.

"Heard the owner and the new bartender at the Rooster are getting mighty friendly," he says.

The others chuckle on cue.

228

"I heard that, too," I slap back.

More chuckles.

"How's the case going?" the Serious Old Fart asks.

"I had a serious dead end this week."

"We know," the Bald Old Fart says. "That Walter Bartol fellow. It was a good lead to follow. Never liked the guy."

I nod.

"You still wouldn't like him. I sure didn't when I went to his house."

"Heard you had a body guard," the Fattest Old Fart says.

I down the rest of the coffee and crush the cup.

"Sounds like you guys are keeping a close eye on me." I turn toward the Serious Old Fart, the one I suspect of calling me. "Did you see me driving around town checking on the properties that had permits that year?"

They shake their heads.

"Anything there?" the Skinniest Old Fart asks.

"Maybe. Too soon to tell. But I'll let you fellows know." I stand. "Gotta hit the road. I'm picking up my mother. Until next time."

I hear a chorus of chuckles.

Ma Comes Home

Ma wants to hear anything and everything about the case as we zip along the Mass. Turnpike. The dog, Maggie, who jumped all over the parking lot when she saw my mother, sits happily in the back seat. Ma's stuff is in the cargo hold along with a box of wrapped Christmas presents. Crap, I have to start thinking about that.

"What were you up to yesterday?" she asks.

I go over my research at Town Hall. Ronnie, the town clerk and the daughter of Andrew Snow's cousin, had everything I needed when I arrived. She let me work in the board of selectmen's meeting room where I could spread out the paperwork on the large table. I used to cover the meetings here, sitting opposite the three-member board. Covering these meetings stopped being important to the Daily Star a long time ago, except when there's a huge controversy, but people are close-mouthed about those if you don't report on the garden-variety meetings.

The files didn't have any big surprises. Recalling my lax nature with Jack, I dutifully studied each one. The newcomers were sure keeping the local guys busy with work that year. They came to town with heavy pockets and gladly paid whatever because it was still a helluva lot cheaper than what they would have spent at wherever they came from. They hired a general contractor to take care of everything from putting in the driveway to slapping on the last coat of paint. Nothing sinister pops out on that list.

As I mentioned, Sam and I did it ourselves. Victor Wilson, of course, built his own garage. Jack took out the permit for his sister's sunroom. His cousin Fred handled the excavation because, as he told me the other night, he likes digging holes.

They installed concrete posts that were poured well below the frost line to hold up the sunroom.

As for septic systems, Woodrow Excavation appeared to have a monopoly, except for the Floozy's mobile home. Bingo. Bobby Collins did the work there. That guy can't cut a break in this case, or maybe I'm just getting soft on losers trying to reform.

"Who is this Fred?" Ma asks.

"He's Jack's cousin. I found out from Ronnie he used to work for Woodrow Excavation back then. Not a very likable guy. But a whole better person than that Walter Bartol."

"Yeah, too bad about him losing his arm."

"Well, the man was drunk when he drove into the tree."

"Oh, that. I meant it gave him a good alibi. We could have wrapped up this case."

"Very funny, Ma."

I skip telling Ma about my romp in the sack with Jack last night. I stopped by the Rooster to flirt a little in the evening. His sister kept poking her head out the kitchen door a few times as if she was some chaperone at a teen dance. Jack came over after he closed up the Rooster and dumped his sister at home. He was all over me last night. I didn't mind. Who knows when we'll do it again? The front seat of his pickup truck is looking more and more like a possibility. Besides, I've never done it in a pickup before.

"Isabel, did you hear me?" Ma asks.

"Huh, no, I was thinking about something."

"About that new fellow?"

I laugh. Man, my mother can read my mind.

"Sorry. What did you say?"

"I was saying I have a new theory about that night Adela disappeared," she says.

Ma has a new theory? Thank God. I am fresh out of theories, except for Victor Wilson holding Adela hostage and then offing her when he was finished with her.

"What is it? I'm all-ears. But I plan to keep my eyes on the road."

"We kept saying there must've been two people who went

to her house that night. Because one person would have to drive her car while the other person took the car or truck they came in. Right?"

"Uh-huh."

"Suppose Adela left by herself."

"Left by herself. What do you mean?"

"I believe we have ruled out suicide because of where the car was found. People searched that area really well. So did you and the boys."

"And we don't suspect she's alive and well somewhere else in America," I offer.

I glance at my mother. She's got a shit-eating grin on her face if that would be possible with my ninety-two-year-old mother.

"What if she went some place on her own?" she asks. "That next-door neighbor did say she heard one car pull out fast. She didn't hear two."

"That's very good, Ma."

"Maybe she got really upset about something someone did or said. Remember the broken dishes?" Ma nods. "We just need to find out who she was meeting."

"Wow. I take that back. That's excellent."

"Now you have to find out who that person is."

"And who had a way to dispose of her body."

Our exit is ahead. I hit the car's turn signals.

I feel myself smiling. Ma came up with a new idea when I was getting ready to call it quits.

"Glad you're home, Ma."

"Me, too."

Up Close and Personal

It's big doings tonight at the Rooster. We have the full menu, hungry and thirsty customers, and a band called the Hunters and Gatherers. I kid you not. Jack says they've played here before. Sam and I must have been away that Friday, or maybe it was during my year of mourning for Sam when I didn't go anywhere fun on purpose. I ask Jack if the band's name has anything to do with the timing of their gig tonight, it being the middle of deer season.

"Maybe," he jokes.

Plus the Hunters and Gatherers have a Rooster-friendly play list. Already tonight, the band has played "Mustang Sally" and "Ramblin' Man." When the guitarists started twanging Charlie Daniels Band's "Long Haired Country Boy," a redneck romp erupted on the dance floor. This may not be the best tune for dancing, but they get it done and shout along with the chorus. Most of the guys here tonight are long-haired country boys anyway, including members of the band, dressed in their flannel or Western shirts with pearl snaps. Their jeans sag at the knees. Pointy-toed cowboy boots or scuffed work boots are the top choice for footwear. With the recent milder weather, the snow has thinned on the trails, so there are no snowmobilers here tonight.

Yes, indeed, Southern rock is big here in the hilltowns of Western Massachusetts.

By the way, the list of lucky hunters has grown a bit this week. People keep checking it out. The apparent winner so far is a Rooster regular.

As usual, Jack waits on the tables tonight. I'm pouring a river of beer, so I'm stationed behind the bar. Eleanor is hit hard in the kitchen.

Midway through the second set, the lead singer of the Hunters and Gatherers announces in the microphone, "This one's for you, Jack."

Jack laughs and sets a full tray of empties on the bar when he recognizes the opening chords to "Good Hearted Woman." He starts clanging that darn cowbell and shouting above the crowd, "No more beer until I've finished dancin' with this woman."

Giggling, I let him lead me to the dance floor, and we go at it. It's an odd song, really, about a woman who will put up with just about any antics of her much wilder man. But it has a nice beat, and for some reason, Jack thinks of me when he hears it. This time, he spins me around three times, and I gasp, "That's a new move."

He's one happy man. I'm one happy woman.

Jack and I walk back to the bar after the song is over. Eleanor stands in the doorway, arms crossed, her lower lip hanging, as her eyes shoot bullets at her brother and me. She mutters under her breath, but the place is too noisy for me to hear what she is saying. Frankly, I don't give a shit.

"Take it easy, Sis. I was having fun with Isabel," Jack tells her. "Maybe you should try it some time."

I'm a little surprised by Jack's tone of voice. Annoyed is a good description. I believe Eleanor is, too, because she spins around and retreats into the kitchen. She sputters words beneath her breath. I hear a loud crash in the kitchen, and when I stick my head in the kitchen, a bunch of dirty dishes are broken on the floor.

"You okay?" I ask Eleanor.

She gives me a drop-dead look and a grunt.

Behind me, Jack clangs that cowbell again.

"Dancin' for Isabel and me is over." He winks at me. "Come and git your beer."

Then Jack slips into the crowd with a tray of shots for the band, his reward, I suppose, for playing Waylon Jennings' tune in that set. I get back to work, paying attention to the guys who sit along the bar and the line that's formed. The Floozy stands three drinkers back. I take the customers one at a time, making

234

pleasant small talk about hunting to the hunters and the weather, which has moderated since our last storm, to those who aren't.

"Hey, Marsha, what'll you have tonight?"

She raises two nail-bitten fingers.

"A Bud for me and a Coke for Bobby."

"Sure enough."

"Bobby says you're a lot nicer than he expected."

I slide the drinks forward.

"That's a relief to hear. Here you go."

She carries the drinks to the table near the front door. Bobby raises his Coke in a salute when he sees me looking his way. Crap, could he really have done it? One scenario Ma and I came up with in the car was that Bobby threatened to take Adela to court over visitation rights. Maybe he said he would bring up all the slutty things she'd been doing. Slutty is my word, by the way. Ma used the word loose. Adela got so ticked off she drove to Marsha's. Bobby didn't mean to kill her, but she struck her head on something. Then he and Marsha buried her.

Oh, boy.

On the other side of the barroom, the band is burning the place down with the Georgia Satellites' "Keep Your Hands to Yourself." I smile thinking of the band's name. I used to tell my new hires at the Daily Star there are two kinds of reporters: hunters and gatherers. Gatherers wait for phone calls and work off press releases. Hunters chase down stories. I wanted hunters. They got it.

I suppose I've been both for Adela's case. But I'm giving myself one more week. Shoot, this would've been a lot easier twenty-eight years ago.

"You off somewhere else?" Jack asks me when he drops a tray filled with empties on the bar.

I smile.

"Just daydreaming," I answer. "Oops, the band's taking a break. Step back, Jack, before you get crushed."

The door opens. Jack's creepy cousin, Fred, makes his way through the crowd of smokers outside. Just my luck, there's an empty seat at the bar.

"Hey, there, gorgeous, set me up with a Bud and a shot of your best rotgut."

I know by now what he drinks.

"Sure enough."

He leans over the bar and gives a shout, "Hey, Eleanor, you in there?"

Eleanor pops her head through the window. The kitchen is closed, but she's got a mess in there to clean, including the broken dishes on the floor.

"Fred," she says, with a bit of a giggle, really a giggle, and then she's back inside.

"You must be the only person in the world she likes other than Jack," I tell Fred.

"She and me go way back. You might say we were kissin' cousins."

I feel like throwing up on him thinking about what that might entail, but instead I say, "Oh, really."

Jack returns with more empties. He's trying to keep up. He says it was a blessing actually when the state stopped smoking in bars. He doesn't have to clean ashtrays although he keeps cans outside for the smokers. Of course, the lazy-ass smokers just chuck their butts on the ground.

The band is back. They're into the music. So are the dancers. And those who aren't dancing, howl and hoot instead when they recognize a song.

Fred tries to get my attention.

"You want something else? The kitchen's closed, but I bet Eleanor might fix you something since you both go way back."

Damn it, I can't help being sarcastic.

Fred crooks his finger. He wants me to move closer.

"How about you and me doin' somethin' together some time?"

I feel myself blush a bit. I know what he means by doing something. Yuck. But instead I make a joke.

"Sorry, I'm not allowed to fraternize with the customers. Company rule."

"Since when?"

"Since yesterday," Jack says behind me.

Fred laughs over his beer bottle. Kin or not, he doesn't want to risk getting kicked out for six months from the only bar around.

Now the lead singer announces, "Here's somethin' for those of you who like to get up close and personal when you dance, but keep it semi-clean folks," and the band plays Patsy Cline's "I Fall to Pieces."

I smile at Jack as he holds out his hand.

"You pay them to play that song?"

"Uh-huh," he says, and then he shouts, "Bar's closed until the end of this song."

We're on the floor again. He pulls me close, and I don't mind who sees or knows we are together. I hear his heart chug. I bet mine does the same.

"Too bad your mother came home today," he says.

"Well, I did tell her I might be late getting home."

He gives me a slow twirl.

"Woman, you're gonna wear me out."

We're just teasing each other. We have no plans tonight. I think last night did him and me for a while. I mean we're not kids anymore.

We're both joking and laughing our heads off still when we return to the bar. Eleanor stands there with her winter jacket zipped to the neck. She's pulled her knit hat to her eyebrows. She stares like she's been waiting hours.

"I wanna go home now," she tells her brother.

"Take it easy, Sis," he says before he turns toward me. "Isabel, you gonna be okay? We have a full house tonight."

"Don't worry about me."

Eleanor gives me a hard bump with her elbow as she walks toward the door. No, she doesn't say "excuse me" or anything like that. She doesn't even grunt.

Fred slides his empty forward.

"This bottle must have a hole in it," he says. "Could you fix it please?"

I reach into the cooler.

237

"You want a shot with that?"

"Nah, I'm fine." When he smiles, I see the family resemblance between him and Jack. But it ends there. "Looks like you and my cousin are getting real cozy."

"We were just dancing."

His chuckle borders on a cackle.

"I'm not blind." He leans forward. "But if you want a man with a little more horse power let me know."

I squeeze my eyes almost shut.

"I'm just fine."

Ma's Surprise

I do get home late, but naturally Ma is up watching TV. I helped Jack close up the place. We kissed a bit and joked about doing it on one of the tables. He said he would carve "Jack and Isabel did it here" on the bottom.

"I thought you'd be out later with that fellow of yours," she says.

"Nah, he hasn't cleaned out his place yet."

"Just bring him here."

"Wouldn't that make you uncomfortable?"

"Uh, how long was it before you and Sam actually married?"

"I forgot about that."

"You sure you wouldn't mind?"

"Might be nice to have a man around the house once in a while."

I shake my head. Wait until Jack hears this.

Saturday

My mother and I do the Conwell triangle Saturday morning although we do it in reverse to break things up. Mira Clark set aside some books she thought my mystery-loving mother would want. She was right.

Outside the library, Ma asked, "Is she still on your suspect list?"

"No, I crossed her off."

"Good. She's really nice. She gets me the books I like."

I smile. Ma's getting softer than me.

At the general store, I hear the old chief is at the VA hospital. The consensus is that it's a blessing for him and his family. He was too much for his wife to handle any more.

While Ma searches the store's shelves, I get a soup bone at the deli counter for the dog, as if that would win her over. Jamie Snow asks how the case is going, and from his voice I surmise he talked with his father about Walter Bartol.

"I haven't given up just yet," I tell him although I am half saying it for my benefit.

The dump was uneventful. I was only there long enough to drop off the recyclables and chuck one small, white bag into the dumpster.

"Big day out in Conwell," I joke to Ma. "Hey, let me show you where that Victor Wilson lives."

Ma's only comment when I drive along the dirt road is, "Well, this is the boonies."

"I think that's the way he likes it."

I stop the car at the end of his driveway. Crap, or maybe not, Victor is unlocking the gate. There's no way I can pretend he doesn't see us. I put the car in park.

"Be right back, Ma."

"Isabel, what are you doing?"

"I'm going to ask him a few questions."

"Suppose he did it?"

"That's what I want to know."

I shut the car door and walk toward the gate. The motor of Victor Wilson's pickup cycles behind him as he studies my approach.

"You again."

He stays behind the gate. I'm on the other side. I wish now I asked my mother to get in the driver's seat as that getaway driver I accuse her of being.

"Sorry to bother you."

"What do ya want?"

"I'd like to ask you a couple of questions."

"About what?"

"Do you remember Adela Collins, the woman who disappeared twenty-eight years ago? Her family has asked me to look into it." My voice is a little shaky because Victor is giving me a major staredown. "I'm asking around to see if anyone might have some useful information."

Silence.

"Did you know Adela?"

"Sure I did. But if you think I killed her, you're crazy."

"I'm not saying you did. Did you ever have a, uh, personal relationship with her?"

He snorts.

"You're kiddin' me, right?"

"Not really. I'm also talking with people who might have, uh, had some work done on their property. You put in a garage and did everything yourself, right?"

He snorts again.

"Isabel, right? I gotta give it to you askin' me that. You got brass balls, lady." He stoops a bit to check out Ma in the car. "Who's that with you?"

"My ninety-two-year-old mother."

His head swings side to side.

"Ninety-two, really?" he says. "Hey, I didn't know the woman. She was kinda outta my league. But you're welcome to come take a peek." He snickers. "But unless ya got x-ray vision, it ain't gonna do you much good. My garage has a concrete slab."

Shit, I believe this guy, and I'm not going soft.

"That's all right. I got what I came for. Thanks a bunch."

I shrug as I walk back to the car.

"Not him?" Ma asks when I slide into the front seat.

I give Victor a wave.

"Nah, too bad. It would've made a great story. Plus, he had the right profile: a guy who's quiet and keeps to himself. He was also packing heat right now, and he wasn't going hunting."

"Another dead end."

"Yup. I believe it's back to Bobby." I frown. "Then there's Jack's creepy cousin. She did cheat with him although Jack didn't find out until much later." I heave a short sigh. "Or maybe this will just remain a cold case."

"I was pretty hopeful at first."

"Me, too."

When we get home, Ma gets to work making kale soup. I have a bowl before I leave for the Rooster. I'm not about to eat any of Eleanor's food tonight. Maybe she'd put poison in it. Of course, I'm only joking.

It's a pretty normal night at the Rooster, steady but not overpowering. At one point, Jack sits on a stool at the bar during a lull in the action.

"Hey, I've some news for you," I tell him.

"Did you solve your case?"

"Nah, not that. My mother said she wouldn't mind if you stayed over."

Jack slaps the counter.

"Hot damn. Really?"

"I was surprised, too. If you don't mind, I'd like to wait a while. You could come for dinner and hang around, so she gets to know you better. Make her feel comfortable first."

"That works for me. We can still come to my place sometimes. I've got my room mostly dug out. You should've seen what I hauled to the dump today." He nods. "I'm thinking

242

of even buying new sheets for the bed."

Jack looks past me. I turn to see old sneaky-foot Eleanor behind me. I jump a bit.

"Sheesh, Eleanor, you scared the shit outta me," I say.

"Somethin' you want, Sis?" Jack asks.

Eleanor shakes her head no.

The Chase

On Sunday, I take my mother to church, of course, and mercifully, God doesn't strike me down dead for all the sinning I've done since the last time I was here. I take Ma out for a late breakfast afterwards. That's when I tell her I have a gift for Jack. I framed three of the old photos I got from the Daily Star. A younger Jack behind the bar at the Rooster is one. The shots from the pig roast are the other two. I plan to drop them off at Jack's while Ma watches the Patriots play today. Besides, I want Jack to show me the progress he's making on his place.

Jack's pickup isn't in the driveway. But I came all this way, so I may as well wait for him. I didn't see his truck when I passed the Rooster. Maybe he ran to the store, which closes pretty soon. I came the back route, so I'm only guessing. Even if Jack went to church, which he doesn't, the service was over a long time ago. There just aren't that many places to go on a Sunday in Conwell.

It's a warm enough day that I can sit on the front steps of the porch and feel comfortable in the sun. This farmhouse is high enough elevation-wise that it has a view of the town and hills. I recall old-timers say that before the forest grew back you could see for miles in any direction. The early settlers had chopped down all the trees. I've seen photos from that time, so for once they aren't spinning tales about the town.

I hear Eleanor's dogs. She's got to be around here somewhere. She's probably taking those mutts for a walk. Nobody can hunt on Sundays, an old rule that's stuck, so she probably wants to give the dogs a good run. I did the same for Maggie when Ma and I came home.

Now that I think of it, I've never asked Eleanor about

Adela. Jack's sister may be slow and unfriendly, but she could've heard or seen something useful. I look down at the top photo on my lap. It's the one where Adela and Jack are having a fun moment, and Eleanor appears put out. Perhaps, it's a case of three's company, but she doesn't disguise her feelings of disgust. That's how I'd describe it. Something's really bugging her.

Eleanor and her mutts eventually emerge from the woods and make their way across the snowy field. The mutts bark and begin to run when they see me on the steps. I'm guessing they don't get many visitors. I will admit to being skittish about dogs, especially ones that look like they're going to bite the hell outta me. I'm hoping Eleanor's mutts are just bluffing, or she calls them off if they aren't. Finally, she whistles to the dogs and grabs the collar of the most aggressive.

"What you want?" she greets me.

"I'm here to see Jack. I have a surprise for him."

"He's at the store."

I eye the dog she holds back. It has sharp, white teeth.

"Are your dogs friendly?"

"They don't know you," she says. "Stay here."

That's exactly what I plan to do while she brings the dogs into her side of the house. Now they're in the sunroom, barking their heads off at me. Eleanor is back. She doesn't offer to let me inside, I notice. It doesn't hurt to be friendly. I believe I'll try it out on her.

"You want to see what I'm giving Jack? They're old photos I framed. You're in one."

Her head tips from one side to the other. I seemed to have sparked her curiosity.

"Me?"

I hand her the photo from the bottom. It's the one I shot of Jack when he bought the Rooster. Eleanor's lips curl ever so slightly when she recognizes her brother. She hands it back.

"Here's one from the pig roast way back when."

She nods as she studies the solo image of her brother. She hands that one back, too.

"This one was taken at the same pig roast. You're in it."

Her smile fades when she sees the photo. Maybe she doesn't like the sour expression on her face or the happy ones on Jack and Adela's. She takes her time studying it. Here is my opportunity. Keep it light, Isabel. Don't spook Eleanor.

"Turns out I took that photo a couple of weeks before Adela went missing. You must've known her pretty well since you grew up together. Jack says you and she were in the same class. You saw her at the store all the time."

Eleanor raises her eyes for a second.

She grunts.

"Your brother told me they were spending a lot of time together the months before she disappeared."

Grunt.

"Jack told me he loved her. I wonder where they would have lived if they got married. Do you think she would have liked it here? This is a nice old house, but she had one, too."

No grunt this time. She hands me back the photo, almost flinging it, but I make a lucky catch.

"I get the feeling you didn't like Adela."

"No," she blurts.

Finally, I get something from her although I believe she means yes.

"How come?"

"She was bad," she says.

"Bad about what?"

"She did it with my cousin. I was gonna tell Jack. I told her that."

"Is that why she came here the night she disappeared?"

Her mouth drops open. Her brows dig inward.

There's no turning back for me.

"You two have a fight about Jack?" I ask. "You didn't want to lose him?"

"Uh."

"Eleanor, what happened?"

Her head shakes. She blinks hard and fast.

"Did she have an accident? Is that how she died?"

And then Eleanor's gone, running toward the woods. Her boots kick up wet snow. Her arms pump. She's wailing.

I set the photos on the porch and chase after Eleanor, past the barking dogs in the sunroom, across the sloppy field and toward the woods. I have a hard time keeping up since she has a head start, and she knows where she's going. I follow her boot prints in the snow into the trees. I haven't any idea what I'll do when I finally find her. I wonder if she'd come peacefully anyways. Right now, I'm more concerned she could hurt herself out there.

I definitely need Jack's help. I slip the phone from my jacket pocket. Damn it, there's no service out here.

"Eleanor, come back!" I shout.

But she doesn't.

I slow my pace. I think the last time I ran this fast I was helping one of the kid's teams. I'm winded, but that's not going to stop me. Besides, Eleanor can't be too far ahead. She's way older than me, for God's sake, and she's not the jock type.

But fear is on her side. She knows I know about Adela.

Crap, why couldn't it be some jerk like Walter Bartol? Or even the old Bobby Collins or Victor Wilson. I would gladly nominate Jack's creepy cousin. But his sister?

I am past the hardwoods and into a thick stand of pines, where Eleanor's boot prints stop. I stop, too. Okay, this woman couldn't just fly or disappear. But as I study the ground, I realize she made a sharp left through the pines.

Eleanor can't be too far away.

Of course, she isn't.

But I realize that too late, when I get a hard whack to my head and I fall to the snow.

Kind of a Mess

I'm told Jack carried me back to his house. He came home to find my car. His sister was tearing from the woods. Eleanor wouldn't say what happened, but he guessed. He made her show him where she left me.

I remember Jack holding me. He kept saying my name.

I was in and out of it, but I told him, "Your sister."

"Yeah, I know."

"No, Adela."

I'm lying in Jack's unmade bed. Chief Ben Jr. already has been here to see me. Jack called him after he got his sister to talk.

An EMT, one of the Rooster regulars, is checking me over again.

"How many of me do you see?" he jokes.

"Just one, thank God," I answer.

My head hurts like hell, and if this guy isn't careful I just might barf on him.

"You've got a good bump in the back of your head. Lucky for you she didn't catch you on the side with that piece of wood. You probably have a concussion, but you're gonna be okay. Do you wanna go to the hospital to get checked out?"

"No hospital. No ambulance. I just want to go home. My mother must be wondering what in the hell happened to me. I have to tell my kids."

"You wanna do that now?"

"No, no, get me home, please. How long have I been here?"

"A couple of hours." He flashes a light in my eyes. "I'll take you. One of the other guys can follow me."

"Thanks." I raise my head but let it drop onto the pillow.

"Where's Jack?"

"He's next door with Eleanor. Chief Ben Jr.'s with 'em. The state cops showed up, too. They're figurin' things out. It's kind of a mess."

"Yeah. What's gonna happen to her?"

"No clue."

Moments later, I zip my jacket and walk outside. The driveway is filled with vehicles, including three cruisers.

I point to the photos on the porch floor. The glass is cracked on the one with the threesome at the pig roast.

"Could somebody bring those inside? They're for Jack. Please?"

"Sure enough, Isabel."

I turn. Jack, Eleanor, and the cops are in the sunroom. Eleanor's head is down. Jack has his arm around his sister. The cops lean forward in their chairs toward them. This is serious business.

Crap, why did it have to be her?

Old Farts' Blessing

It's too early for my night owl mother to be up, but I do know who is awake at this hour. I leave a note for Ma: "Gone to see the Old Farts."

I haven't been out of the house much since that Sunday almost two weeks ago. First, there was that knock to my head, but then I just felt funny seeing anyone, except my mother and the kids. Ma has been thoughtful, of course, making me enough kale soup to grow hair on my chest, as we Portagees like to joke. She admonishes me when I say I should've quit the case.

My mother put it best when she said, "The good news is you solved this case. The bad news is you solved this case."

Andrew Snow came over the Monday after it all went down. I felt awkward taking his money, but he said I deserved it. There were tears in his eyes.

"It's not what I expected," he said. "But at least we know what happened. I'm grateful for that."

Andrew did say he's heard from someone in the next town over who wants to hire me. Another hilltown mystery. Another cold case. I can't think about that now.

Of course, the papers and TV stations went nuts over the story. The news went national, I heard. I'm not surprised. This story has so many great elements like the former reporter who covered a local woman's disappearance solving the case twenty-eight years later. My landline rang constantly for a few days although I ignored it. I did do a brief interview for the Daily Star, for old time's sake, but I downplayed any heroics on my part. I called for compassion.

Who really knows what happened twenty-eight years ago?

As for the town of Conwell, I suspect people closed ranks

and were typical tightlipped Yankees with the press. They, at least the natives, would be torn up about the case. Now maybe Bobby Collins can finally get everybody off his back.

As I step through the store's side door, one of the Old Farts says, "She's here," as if they've been expecting me all along.

I take my usual spot next to the Fattest Old Fart. He reaches his arm around me and gives me a half-hug.

"How's your noggin?"

"As hard as ever," I say.

"You did good, Isabel," he says.

I sigh.

"Why did it have to be Eleanor?" I say for the millionth time.

The Old Farts hum low in their throats.

"I would never have thought it myself," the Serious Old Fart says for everyone. "None of us did."

"Eleanor strangling Adela?" the Bald Old Fart beside him says. "Unbelievable."

The Old Fart with Glasses looks over his shoulder, I suppose, to see if Jamie Snow is in earshot.

"That was awfully decent of the family to ask the judge for clemency," he says.

Yes, it was mighty noble of the Snows. My understanding is she won't serve time, except at home. Yes, she admits to choking Adela Collins to death, but it was precipitated by a fight that got physical, with Adela starting it, at least according to Eleanor. That's when her necklace broke. Eleanor found it on the floor under her kitchen table later and hid it beneath her mattress. Why she placed the locket at Adela's grave is beyond me and everyone else. I wonder if she understands why. She told Chief Ben Jr. she didn't want it anymore.

And you probably guessed correctly the baseball cap found in Adela's car belonged to Eleanor. Yeah, her head is that big.

Jack recalls his sister's face was bruised and scratched when he came home from his fishing trip, but from his recollection she claimed one of her dogs accidently knocked her down.

The Fattest Old Fart shakes a fat finger.

251

"We all know Eleanor is real slow, but she sure figured out how to clean up things," he says. "Driving Adela's car to that logging road and then hiking back in the dark along a snowmobile trail. Then she used the bucket on the farm's tractor to bury her body where they were building that sunroom. I scratch my head about that."

I heard the ground beneath the sunroom has already been excavated. I bet the Old Farts heard, too.

Now Adela's remains are in her grave.

The Fattest Old Fart nods to the Skinniest Old Fart, who gets up to pour me coffee.

"How do you take it, Isabel?"

"A little milk, please."

He hands me the Styrofoam cup.

"Sorry, the espresso machine's getting fixed," the Skinniest Old Fart jokes. "We should have it back next week."

Yup, there's a chorus of chuckles.

"Oh, you guys."

Jack

Later that day, I'm in the cellar sorting through Sam's tools. With the snowstorm that moved in this morning, I have nowhere to go. I have a buyer for all the machinery. The boys and Gregg are not interested although they did move the big stuff to one spot for me. I'll hold onto the hand tools, like the German planes and Japanese saws Sam prized, but getting rid of the power tools will reduce the shop's size greatly. It will mean I can get an entire winter's supply of firewood in here from now on and avoid that chore mid-January.

Plus, I could use the cash with Christmas being two weeks away. Yeah, Jack didn't have to tell me, but my job at the Rooster is over. The Rooster has been closed since that Sunday.

On the floor above me, Ma talks with a man. I recognize Jack's voice. The conversation is so brief he's out the door before I get upstairs.

"What did Jack want, Ma?"

She holds an envelope.

"He says it's a check."

I peek out the window. Jack walks toward his pickup through the falling snow. His hand is on the door as he gives a backward look. Shoot.

I grab my jacket from a chair and rush outside.

"Jack, Jack!" I shout.

I run until I can catch up to his pickup. He looks a bit startled when I knock on his window, but he stops the truck. He rolls down the window.

"Jack, where are you going?"

The man is uncomfortable. I read it all over his face. There's no Jack Smith grin or mischievous twinkle in his eye.

I don't blame him. It's been a mess since his sister's arrest.

Jack finally speaks.

"How are you, Isabel?" he says. "How's your head?"

I stick my arms through the sleeves of my jacket. The snow is coming down harder.

"My head's fine," I answer. "But things could be better."

I haven't seen Jack since that Sunday. He called that night to ask how I was and to apologize. I haven't heard from him either, although according to my phone, he hung up three times before I answered. I called back, but each time his phone went to voice mail.

Jack's hands are on the steering wheel as if he's ready to peel out of here.

"How's your sister?" I ask.

"She's okay. She's home and she's got her dogs. She's got me. That's enough for her."

"I'm relieved they didn't put her in jail."

"Me, too. There's really no other place for her." He pats the steering wheel. "Listen, Isabel. I don't blame you for what happened." His voice drops. "I'm just having a real tough time dealing with all of this. I haven't been able to think about anything or anyone else."

"I understand," I tell him, which is about the stupidest thing people ever say. Really, how could I understand? But I'm trying. "I heard you're reopening the Rooster."

"I need the money. Those lawyers are expensive," he says. "I gotta find a cook. I'll hold off on music for now. It just doesn't seem right."

I read between his words, or I'm trying at that, too.

"Jack."

"Yeah, Isabel?"

"If you ever wanna come by and just talk, that'd be fine."

His head bobs in a steady beat.

"I just might, Isabel Long," he says, and after a pause, "Let me think about it."

I say good-bye and through the falling snow run into the house. I want to get inside before Jack sees me crying. I'm already bawling my head off when I reach the front door.

Behind me, his pickup makes its way up the driveway's steep incline.

Now I'm inside and leaning against the front door. Ma sits in her chair with her pets. The TV is on low. She's wondering what she could do for me. We Ferreiras are not an emotional family, but I am breaking into little pieces in front of her.

Okay, Isabel, get a hold of yourself. It was only a fling, but a fun one. Jack's the only man you've been with outside of Sam in how many years? He owns a bar. He was your boss. His sister killed a woman, and she might have done the same to you.

But there is something I really like about Jack.

"Ma, I'm gonna go upstairs for a while and lie down," I tell her.

She leans forward in her chair as she stares out the window.

"You might not want to, Isabel," she says. "I believe you've got company."

"Company?"

I go to the window. Jack's returned. He parks his truck and steps toward my front door. I swipe the tears from my face with both hands.

I don't wait for him to knock.

"You came back."

"Well, Isabel, I thought it over."

He makes a grin, a shy grin, an uncertain grin, a grin I haven't seen before. He runs his hand over his hair.

I smile.

"Aw, Jack, I'm really glad you did."

Fantastic Books
Great Authors

CROOKED
CAT

Meet our authors and discover
our exciting range:

- Gripping Thrillers
- Cosy Mysteries
- Romantic Chick-Lit
- Fascinating Historicals
- Exciting Fantasy
- Young Adult and Children's
  Adventures
- Non-Fiction

Visit us at:
www.crookedcatbooks.com

Join us on facebook:
www.facebook.com/crookedcatbooks

Made in the USA
Middletown, DE
13 May 2019